DAWN OF
BROKEN
GLASS

DAWN OF BROKEN GLASS

GORDON
ANTHONY
BEAN

Guardian of Forever
Publishing

Guardian of Forever Publishing

Cover design by Emma Dolan
Cover photo: istockphoto.com/Fitzer
Editor: Allister Thompson

Print ISBN 978-0-9918275-4-1
Ebook ISBN 978-0-9918275-3-4

Printed in the United States of America

17 16 15 14 13 5 4 3 2 1

Library and Archives Canada Cataloguing in Publication

Bean, Gordon Anthony, 1967-, author
      Dawn of broken glass / Gordon Anthony Bean.

Issued in print and electronic formats.
Dawn of broken glass.
ISBN 978-0-9918275-4-1 (pbk.).-- ISBN 978-0-9918275-3-4 (pdf)

      I. Title.

PS8603.E35234D38 2013   C813'.6   C2013-902214-7
                                                 C2013-902215-5

I dedicate this book to my wife Greer and my daughter Alexa
who keep me out of the shadows.

PROLOGUE

November 10, 1938. Hanover, Germany.

The child grabbed his new camera and ran upstairs to play with it. Just the week before, he had discovered the hidden crawlspace upstairs behind his bedroom closet. His eager subsequent exploration revealed a child's dream: a passageway between the walls where he could eavesdrop on virtually every room of the house through air ducts, floor grate or carefully-built peephole. The child even found a tunnel from the cellar that led out to the woodshed behind the house. On this day, though, his twelfth birthday, he was going to hide in the passageway and take hidden pictures of his family, who were in the den spending quality time together. The boy reflected on his vantage point, which was above eye level, and eavesdropped. A small hole in the plaster of the wall allowed the boy to look through, yet remain virtually unnoticed. He smiled and took his place at the hole, his camera at the ready.

His father was seated at the Bechstein family piano, playing an old Yiddish folk tune that his mother and sister happily sang. His older brother sat on a chair in the corner, sullenly reading a pulp novel, trying to look as disinterested in the rest of the family as possible. His father was a large man, standing a towering six foot four, with broad shoulders and a barrel chest. In his youth, he had done some semi-professional boxing, but had soon opted for a quieter and safer desk job at his father-in-law's import/export company. He didn't complain, since it allowed him to travel, to become financially comfortable, and still be around the family he loved. His kindness shone in his eyes and strong face. There wasn't a day that went by that the father did not marvel at how his youngest son was the spitting image of him. Josef smiled as he thought of how lucky he was to have such a caring and devoted father.

The boy looked down at his mother and sister. Even though he was only a child, Josef knew that they were truly blessed with natural beauty. Wherever he went with his mother, he noticed how men stopped what they were doing and stared at her. Although only fifteen, Elizabeth was starting to get the same reaction from young men. Both mother and daughter were fair of skin, almost alabaster, with rich green eyes and pale gold hair. They were tall and slim, and carried themselves with bearing and grace. Of course, Josef could see beyond their beauty. His mother was a brilliant woman and taught physics at the University of Hanover, while his sister, although still many years from a career, was already one of the top students in her grade. He also marveled at how beautifully they sang....

The boy's older brother, Michael, was clearly different from the rest of the family. A brooding youth of seventeen, he was quiet, sullen and preferred to be alone rather than partake in family gatherings. He was of medium height, with skin and hair coloring somewhere between the mother's fair looks and the father's dark. Michael had black eyes that seemed as if they could penetrate a man's soul just by looking at him. He did poorly in school and frequently got into trouble, although Josef had the feeling that if Michael ever applied himself, he would shock everyone. He knew that Michael was surprisingly clever, and the rare times Michael actually applied himself, Josef was amazed at his brother's astounding analytical mind.

One day, while Michael was out, Josef crept into his brother's room and was digging through his drawers and closet, looking for anything interesting, when he found a sketchpad hidden at the back of the closet under several old shirts. He could not believe his eyes when he gazed upon the dark and beautifully rendered charcoal drawings. Some were so detailed that the creatures of myth and legend contained within actually seemed alive, clawing their way free of the page's confines. Josef had nightmares for weeks with the vivid images seared into his brain. The other thing that Josef noticed about his brother was that he always seemed to be lost in a book, preferring to read than be around other people. He had few friends, and instead of playing sports, he read voraciously, often on diverse and eclectic subjects such as science, mythology, arts, literature and even arcane books of folklore. The one aspect of Michael's persona that Josef did understand was his choice of girlfriend. Rachel was of medium height and slim, with pale skin and large blue eyes. Her hair was raven black, and as Josef seemed to shun others, Rachel was the opposite, drawing people in with her warmth and charm, making everyone feel instantly at ease in her presence. Josef sometimes secretly wished he were Michael, just so he could get her to look at him with such adoration, even for a moment.

Josef began snapping pictures, the flash lighting up the narrow passage in which he had sequestered himself. He noticed his father look up in his direction and wink. Almost simultaneously, Michael looked up to where Josef was hiding and scowled and shook his head disapprovingly.

The family's singing stopped abruptly when a series of barks from the family dog, followed by the sharp crack of a gunshot, resonated from outside. Josef's mother looked at her husband, her eyes wide and fearful.

"It's happening, isn't it?" she half whispered. He looked back at her sadly. The acts of violence towards Jews around their town had been increasing for a long while and while everyone was hoping that things would blow over, they all suspected that the worst was truly yet to come.

"Michael," the father said in a hushed tone, "go upstairs and get your papers. Find Josef and take him through the passageway from the cellar to the shed out back. From there, wait until you are sure that you have not been seen by anyone and then run through the woods and don't look back. Do you understand?" Michael nodded solemnly. "You need to do whatever it takes to stay hidden and don't stop until you are out of Germany. We will meet up again at your Aunt Hanna's house in London. Anna, grab the papers for you and Elizabeth and do the same. Make sure that you go by a different route. You have a better chance of getting away unseen if you travel in smaller groups."

"But father," Michael began, "what is going on?"

"Go now, my son," his father begged. "The Germans are coming and will likely arrest us or worse. Don't worry about me. They won't see me as a threat as I am too old to fight, but you are a young male, and I fear they will likely shoot you on sight. You must protect yourself and Josef. As for you, Anna," he said, his voice trailing off, the look between him and his wife speaking volumes.

"I will stay and fight, then," Michael hissed through clenched teeth.

"No," his father growled, "you will do as I say. I will try to persuade them that the rest of you are away and that I am an old man and of no threat. I will see you all at Hanna's as soon as I can. Now, please. Just do as I say."

Michael turned without another word, raced up the stairs to Josef's room and noticed the closet door wide open. He walked into the closet and peered into the entrance to the crawlspace. He was about to call Josef's name when he heard a crash from downstairs followed by angry shouts. He quickly entered the passageway and closed the panel behind him. He had to crouch down to his hands and knees, and he grimaced when his fingers brushed against something warm and fuzzy that moved when he touched it. He crawled down the passageway as fast as he could, brushing aside cobwebs as he went, hoping he could get to his brother and get away before something bad happened to them.

Downstairs, the door was kicked in and three men entered. The men were dressed in stiff brown uniforms and brandished handguns. *The Sturmabteilung*, the father thought, as the fear knotted his stomach.

"What do you want?" he asked hoarsely, trying to show enough courage that his wife and daughter wouldn't worry. "We have done nothing wrong."

"Quiet," the soldier yelled, striking him across the face with the butt of his gun. "Your whole race is what's wrong. Your kind killed Ernst vom Rath and there will be payback." From his hiding point, Josef watched his father drop to his knees and put a hand to his face where the soldier struck him. Although he was terrified for his family and wanted to run, he knew somehow that he had to bear witness to what was happening and that he should have a record on film, so he kept taking pictures. Elizabeth hugged her mother and began to weep.

The youngest of the soldiers ran over to Elizabeth and grabbed her by the arm, pulling her away from her mother, who cried out in fear. The soldier was barely eighteen, with thin blond hair and pale, watery blue eyes. His lean face was slightly pockmarked from past acne and he had a scar running down his left cheek. He was lean and wiry, and he moved furtively like a jackal. He leered at Elizabeth and gave her a backhanded slap across her cheek. He then grabbed her by the blouse and tore it open. She screamed in terror, tears welling up in her eyes as she shamefully tried to cover herself.

Her father leapt to his feet and charged at the soldier who had struck his daughter, sending him sprawling. He began striking him powerfully in the face, breaking the young man's nose and covering his fists with blood. The soldier who initially struck the father turned and fired a shot directly into the back of the old man's skull, sending a crimson spray of blood and brain matter all over the youngest soldier. The father fell forward, twitched briefly, then was still with the blood pooling all around him and on the soldier.

"Papa!" Josef screamed. The third soldier, the eldest and highest in rank, turned to the wall and sneered. He aimed his gun and fired five consecutive shots into the plaster of the wall. Seconds ticked by as if they were frozen in time. Then, from two of the holes, blood began to slowly trickle down the walls.

Anna cried out for her youngest and was quickly and forcibly restrained by the soldier who had shot her son. He ripped a section from her shirt and forced it into her mouth. The soldier who had killed her husband did likewise to Elizabeth. The youngest of the soldiers stood and grinned maliciously, wiping the father's blood and brain matter off his face and out of his eyes and attempting to staunch the flow of his blood from his mangled nose and mouth.

Michael reached Josef where he lay on the dusty passage floor, whimpering and shaking as dark blood pooled around his trembling body. Michael knew from his brother's wounds and the sheer amount of blood that he did not have much time left. He cradled his dying brother in his arms, holding him close as tears sprang to his eyes. Josef looked up at Michael with pleading, fearful eyes, wanting some sort of reassurance. Michael felt his own tears start to flow for his sweet younger brother who would never get to enjoy the wonders life had to offer. As Josef's eyes clouded over and his form grew still, Michael felt the rage grow within him. He looked through the peephole and witnessed the horrors the soldiers had inflicted upon his parents and sister. He swore he would avenge his family and that these men would pay tenfold for what they had done. He stayed only long enough to witness the soldiers savagely shoot his mother and sister dead where they lay after being brutally ravaged.

Michael grabbed the camera, took a few more pictures of the soldiers and his dead family and then quickly and quietly exited the house through the passageway. He climbed out of the shed and wheeled his bike into the woods. Once well past the house, he drove away through the cool night, stopping only at his girlfriend Rachel's house to describe the horrors he had witnessed. He warned them that the soldiers would surely be coming for them, but Rachel's father refused to leave. Against her parents' wishes, she joined Michael and they fled the city together, leaving Germany and their lives behind them. Michael swore on his family that the men who did this would pay, even if it took his whole life to make it happen.

CHAPTER 1

The Present

The wind blew frigid blasts of snow and sleet across the near-deserted streets of Boston's Back Bay district. Even though it was barely three in the afternoon, most stores had closed down hours earlier in anticipation of the nor'easter expected to break all modern records for snow accumulation. The tops of the buildings were nearly obscured by the maelstrom above, so much so that they appeared to bleed into the dark and angry sky.

A lone figure walked up Boylston, heading towards the Green Line T stop. His destination was North Station, where he hoped to catch the commuter rail to the northern suburb where he lived. He hated going into the city, and the only reason he had even bothered with the storm of the century looming was out of self-preservation. Ryan Carson knew that if he didn't pay Joey Falazzi the five large that he owed for a string of gambling losses, Joey, or one of his men, would come after him and inflict a world of hurt.

Coming into the five thousand was no easy task for Ryan, either. His life had taken a serious downturn in the last few months. His wife had divorced him, claiming she loved him too much to watch him waste his life and talents away. That didn't stop her from leaving and taking up with that arrogant prick professor friend of hers, though, and Ryan still felt a surge of rage every time he thought of her. Ryan knew that he was meant for better things, but every time he felt like he was making some forward progress, some event would cause him to come crashing back to the bottom. He was a writer, in spirit, if not in profession. The great American novel on which he toiled was still unfinished, and every time he attempted to get it back on track, something would always come along and take priority.

In order to make ends meet, Ryan waited tables at a busy restaurant/bar in Lowell. The workload was hectic, and often, financial responsibilities forced him to work a second shift. Chrissy, his ex-wife, was a student. A perpetual one, Ryan thought sarcastically, and it forced him to work extra hours to ensure that she always got her alimony money, which she seemed to piss away on clothes, tuition, books and anything else she felt she needed. He worked his ass off getting nowhere in life while she worked to better herself…all on his dime. As college students are wont to be, Chrissy saw the world through the eyes of an innocent and couldn't begin to fathom why Ryan would wait tables when he should instead be focusing on fine-tuning his writing skills. Ryan was always a realist and knew that skill and talent alone did not always pay the bills. He was also the eternal optimist and was convinced that good things would eventually come his way. He held on to these beliefs with such conviction that he often bet large amounts on high profile sporting events in the hope of supplementing his weekly cash flow. Plus, he was simply tired of working the equivalent of two jobs to keep his own head above water.

The event that changed things beyond the breaking point for Ryan came when his father suffered a massive stroke which partially paralyzed him and necessitated the need for a live-in nurse. Medicare simply did not cover enough of the costs and Ryan's father's meager savings diminished very quickly. Ryan helped out where he could, but it was just not enough. Without proper medical care, his dad would die. Ryan did not know where to turn and out of desperation jumped at a chance for a fifteen-to-one shot at a prize fight. He knew of the fighter and the promise he held, and even though the odds were long, Ryan felt confident enough that he wagered five thousand dollars through his longtime bookie, Joey Falazzi. As always, luck was not with Ryan and his fighter was knocked out in the first round. Joey called on him the next day requesting payment. When Ryan told him that he did not have the money, Joey gave him three days to pay and patted him gently on the cheek, reminding him that there would be consequences if he did not. He reminded Ryan that their long-standing relationship could be pushed only so far, and that he expected complete payment within the designated time period.

The next day, Ryan withdrew his entire savings and sold his coin collection, the one his father had helped him start when he was a child. Even that was barely enough to pay off his losses. Selling the coins was like dying a little bit inside, a piece of his lost youth and innocence that was gone forever. Work had kept him busy enough that he wasn't able to pay Joey until the last day, a day that began by Joey leaving a very gentle reminder on Ryan's answering machine that payment was due by noon or he should expect company. Ryan cursed when he heard that the storm had changed course and that it would hit Boston hard, burying it for the next few days. With grim determination, Ryan drove to the Andover train station and caught a morning train into the city, where he arranged to meet Joey and pay him in full.

Joey took the money but did not thank Ryan. He reminded him, once again, that their friendship could be stretched only so far and that in the future all bets needed to be cash up front. "Better than a bullet in your head, right?" he smiled, patting Ryan on the back and sending him on his way.

As Ryan boarded the train home, he reflected on his life. He had shown serious promise in high school, winning award after award for his prose and poetry. Somehow, though, fate always seemed to have other plans for him and had taken him in one direction after another, never allowing him time to focus on his goal. As the train sped north, Ryan vowed that he would start fresh and that today was the first day of the rest of his life. *Tabula rasa*, he thought, *a blank slate where new beginnings are free and unencumbered by the past.* Of course, fate had other plans and as Ryan thought of how he would make his new start in life, a long black limousine was pulling up in front of his building. The occupant stepped out of the car, looking at the shabby building with disgust.

He walked purposely inside, knowing full well that one way or another he would not be leaving alone.

*   *   *

Ryan arrived home at his small one-bedroom apartment in Andover, exhausted and soaked. It had taken him nearly half an hour to brush the snow off his car and clear a path out of the snow- and ice-covered parking lot to begin his drive home. By the time he got there, he was tired and thoroughly pissed off. All he wanted was to turn on the fireplace, make a cup of hot chocolate, curl up on the couch and watch a movie on television.

When he got to his apartment he noticed that the front door was slightly open. He prayed that he hadn't been robbed. He didn't have anything really worth stealing but the invasion of his personal space was enough to make his blood boil. After the day he had, he didn't need any more grief. Balling his hands into fists, he swung the door open and stepped in. Inside, he noticed a man seated in his living room, casually smoking a cigar as if he belonged there.

"I hope you don't mind, Ryan," the man said matter-of-factly, "but it was cold outside so I let myself in." Ryan noticed the thick accent and tried to place it. It sounded Arabic, but only barely.

Ryan gauged that the man was in his late thirties, with a thin but wiry build. He stood a bit over six feet tall and wore a long black trench coat over a dark green turtleneck sweater and jeans. He had closely cropped black hair, green eyes and an olive complexion. Ryan's first impulse was to run, but something kept him rooted in place. There was a good chance that that the man was here to break his legs on Joey Falazzi's bequest as a reminder not to ever mess with him or his livelihood.

"W-who the hell are you?" Ryan stammered, hoping he sounded braver than he felt.

"Please have a seat, Ryan," the man replied while gesturing to the chair across from him. "You don't know me, but I am very familiar with you."

Very familiar with you. Something about the way he spoke sounded off, almost as if English were not his native tongue but was using it for

Ryan's benefit. Ryan took an involuntary step back towards his front door and the hallway outside his apartment.

"If you don't start with who you are and how you got into my house, I'll call the cops," Ryan said, keeping his eyes on the man.

The man grinned widely, exposing shockingly white teeth. "Sit... please. If I wanted to do you harm, you would already be dead. I can assure you of that. You are quite safe with me. I have a story to tell you, one that is in your best interests, and if you are patient and are willing to listen, there is a chance you can become exceedingly rich beyond your wildest dreams."

Ryan sat down on a chair as far from the man as possible. He leaned forward slightly. "I'm listening, but start at the beginning."

"As you wish," the man said, smiling, "First off, allow me to introduce myself. My name is Jason Froemmer. It is not the name I was born with, but it is who I am these days. Either way, it does not matter. You can call me Jason and that will suffice. I am currently in the employ of your grandfather and have been so for many years. You might say that I am like a consultant and help him solve problems." He leaned forward and extended his still gloved hand, which Ryan shook.

"You work for my grandfather?" Ryan asked, his brow furrowing as he looked at Jason. "My grandfather died four years ago from congenital heart failure."

"Not your mother's father, Ryan, your father's father. Your paternal grandfather."

"My father didn't talk too much about his father. All I ever heard around our house was that there was some dispute between them when I was just a child, and they never spoke again. In fact, my father told me that my grandfather has been dead for nearly twenty years."

"I would like to tell you that your grandfather is indeed still alive, and that the reason your father broke ties with his father partially accounts for why I am sitting in front of you right now." Jason grinned widely again, his eyes slightly darkening. Ryan felt a chill grip his spine. Every instinct he had screamed out, warning him to turn and run while he still could. Something about Jason seemed off, but he couldn't put his finger on it. Ryan forced those thoughts back and decided to at least hear what Froemmer had to say.

"All right," Ryan continued, pausing just long enough to regain some of his composure, "assuming my grandfather is still alive, what could he possibly want with me? More so, how does he even know anything about me? He hasn't contacted me once since I was a kid. Why should I be so damned eager to hear what he has to say now?"

Jason smiled. "He assumed that you would feel this way. According to him, the two of you are very much alike." He reached into his pocket, pulled out an envelope sealed with wax and handed it to Ryan. Ryan opened the envelope and took out a letter. Stapled to the letter was a check for twenty thousand dollars. The letter read:

Grandson:

I know that it has been many years since we've last spoken. Believe me, it was not by choice. Your father and I had a falling out over very different beliefs and ideals and he asked me to keep out of your lives. I could do nothing to persuade him otherwise. In the end, I acceded to his wishes and left you on your own. Although I could not share in your lives, I still had the means to follow them. You've had a guardian angel looking over your shoulder without ever knowing it.

I have a lot to tell you about myself, your family, and your heritage. Jason will fill you in on the basic details, and should you be willing to learn a bit more and fulfill our destiny, I will explain the rest later. I guarantee, it is in all our best interests.

For now, please use the attached check to ensure that your father continues receiving the medical attention that he needs. After all, even though we have not spoken in many years, he is still my son. Please do not tell him where the money came from. He is a proud man and would sooner perish than to feel beholden to a man who shames him.

I look forward to finally meeting with you.

Regards,

Michael Carson

Ryan looked up at Jason. "What kind of crap is this? Who the hell does he think he is, anyways."

"Very well," Jason replied and leaned back in his chair, "your grandfather assumed you'd be…reluctant, and allowed me some latitude in explaining why he wants you to come see him so badly. So, why don't I start from the beginning? Your grandfather was born in Hanover, Germany, shortly before the Nazis came to power. His family was not only well respected in the community, they were also well liked. In some ways, you can say they were a picture-perfect family. Both parents were professionals, and all three of their children were very talented. The Nazis ended that family's dream with a brutal attack on Kristallnacht, the night of broken glass, when Goebbels' pogrom against Jews was put into effect. This was done as a knee-jerk reaction to the murder of vom Rath. It boiled over into the German population, which was an already unstable powder keg, and was the start of what developed into Hitler's 'final solution.' Amidst the chaos that ensued, your grandfather escaped the massacre of his family and fled from Germany, and along with his girlfriend headed to England. The route to England was not an easy one, and your grandfather barely made it alive. Sadly, his girlfriend was shot en route by a German patrol near France. In a short span, your grandfather lost everyone who ever mattered to him in the world.

"He finally reached his aunt's house in the heart of London. She took him in and gave him a home, where he stayed for the duration of the war.

His memory of that night in Germany haunted him, and he frequently woke up screaming. He has night terrors to this day. Your grandfather eventually got his life back together and met a young lady while vacationing in New York. They fell in love and got married. To be more accommodating to his young bride, your grandfather pulled up roots and moved to New York. Part of his break from the past was in changing his name to one that had an American feel to it. In a sense, Michael Karstein died that day so Michael Carson could live.

"Living in New York was very good for your grandfather. He cultivated friends who were very influential in the city. He charmed them with his sense of humor, his brilliant mind and the ability to weave a fanciful tale. He was very charismatic, and when he spoke, people stopped and listened. His friends and wife urged him to write down some of his stories. He reluctantly agreed, but only if he could write them under a pseudonym. Your grandfather valued his privacy above all else, and had no desire for the fame that writing could bring. Nevertheless, he did write and sell novels under his pen name. The books became immensely popular and gave your grandparents wealth they never dreamed of.

"Your grandfather also is a very shrewd man, and he quickly took his royalties from his novels and invested them in several companies which he felt had vision. Within a few years, he had enough money that he no longer needed to work for the rest of his life. He was so wealthy, in fact, that his children or even his grandchildren would never need worry about anything in their entire lives."

Ryan stood up and walked over to the fridge in the galley kitchen adjoining the living room. "Would you like a beer, Mr. Froemmer?" he asked as he withdrew a Sam Adams Cherry Wheat from the fridge.

"Thank you, but no, Ryan," Jason said with a dismissive wave. "I do not drink but would love a cup of tea if it isn't a bother. And please, call me Jason. After all, you may soon be my employer."

"What do you mean by that?"

"All in good time, Ryan. Patience is indeed a virtue, and patience is what you will need in abundance for what we have ahead of us."

Ryan nodded and put on the kettle. *All in due time*, he thought. He found some Twinings Earl Grey in the pantry and within a few minutes handed the steaming mug to the mysterious stranger seated across from him. He noted, with slight amusement, how Jason never took off his coat or gloves, even though the apartment was in fact quite warm. He also wanted answers, and he did not like being played. He decided to go along for the moment but to maintain a reserved skepticism. Plus, he reasoned, he did not wish to anger the man. Ryan sensed that doing so would prove to be a huge mistake.

Jason took a sip of the tea and continued. "Things were going well for your grandfather. He had wealth, a degree of power, a beautiful wife and home and a bright future. Eventually, he had a son who became his whole world. That son, Josef, was named after his deceased brother and would eventually become your father. Then, one day, when your father was around ten years old, your grandfather and his wife were walking home from the theatre when a man stepped out of an alley with a gun pointed at your grandfather, demanding all his money. Your grandfather was no coward, but he valued his family above all else, so he reluctantly handed over his wallet, hoping the thief would take it and leave. Instead, he shot your grandfather and dragged your grandmother off into the alley. Luckily the bullet only grazed your grandfather's forehead, and he regained consciousness a short while later to his son shaking him and crying. From the alley he could hear the screams of his wife. Without a second thought, he ran into the alley and threw himself onto the thief. Your grandfather tore into the thief like a madman, hitting him until the thief was no longer moving. He then carried your grandmother out into the street and hailed a police car, which rushed her to the hospital. Your grandmother died en route to the hospital in your grandfather's arms. The police saw the incident as a violent mugging and that your grandfather was only trying to protect himself and his family. He was never charged in the death of the thief.

"After that, your grandfather became withdrawn. He became a social recluse, venturing out only to go to the local market or wherever necessary to ensure your father's well-being. He was a man who had lost his way. He eventually returned to religion and began attending services at the local synagogue on a daily basis. He learned Hebrew and Yiddish and began poring over ancient Torahs and any other books he could find. He became a student of the Kabbalah and began to delve into ancient mystic writings. One day, in an old book, he made a very important discovery which led him to a whole set of older, more arcane literature and knew that he had found what he was looking for. To him, it seemed as if the last few years had been a daze and that he finally had crystal clarity as to his next steps."

"What did he find?" Ryan asked, drawn into his family history and needing to know more.

"Those details, Ryan, I will leave for your grandfather. I don't wish to spoil all of his surprises. " Jason grinned, and the way he looked at Ryan reminded him of how a predator would view its prey.

He was holding something back, Ryan thought, something that would keep him from going with him to see grandfather.

"As I was saying," Jason continued, "your grandfather found his calling. He packed up his and Josef's belongings and moved to a quiet town in northern Maine where he had a large mansion built. As the years wore on, your grandfather added to the house, building new wings and expanding further across his property. With each new renovation, he hired a different group of contractors and had them flown in from out of state. Other than your grandfather, no one has seen the entire house from the inside, myself included. From what I have seen, it's spectacular. He has one of the most comprehensive libraries on mythology, folklore and arcane lore, among others, in the world.

"But that, Mr. Carson, is the end of my tale. The time for destiny is now and you must choose. You can send me on my way, and trust me when I tell you that our paths will never cross again, or you can take a leap of faith, meet your grandfather and forge a new destiny for yourself."

"How long do I have to decide?" Ryan asked, a million thoughts racing through his mind.

"You do not have time." Jason stared directly at Ryan, his dark eyes seeming to bore into his brain. "You must decide now. I leave in five minutes, with or without you."

Ryan looked at Jason and knew he was very serious. He also suspected that if he refused, the police would find his corpse with a bullet hole in the forehead. Every instinct screamed in his brain that this was a bad idea, but the more he looked at Jason, the more he found that he was curious about his grandfather and wanted to go with him. "I'm in. Give me ten minutes to pack."

"Not necessary, Ryan," Jason replied, grinning, "We anticipated your acceptance and have a new wardrobe waiting for you at the estate. Come. Grab your coat, young master Carson, your car awaits."

CHAPTER 2

Buenos Aires, Argentina, 1962

The man exited the smoky nightclub and out into the darkened streets. He stood for a moment to adjust his hat and began the mile long walk towards home. He smiled and began to whistle an old tune, one that he hadn't thought of in years. It was funny how cognac and brandy always made him think of the old days when he was a man people feared and respected, not some harmless old bakery owner.

His walk was a long one, but he didn't mind. The fresh air helped take the edge off his intoxication. Also, he admitted, albeit only to himself, his wife did not allow him to drive if he was going out to the clubs. He cursed himself for becoming so tame and docile. There was a time when he had scores of lady friends, and took those he couldn't have voluntarily. He grinned again, remembering his conquests of old.

The path to his small cottage took him down several dark and deserted streets. The steady click of his shoes echoed dully in the night air. He wished the town would install streetlights of some kind. The road was too dark, so much so he could barely see the homes from the street.

"Wilhelm..." a voice sounded, off in the distance. The voice whispered, raw and rough, like stones being scraped over gravel, the sound emanating from all around him.

The man whirled about, searching for the source of the voice. He had not heard that name in decades, since before he had come to this South American country. "Who's there?" he asked nervously.

"Wilhelm…" The voice came again, swirling around him like mist, caressing him with its chilling touch.

"Who are you?" the man yelled. "You have me confused with someone else." He turned around again but saw no one lurking within the shadows. "I don't know who you want, but it is not me. I am a peaceful citizen. If you come any closer, I will call for the police."

"Wilhelm…" the voice continued, closer yet still indistinct. The man felt the air moving around him, caressing his skin with dark and foreboding promises.

"What do you want?" the man replied, the fear and adrenaline purging the effects of the alcohol from his system, his faculties honed to a razor sharp edge.

"Retribution," came the reply, cold and sharp in the still night. And then it was gone. The man felt the streets relax, as if a huge oppression had been lifted and absorbed back into the eager darkness.

The man ran home as quickly as he could manage through the darkened streets. Upon reaching the small, unassuming house he shared with his wife these last seventeen years, he began to once again feel a sense of foreboding. There were no lights on in the house, a fact the man found disconcerting. Even though he knew his wife would be long asleep, she usually left a light on for him so he wouldn't bump into anything when he got home.

Retribution. The word struck a nerve with him. He had led a quiet existence the last seventeen years under an assumed name. There were no enemies that he was aware of. His papers were flawless and had not given him one bit of trouble since he came to the South American country. Even so, the word chilled him to the very core.

The man climbed up the stairs and let himself into his home. The air was still and the familiar smells of baked strudel and the night's dinner still lingered in the air. But there was something else as well, light and barely distinct, a faint coppery scent. He recognized the smell, for it was burned in his brain for eternity. A lifetime ago, it was all around him and he had once reveled in it and the power that came with his dominance over life and death. Now, it merely made him very afraid. He went to the light switch to throw some light in the room, but it didn't respond. He clicked the switch up and down a few times, almost as if the extra effort would change the fact the lights were out. Silently cursing, he walked further into the house, the sense of claustrophobia squeezing him until it became oppressive and he couldn't breathe. The coppery smell got stronger as he went further into the house. At his bedroom door, he paused.

"Alice?" the man called out, "are you all right?" He did not expect an answer, nor did he receive one. The darkness in the house got deeper and more oppressive, becoming almost tangible. He swung the door open and froze as he surveyed the room. In the shadows he saw pieces of his wife strewn all over the floor, walls, and ceiling. Blood and viscera dripped from coagulated clumps hanging on the light fixture. Organs lay in small piles, spread haphazardly about the room. The man bent over and vomited. He had seen so much death, but in the past, at the camps, it didn't matter. He never considered them people. But Alice was different. She softened his rough edges and accepted him no matter what he had done. She had also willingly fled to Argentina with her husband, no questions asked. For her life to end in such a manner was sheer horror. The man tried in vain to suppress his tears. He needed to get away and fast.

"Wilhelm…." The voice resounded, louder than before, yet still raw and gravelly.

The man turned around, sobbing and spitting out the last trace of bile. Behind him, cloaked in the shadows, was the tallest man he had ever seen, over seven feet tall and muscular, with a faint luminescent glow that outlined his form from the shadows around him. He could not discern any of the stranger's features, and he wasn't sure if there were even any. The stranger smelled strongly of damp, rotting soil and something else that seemed rooted in his memory, yet still lay just beyond his reach. The man heard the stranger take several deep, ragged breaths before he uttered a single word and then advanced on the man. The word was "retribution." Wilhelm had time to emit one quick scream before everything went black.

CHAPTER 3

After the ride north from Boston, Jason had dropped Ryan off in front of the large mansion. He had business elsewhere, and he knew Michael wanted several days alone with Ryan before they could begin. Jason had acceded to his employer's wishes, as he always had, at least outwardly, but in reality he had no desire to be away from the mansion. He would watch from the shadows, as always, and make sure things stayed according to schedule.

The snow was coming down in driving sheets, with the cold easily slicing through to his very core. Ryan hugged his coat about him, dodging patches of ice as he maneuvered carefully along the walk and up steps treacherous with water-covered ice. One thing he realized right away was that the home had very few visitors for, if they did, surely someone would have made the walk and stairs somewhat manageable. When he reached the massive double doors, he paused to take in the sheer grandeur of the mansion. The tall, polished white stone columns at the top of the stairs, rising up at least thirty feet to the overhang on the roof, lent an air of opulence and prestige. Unlike most New England homes, the mansion was made of stone, a slate grey, which was designed to blend in with the landscape. In the middle of a winter storm such as the one that was currently raging, the home became virtually invisible and indistinguishable from the land surrounding it.

Ryan pushed the doorbell and listened as the tone echoed throughout the house. After a few minutes, he heard footsteps approaching the door from the other side. A small, wizened man opened the door and gazed at him with heavy-lidded eyes.

"You must be young master Ryan," the man remarked as he turned back into the house. "Please follow me."

Ryan followed the butler into the sprawling foyer that led into a great hall boasting cathedral ceilings, gorgeous hand-crafted furniture and a richly textured Persian rug in the center of the marble floor. From the hallway, he noticed several rooms furnished in a mostly Victorian motif. The butler led him silently up two flights of stairs and through another long hallway until he came to a stop outside a double door. He then removed a key from his pocket, unlocked the doors and swung them open.

"Your rooms, sir," the butler said while handing over the key to Ryan. "Dinner will be brought up in an hour. Please take advantage of the time to freshen up and relax. The master of the house will expect you first thing tomorrow morning." Without another word, he turned and left Ryan standing at the door.

Ryan walked into the rooms and was stunned by the beauty. The main bedroom had a large, covered four-poster king-sized bed. The sheets were silk and the comforter was pure down. On the floor was a handcrafted oriental rug that filled most of the room. The furniture was polished, hand-carved mahogany, and looked as if each piece had been made individually to ensure their perfection. Overhead, in the high, vaulted ceiling, a skylight covered the area over the bed. Ryan stared in wonder at the storm raging above him and marveled at the rawness of nature unfolding above him while he stood there warm and safe. Somehow, from inside, it all felt so surreal. In the far corner of the room was a built-in fireplace of red brick with a black granite mantle. The fire had already been laid out and was burning nicely, casting a comfortingly warm glow throughout the room.

Off the main bedroom, to the right, was the large bathroom. The countertops and floor were done in a dark black marble, with tiny silver threads throughout the stone. There was a glass-enclosed shower built entirely of terracotta tile. Next to the shower in the corner of the room was a large raised tub. At the foot of the tub and built into the wall was a plasma television. Ryan noticed the openings at each corner of the tub and guessed that they were for the Jacuzzi.

He then walked to the small room off the back of the master bedroom. This was a multi-purpose room that served as den, library and office. There was a sixty-inch plasma television mounted on the rear wall, with three black leather couches surrounding it in a semi-circle. Also built into the wall was a console containing a Bose audio system and a Blu-ray/DVD player. Between the couches and the television was a mahogany coffee table with glass inlaid in the top. Several large leather-bound books were placed atop the coffee table along with several remote controls to control the electronic equipment as well as the overhead lights. On the eastern wall was a bookshelf running from floor to ceiling the entire length of the wall. The bookshelf was filled with books of every genre, from fiction to nonfiction to do-it-yourself manuals. The number of books on mythology and arcane lore fascinated Ryan. The western corner of the room held a laptop atop a large computer desk. The computer was attached to a large 36" LED monitor. Ryan grinned as he realized that these rooms made his old apartment look shabby by comparison.

The butler came back exactly one hour later with a tray containing prime rib au jus, Monte Carlo potatoes, fresh cut asparagus and a demi-liter of Cabernet Sauvignon. Ryan thanked the butler, Willis, as he learned when the butler arrived with his food. He carried his tray over to the coffee table by the television and settled in to watch a film. He didn't realize just how tired he was from the trip until he finished eating, because he fought to keep his eyes open. He finally realized that he wasn't following the movie so he just gave in and leaned back into the soft leather of the couch, swearing he was just going to rest his eyes for a minute or so. Sleep quickly took him as all conscious thoughts faded away into the enveloping darkness.

Ryan awoke hours later feeling as if he had been asleep for a week. From the corner of his eye he noticed a figure sitting quietly on the couch to his right. As he jolted awake, the figure came into focus and for a moment, a brief moment, he felt like he was looking at himself, or how he'd look if he had aged fifty years.

"Good morning, Ryan," the man said in a voice barely above a whisper, which held traces of a European accent. "Welcome to your new home. Allow me to introduce myself. I am your grandfather, Michael Carson." He got up slowly, leaning on a beautiful black cane with a silver wolf's head on top, and walked over to Ryan. He eased himself slowly into the seat next to Ryan, grimacing as he moved. "We have a lot of catching up to do, and only a few days in which to do so. I recommend we do not waste any time."

"What do you mean by 'only a few days to do so'?"

Michael looked sadly at Ryan. "I've got very little time left. I'm dying, you see. Hence the reason I had Jason come get you with such haste. I have an inoperable brain tumor that has grown between the two lobes of the brain. I've been seen by the best neurosurgeons in the country and they all had the same opinion that any attempt at surgery to remove the tumor would cause a fatal hemorrhage. Chemo has kept the cancer at bay for the last year or so, but lately it has started growing at an exponential pace. The head of Mass General's oncology department has learned not to sugar coat things with me. He told me I had at best a week left and to consider getting my affairs in order. So I did, in a fashion. I brought you here to set things right, to tip the scales back to the way they were meant to be before I go."

Ryan looked at his grandfather with concern. "Why did you wait so long to get in touch with me? And how can I set things right? I'm sorry, but I have no idea what you're talking about."

"All in due time, my boy," Michael responded while gently patting his grandson on the knee. "We have much to discuss and I'd rather do it over breakfast. With the chemo being finished, I've found somewhat surprisingly that I can enjoy food to a degree. Please, follow me."

Michael led his grandson from the room and to the wall at the end of the hallway. He tapped the wood paneling twice at about the height of his right shoulder. To Ryan's surprise, the wall slid away, revealing a hidden elevator. Michael looked at Ryan and grinned. "This house is full of hidden doors, passageways and even surprises. I am the only one who knows where they all are. Not even Jason knows all the house's secrets.

I will show them all to you, but you must not divulge their locations to anyone. After all," he grimaced, "I prefer to keep some things from Jason. While he serves a purpose, I have learned to be very careful with who I trust implicitly. Come on then, grandson, breakfast awaits."

After a hearty breakfast, Michael led Ryan to another hidden door at the back of the house. He walked to the fireplace at the far end of a large den and pulled forward one of the bricks. The fireplace slid silently to the right, revealing a stone staircase that spiraled downwards into the gloom. Michael noticed his grandson's amazement and winked. "If you think that is impressive, wait until you see what's below."

Michael seemed to stand a bit straighter as he confidently walked to the staircase and began descending the smooth stone steps. Ryan followed cautiously, keeping his hands against the wall as they descended into the darkness. Michael pulled a small remote from his pocket, typed in a code, and the fireplace closed up above them, plunging them into total darkness. The only visible thing was the remote that glowed with a faint fluorescent green. Michael then hit another button and the stairway suddenly lit up with fluorescent lights overhead. As they descended, Ryan noticed that the air was noticeably cooler and held a faint dampness. Eventually, they reached the bottom and Michael directed Ryan to the touchpad on the wall. "What we have here," Michael said, "is the ultimate in modern technology. To pass beyond this point, one would need both my palm print and a retinal scan of my left eye. The scanner also does a rapid temperature scan on the palm and eye. This ensures that someone can't kill me and take the hand and eye and try to trick their way through. After today, you will be set up for this as well."

"What's with all the security, Grandfather?"

"Patience, my boy, and all will be revealed." Michael placed his palm against the touchpad and a green light scanned from the bottom of the pad to the top as it read his palm. It beeped once and rose up to reveal a small camera lens behind it. Michael placed his left eye in front of the lens as the light came on and took his retinal scan. After a few seconds this, too, emitted a beep and the wall in front of him pulled back and slid across to the right. Michael stepped through the opening, followed by Ryan. This door also closed behind them and fluorescent white lights came on, bathing the room in a sterile white glow. Michael motioned to two chairs in front of a large console, on which was mounted a large plasma monitor which filled the wall. "Please, have a seat." They each sat down and Michael touched a button on the console. He monitor came to life and was divided into eighteen separate images, each one shrouded in darkness. "Now comes the fun part." He grinned at Ryan, his eyes twinkling. "Below the house is a huge maze, several miles long. Each image represents an area in the labyrinth below the house. Each area is unique and has its own…challenge."

Michael pointed to the screen in the upper right corner. "Please notice what is on this screen," he said as he hit a key on the console. The room on the screen illuminated slightly, and Ryan noted a huge humanoid shape hidden in the shadows.

He jumped up. "What the hell is that thing?"

"Have a seat, Ryan," Michael replied, smiling, "you're perfectly safe here. The answer to your question is a *golem*."

Ryan looked over at his grandfather. "First off, what is a *golem*, and why is it here in your house?"

Michael looked down and sighed. "Both questions require long, complex answers. To reassure you, though, the *golem* is not in the house. Rather, it is in the maze below the house. It cannot gain access here. Maybe I should explain what the creature is and then the reason as to why I created it. The term *golem* comes from the Hebrew word, *gelem*, which means raw material. I first learned about creating the *golem* through the Kabbalistic book called *Sefer Ha Yetzera*, the book of formation. You see, there are a number of elements and steps used to create the *golem*. These include the ritual cleansing and high qualifications of those creating the creature, the use of a specific soil, from which I took clay and earth from the graves of my family, the use of a verbal ritual to form the soil, and a concluding word or Name; all this is used to activate the creature.

"After kneading the clay and the earth from my relatives' freshly dug graves with purified water, the first stage of creation involved forming the limbs of the creature. The limbs included the torso and the head.

Each limb has a corresponding letter, as mentioned in the book of formation, and this letter is combined with every other letter of the Hebrew alphabet to form pairs. Then a more general permutation is done for each limb separately, using each letter with every other letter of the Hebrew alphabet. This is called the '221 gates'. Then, for each limb, you combine each letter of the alphabet with each vowel sound. This completes the first stage, which is the formation of the creature's body. In the second stage, you need to combine each letter of the alphabet with each letter from the Tetragrammaton (YHVH) and pronounce each of the resulting pairs with every possible vowel sound. Now the use of the Tetragrammaton becomes the activation word.

"I decided to take this to the next level. In order to do so, I pronounced the 72-part name of God over it. This became particularly dangerous, as this Name is one of the most powerful Names a Kabbalist might use. It is made out of 72 triads of letters, and is derived from Exodus 14:19 through 14:21, each line of which has 72 letters. To create the first triad, you need to put together the first letter of 14:19, the last letter of 14:20, and the first letter of 14:21. The second triad is composed of the second letter of 14:19, the second to last of 14:20, and the second letter of 14:21. You continue until all 72 triads are complete. The difficult thing was that if the Name was invoked in a state of impurity or uncleanliness, I ran the risk of being struck dead. As a result, I spent years working to cleanse and purify my soul. When I finally created the creature and invoked the name of God, my soul was pure, or so I thought. The problem arose because of the grief which I have carried my whole life. The creature was activated, yet I only had limited control over it. My pain fueled it, making it stronger and more unpredictable than I ever could have anticipated. As I grow older and weaker, it grows stronger, driven by a never-ending rage at the pain that sparked its existence. I fear that when I die, the creature will break free and be unstoppable. That is where you will come in, Ryan."

"You want *me* to stop it?" Ryan asked, his eyes widening.

"No, of course not," Michael replied. "I intend to transfer control of the creature to you. I am too old to stop it…I simply do not have the strength. But you, my boy, you can. The *golem* will be stopped if it completes the task for which it was created. You will need to oversee the completion of this task or we run the risk of the creature getting loose and becoming an unstoppable killing machine in the world."

"But why was it created in the first place?"

"A picture," Michael whispered, "is worth a thousand words..." He pushed some buttons on the console and the screen flickered and changed. The eighteen screens each showed separate images, some black and white, others in color, which faded out to be replaced by new images every few seconds. Even though the images were different, they all conveyed the true horror behind them. Michael explained to Ryan what he was watching and by the time the two men had seen the slide show to the end, Ryan had tears in his eyes and heaviness in his heart he had never experienced before in his life. The horror...all those innocent lives...all those dreams and hopes...dashed...lost. The images consumed him and his family's past hurtled forward to sit center stage with Ryan's present. He looked towards Michael, noting the wetness in the older man's eyes. "What do I have to do?" he asked numbly. He knew at that moment that things would never seem the same again.

"You must complete what I started, Ryan," the old man whispered, the pain evident in his eyes. "You must help the *golem* complete what it was created for. Because this will destroy it and it will allow my soul and those of everyone I have ever loved to finally be free. When I built the creature, I was younger and hungered for vengeance. Age and encroaching death will soften a man's hatred. But what has been set in motion cannot be undone. Stay the course, no matter how difficult it seems, and things will end and the creature will simply cease. Do nothing, and it will unleash an evil on the world unlike anything it has ever seen."

*   *   *

Upstairs, in his private room, Jason lay on his bed still and unmoving. The small device he had slipped into Ryan's pocket was transmitting perfectly. He could hear everything. Satisfied, he sat up and smiled. Things were falling perfectly into place.

CHAPTER 4

Jason Froemmer stood outside the well-maintained ranch house in Modesto, California and adjusted his tie. The sun had just dropped from sight behind the rows of houses and there was a faint pinkish hue to the slowly darkening skyline. *Dusk,* Jason thought as he smiled, *the perfect time to start the hunt.* The family that Jason and Ryan were watching was either sitting for dinner or was just in the process of finishing. He didn't want to dawdle since he had a very busy schedule over the next three days, yet each visit needed to be handled professionally, and the timing needed to be perfect. He had nine families to visit, three a night, spread out over the United States, Canada and South America. Thankfully, there were none in Europe. Those had already been taken care of years ago. He knew that his employer held him in the highest trust, so much so that he allowed Jason to be in charge of the entire acquisition phase of the project. Of course, Jason grinned, his employer would do as he wanted anyway. It was a great relationship, but the old man was nearly gone and Jason needed to consider the future. He looked over at Ryan and wondered if he were made of the same stuff as his grandfather. He bore watching, since Jason had been unable to get a good read on the young man. Jason had played this role before and he understood that Ryan was a crucial component as part of the grand design, and that feigning complicity would be to his advantage. These next three days would give him a better handle on Ryan, and should he not prove to be the right fit, well, accidents were easy enough to stage. Of course, the targets needed to be secured first. Until then, it was to be business as usual.

Jason rang the bell and listened for the approaching footsteps. The door swung open to reveal a pleasant looking woman in her late thirties. She had mid-length brown hair, light brown eyes and an athletic build that was verging on going soft. She wore a simple blouse and a pair of faded jeans. She looked up at Jason, raised an eyebrow and asked, "Yes? Can I help you?"

Jason broke into his most charming smile and extended his hand. "Good evening, Mrs. Martin. Allow me to introduce myself. My name is James Rossi, and I represent a new reality series in production from Fox. We are in the casting phase and were given your family as potential players."

Mrs. Martin looked dubiously at Jason. "How did your network get my family's name? We never signed on to do a series, or any reality show for that matter."

Jason smiled and continued. "Actually, no, you haven't. You see, this series is something different. It's completely unscripted and based on contestants picked out at random. I'd love to explain it in further length, and, of course, you can always decline." He reached into his front breast pocket, extracted a very professional business card and handed it to her. "May I come in?"

Mrs. Martin looked at the card, and then back at Jason, who stood back, establishing an earnest yet non-threatening stance. "Alright, Mr. Rossi, I'm curious. Please come in." She stepped back from the door and beckoned them in. Jason walked into the house, taking in the classic décor and noting the woman's impeccable taste. She walked over to the couch and motioned for Jason to sit on the sofa directly across from her. "So tell me, Mr. Rossi, what does a new reality series have to do with me?"

"I'll be glad to go into the details," Jason replied, "but this involves the whole family. Are your husband and son home?"

"I'll go get them." Mrs. Martin hurried off and returned shortly with her husband, Derek, and son, Carl. Introductions were made all around.

"Mr. Martin," Jason said smiling, "so good to meet you." He shook

Derek Martin's hand and quickly appraised him from the file he had committed to memory only hours earlier. Derek Martin was forty years old, born in Argentina and moved to California to go to school at Stanford, where he got his MBA. There he met Ellen, married, and had a son, Carl in 1985. Derek stood a little over six feet tall, of lean to medium build. His blond hair was beginning to thin and grey around the temples. Nevertheless, he was in excellent physical shape and would be a great challenge for what lay ahead. Jason turned to the son and shook his hand as well. "It's a pleasure to meet you, Carl." Carl had his father's looks and build. From Jason's notes he knew that Carl was heading off to UCLA on a football scholarship in the fall and that he was considered to be a top prospect, with aspirations towards the NFL.

"So what can we do for you, Mr. Rossi?" Derek asked, sitting down.

"Well," Jason began, leaning back slowly to create effect, "Fox is preparing a top-secret reality series for families, and through careful market demographics, your family was selected as one of the families eligible to compete." He paused and let that sink in.

"What is the series about, Mr. Rossi?" Ellen asked. Her curiosity was already piqued.

"The specifics, unfortunately, must remain top secret. But," Jason said, leaning forward, "what I can divulge is that it is somewhat of a treasure hunt. Picture a cross between *The Amazing Race* and *Survivor*. The real kicker is that we've increased the grand prize typically given on most reality shows to $15 million to the winner."

"Fifteen million," Carl shouted, standing up quickly, "where do we sign?"

"Hold on a minute, son," Derek said in a cautionary tone, "we don't know anything about this." He turned to Jason. "Do you have any identification to support who you are?"

"Of course," Jason replied, pulling out his wallet. He had all the necessary documentation prepared well in advance of this visit, and a well-paid former associate who worked at Fox who would corroborate his story. He handed a business card to Derek, identical to the one he had given to Ellen, showed Derek the driver's license he had made to support his identity, and pulled out a formal contract, which he placed on the coffee table.

"I understand that you can't divulge exactly what the show is about, Mr. Rossi," Ellen said with a hint of excitement, "but my question is, while this is rather exciting, can we think things over and get back to you?"

Jason stood up and collected the contract from the coffee table. "I'm truly sorry, Ellen, but I need an answer now. This offer is a one-time-only arrangement. If I don't get your signed contract now, the window of opportunity closes and we choose the next family on the list. What will it be? To further entice you, each family is compensated $2,500 a week while they are still in the game."

"I'm in." Carl stood and moved towards Jason. "Where do I sign?"

"That's great, Carl," Jason replied, "but it has to be an all or nothing deal, meaning it's the whole family or not at all."

Ellen leaned in towards her husband, a flush of eagerness shining in her eyes. "What do you think, Derek?"

"First, of all, Mr. Rossi, how long will we be obligated to participate, should we choose to agree? My wife and I both have our careers to think of and Carl starts school in the fall. And can we withdraw if we are so inclined?"

Jason sat down, leaned back in the chair and clasped his hands behind his head. "It's like this, Derek. The series runs for two months. The winning family gets fifteen million dollars, second place gets one million dollars and third place gets two hundred and fifty thousand. All other families get the monthly stipend I just mentioned. And in answer to your second question, no one leaves the game until they are eliminated. We will arrange everything with your companies, so don't worry about anything. So then, Derek," Jason said with his warmest smile, "what will it be? Are you in?"

Carl looked over at is father, silently pleading with him to agree. Derek looked from his son to his wife, who also sat by quietly, waiting for her husband to make a decision. "I'm sorry, Mr. Rossi. We are really not the kind of people who would just drop everything and run off to do a TV show. But we do appreciate the offer."

"Dad," Carl yelled, "Mom and I want to do this."

Derek turned to his son as Jason turned his back on the family. He pulled a tranquilizer gun from his jacket pocket while the Martins argued.

"Oh yes," he said as he turned around, "there's just one more thing."

"And what's that, Mr. Rossi?" Derek said without taking his focus from his son.

"Say goodnight, Gracie," Jason remarked as he took down both Ellen and Carl in two rapid shots, dropping them both where they stood. Derek's head jerked up as he heard the muffled shots, his eyes widening when he saw the gun in Jason's hand. With sheer instinct behind him, he charged Jason, who calmly fired a single shot, the dart striking Derek squarely in the chest, knocking him out before he even hit the floor. He fell forward onto the coffee table, splitting it down the middle.

Jason pulled his smartphone from his pocket and typed in a few comments to a private journal app. He then called out to the van and signaled to Ryan that all was set. Ryan came in a few minutes later. He froze when he saw the Martins lying unconscious in the living room, Ellen sprawled back in her chair, her head slumped to the side, Carl lying face down on the carpet, and Derek draped over the broken coffee table. Jason looked hard at Ryan, knowing this would be the moment of truth, whether he'd continue with the plan or whether he would become a liability.

After a dazed moment, Ryan turned to Jason and with shallow breath, asked, "So, where do we begin?" Jason smiled. Ryan was falling in line as easily as his grandfather had so many years ago.

After the Martins were placed in the back of the van, carefully secured with black hoods over their heads, their wrists and ankles securely tied, Ryan climbed into the passenger seat and looked over at Jason.

"You did good, kid," Jason said, lightly patting him on the shoulder. "Are you sure you're up to what we have ahead of us?"

Ryan looked over to Jason and shook his head solemnly. "After what grandfather told me and my promise to him, there are no other options. Besides, if I don't do this, the results could be catastrophic."

Jason nodded silently, started the white, nondescript van and headed to the small private airport where their plane was kept, careful to keep within the posted speed limit.

Ryan closed his eyes, hoping to get some rest. It had been a long night and they still had work ahead of them. He felt resigned that what they were doing made sense, yet something was gnawing at the back of his mind. Something felt wrong and whenever he tried to clear his mind and understand the feeling, the feeling slipped away. In his mind, he kept hearing his grandfather telling him that the path they were on needed to reach its conclusion, and the whole time Jason was there behind his grandfather, smiling.

Chapter 5

"We're here," Jason said to Ryan as he pulled the car over to the curb. He had purposely chosen a five-year-old grey Honda Accord to steal because it offered complete anonymity. The task ahead was by far their most difficult, and he wanted to ensure that if it went wrong, they'd be able to get away by blending in. He stopped the engine and looked directly at Ryan. "Our mission today will not be like the others. Today, we do not go in using false identities and a phony story to gain their confidence and catch them off guard. The guy we're looking for today is a real bad seed. He is an active and often vocal member of the Vermont chapter of the most violent group of white supremacists in the country. He has been charged with three separate murders, two young black men and a gay woman. For each charge, he had several people who corroborated his claim that he was elsewhere, and each time he got off with split juries or dropped charges. He is very influential and very smart. Are you following me so far?"

Ryan nodded. He took out his pack of Marlboros and pulled out a cigarette. His hand shook as he lit it.

"Are you sure that you'll be all right? I can't afford to watch your back and do what we came to do. Tell me now, Jason. If you can't handle it, I have to know." Jason put his hand on Ryan's shoulder and looked him straight in the eyes. "This is the last pickup. I saved him for last so I could gauge how well you handle yourself. You've done great so far, kid. I believe that you have what it takes to help me wrap things up here. Once we finish, we'll grab a bite to eat and hit the road. We can be back at the mansion before dawn."

Ryan swallowed once and nodded. "Okay, Jason. Let's do this. How you want to proceed?" He took a long, soothing drag on his cigarette.

Jason pointed to a cottage at the end of the road. It was a very nondescript home, neither upscale nor broken down. The home was set back far from the road, with a long gravel drive leading up to the barn which sat next to the house. A walk branched off from the driveway and led up the house, which was a two-story cottage, rather plain in appearance. It was painted white, but that had clearly been several years back, and now the color was dull and dirty and was beginning to peel in several places. The blinds in all the windows were drawn, making it impossible to tell if there was any activity inside the house. The sky was cloudy, effectively blocking the moon and causing the whole property to appear plunged in darkness. The barn was painted red and the huge double doors at its front were both painted white. Like the house, it was well weathered and worn and also looked to be sealed up tight. Jason pointed to the cameras carefully hidden in the surrounding trees.

"As I was saying," Jason continued, "our target is very smart and very dangerous. His name is Paul Kaufmann, and he has been spreading his vitriolic messages of hate for decades. As you can see by the cameras, our Mr. Kaufmann is also very paranoid. The problem is we do not know if he is alone in there. Every private investigator I've had tailing him has come back with the same thing. He's a loner and prefers to avoid others, even members of his own brotherhood. Now remember, we are only looking for him. Anyone else that we come across must be considered collateral damage and must be eliminated."

Jason pulled a photo from his pocket and handed it to Ryan. "This is Kaufmann. He is thirty-nine years old. His hair is thinning and light brown. He stands about five foot ten, with a thin, wiry frame. He typically wears round, wire frame glasses, plaid shirts and jeans. He also usually has a gun or two on his person and is keenly aware of his surroundings.

Surprising him will be difficult. For that reason, we go in and take him by force. One other thing: he is an avid hunter and is no stranger to firearms. For those reasons, your role is to offer me backup. I will take out Kaufmann and anyone else who may be around. All I ask of you is that you keep a watchful eye as we go in and make sure no one catches us by surprise. You got that, Ryan? I don't want any heroics."

Ryan nodded. Jason handed him a pair of thick glasses, which he put on. They fit snugly over his eyes. "These glasses are state-of-the-art military issue and will allow you to discern heat signatures, so that they cannot sneak up on you in the dark. I will cut the power to the house and then we go in. While Kaufmann is blinded, we take him." He put his gloves on and pulled the black mask over his face. He then donned the heat sensor glasses and turned them on. Ryan followed suit. Jason gave Ryan a gun fitted with a silencer. It looked like a Walther he had once seen in a movie, but he wasn't sure. He made a mental note to ask Jason when they were done. *If we complete this last pickup*, he thought grimly.

Jason crossed over to the first tree and stood directly under the camera. He took a thin tube from his jacket pocket and sprayed a misty black substance over the lens. "It works like a filter," he explained to Ryan in a hushed whisper. "The color of the spray is identical to our outfits. To the viewer, if any, it will appear as a normal dark evening. Our motion will not even be detected." He then proceeded to the other trees on the property and sprayed the remaining four cameras. He then scrambled to the side of the house, moving from tree to tree until he got to the wall. Ryan followed carefully, matching Jason step for step. They worked their way around the wall heading to the back of the house. When they came to the main power line that ran up the corner of the wall, Jason swiftly pulled out a small metal box and placed it over the wire. The light turned green and he grinned at Ryan. "New technology. It will scramble the signal for the alarm without affecting the power. And when I tap my remote, it will shut down all lights in the house, giving us our window to take Kaufmann."

They worked their way around the rear of the house until they came to the back door. There was a screen door on the outside with a heavy oak door on the inside. Jason climbed the three chipped cement steps and took out another tube from his pocket, which he proceeded to spray over the hinges.

"Oil," Jason whispered, "so it won't squeak." Although he could not see Jason's face with the mask and night goggles, Ryan was sure the older man was grinning and thoroughly enjoying watching Ryan squirm. Jason tried the screen door and found it unlocked. He expected this. He swung it open slowly and tried the wooden door behind it. This door was locked, and the deadbolt lock was both new and expensive. Undaunted, Jason removed a small case from his jacket pocket and removed two thin metal rods. He went to work on the lock, and shortly a small click was audible in the still night air. He then pulled out his gun and motioned for Ryan to follow suit. He slowly turned the knob and opened the door into the kitchen. The room was both dark and deserted. Ryan felt his heart hammering in his chest and sweat already building up under his mask. He realized just how scared he was. He was in way over his head and wished he had never laid eyes upon Jason.

The kitchen was old with grimy, stained linoleum floors and worn powder blue laminate countertops. The shelves and cabinets were wooden and were badly in need of being refaced. The sink was a single basin, and in it were dirty dishes piled higher than the rim of the sink itself. The table was old and round with four chairs placed around it. The top was made from dull Formica and looked to be at least thirty years old. The chairs were stained and worn, and had visible tears in the Naugahyde cushions. A full ashtray and nearly a dozen empty beer bottles covered most of the table.

Directly across the room was an open archway that led to the living room and the rest of the house.

Jason motioned for Ryan to follow him as he tiptoed across the kitchen. He crossed the room without a sound, but Ryan was not as silent. The floor creaked as he was midway across and he froze in mid-step. Jason turned and motioned with a raised fist, indicating to Ryan to stay where he was. Turning swiftly, he scanned the living room and the hallway that branched off, and then motioned Ryan forward. Ryan managed to cross the rest of the kitchen in complete silence. He felt the mask absorbing the moisture from his perspiration. He had never been as nervous as he was at this moment, and that included his first encounter with Jason.

Jason entered the living room, motioning for Ryan to stay back. He pointed to a big man who was sound asleep on the living room couch. The man was mid to late twenties, had long dirty blond hair, and a long, ragged beard. He was wearing stained jeans and black t-shirt and Ryan estimated his size as at least six foot four, and well over two hundred and fifty pounds. Jason approached the man, drew out his pistol and fired once directly into the man's forehead. The silencer made only a small *whup* and the man buckled once and lay still. The couch behind his ruined head was covered with a spray of blood, brains and bone shards. Blood welled up into a pool on the seat cushion and began to drip down to the faded carpet below. Ryan was frozen in place as he witnessed how easily and clinically Jason had just killed that man. He could not believe just how black the blood looked in the dark room, and how the man's dead body lost its heat signature through the night goggles as it cooled down to room temperature.

Jason turned and quickly moved from the living room. It led to the front door on the right and just to the left of that were stairs heading to the second floor. The remaining rooms on the ground floor consisted of a small bathroom and a den, both of which were empty. Jason slowly started up the stairs, careful to keep the creaks to a minimum. Ryan followed closely. At the top of the stairs was a landing with four doors branching off a short hall.

The first door to the left of the staircase was partially ajar. Jason gently eased it open and quietly stepped in. Ryan remained on the landing, where he had a good view of the inside of the room and of the other three doors. Jason looked around the darkened room and noticed a dresser to the right of the door and a bed to the left. On the dresser were a wallet, some keys and a small automatic handgun. He noticed a man lying naked on the bed, sleeping above the thin covers. Jason frowned as he saw the large red tattoo of a swastika on the man's left arm. He motioned for Ryan to stay where he was and then advanced to the sleeping figure. He pulled one of the sleeping man's pillows out and placed it over his head. In a fluid motion, he pressed his gun firmly into the pillow and fired two muffled shots, killing the man instantly.

He turned without a sound and joined Ryan on the landing.

Jason motioned for Ryan to stay where he was as he tried the next room. Inside was a small empty bathroom. Jason continued on to the first door on the right of the landing. He paused at the door and put his ear to the wood. He motioned for Ryan to come closer and whispered, "Someone is awake in there. I want you to be ready for trouble. Think you can handle that?" Ryan nodded weakly, the perspiration on his brow sweating through his mask.

Jason gently slid open the door and quickly crept in. The room was of similar layout and furnishings as the first bedroom, except for the occupants. Luck was with them; the lights were out. A couple was having rough sex and seemed totally focused on what they were doing. Jason crept closer, slowly raising his gun. Suddenly, the woman who was under the man's thrusting form noticed Jason and started screaming. The man reacted quickly, turned around and jumped off the woman, who was frantically grabbing the blanket to cover herself. The man moved towards his pants, which were on a small chair by the bed and pulled a gun from the pocket. Jason shot him cleanly through the forehead before the man could even get off a shot. The woman, meanwhile, was shrieking hysterically, loud enough to wake the whole house. Jason fired two shots into her head and she slumped back against the headboard.

Shots came from the hallway and Jason rushed out to see Ryan standing there trembling, holding his smoking gun. Paul Kaufmann lay sprawled on the floor a few feet away. Jason cursed bitterly, rushed over to Kaufmann's side and noticed with relief that the man was still alive. The first shot went clean through the man's shoulder and the other had grazed his skull, effectively knocking him out cold. Jason breathed a sigh of relief, because this was the only one in the house they wanted to keep alive. "Did you check the room yet?" he asked Ryan, who indicated that he hadn't. "Stay with Kaufmann, and I will take a look."

Jason slipped quietly to the doorway and peered into the room. It looked empty. He entered the room and noticed a heat signature coming from the closet. He moved quickly to the closet and while standing aside pulled the door open. Three rapid shots rang out. Jason turned in to the closet and grabbed for the wrist of the woman who had just tried to shoot him. He applied pressure until she let the gun drop. She was thin, late thirties with pale blond hair and ice blue eyes. She was still pretty and must have once been a real head-turner in her younger days, before a hard life had leached her youth away.

"Who are you?" she sobbed. "Please, don't kill me."

"Wrong place, wrong time and wrong company," Jason replied coldly as he shot her in the forehead.

He left the woman's body in the closet and went back to see how Ryan was doing. He noticed that Ryan had bandaged Kaufmann's wounds and had tied him securely by the hands and feet. He felt a small surge of pride at the kid's initiative. "Let's go," he muttered to Ryan, "we have to get out of here before the police arrive." Their guns had silencers, but the supremacists did not, and even in a backward Vermont town like this, someone was bound to hear the shots and call the local police.

Jason grabbed Kaufmann, slung him over his shoulder and hurried down the stairs with Ryan close behind him. As they loaded their captive into the trunk of the Accord, they heard the faint whine of sirens off in the distance. By the time the police arrived at the farmhouse, Jason and Ryan were well on their way back to the mansion in Maine.

CHAPTER 6

Salzburg, Austria, 1971

A cool breeze blew across the Mozartplatz. John Marks and his wife, Greta, had just finished a romantic evening celebrating their thirtieth wedding anniversary at the Café Stadtalm, where they had sat out in the garden, with the stunning view of Salzburg below, after having watched the May Day celebrations in the street. They walked slowly, cherishing the cool night air as they each reflected quietly on the last thirty years. Although it was only May 1st, neither of them felt the cold since the fine bottles of Austrian wine they had consumed with dinner gave them both an extra bit of warmth.

John looked around at the century-old baroque inspired buildings and marveled at the beauty of Salzburg. This was one of the few places where the night's charm was enhanced by the Mönchsberg, lit by candles, adding a gothic charm to their surroundings. He knew he had made the correct decision to come here in 1945, after the war ended, and he knew that Greta felt the same way. There were times he reflected back on the war and the atrocities they had committed to keep with the Führer's final solution, but those days were long past and the victims long dead. Life was for living and John did not wish to reflect too long on past events. He was proud of his role in the SS-Totenkopfverbände, and knew he brought great pride to the Fatherland. Sadly, his two sons, Klaus and Rudolf, were not so inclined, and after many years of heated arguments, both had cut ties with their father, calling him a murderer, ashamed the old man could not feel even the smallest bit of remorse for his wartime acts. They never told John where they went but did speak with Greta and told her they had moved to America and that they wanted their families to grow up free from their father's hatred.

John and Greta walked to their car, still aglow from the enchanted evening. John walked around to Greta's side and unlocked the door on their Mercedes. He swayed slightly from the wine and hoped Greta did not notice. She always scolded him when he drank, especially when he had to drive back to their home near Saalfelden. As he eased himself into the car, sliding gently across the soft leather, his wife looked at him gravely. "John, are you alright to drive?"

"Of course," he replied, trying not to let anger enter his tone and spoil their evening. "I only had a little wine." He gave his wife a reassuring pat on her knee.

John started the car and it roared to life. He always bought the best of everything, a habit he had acquired since the war, when he had become extremely wealthy from pilfering the houses of those he had sent off to the extermination camps. The gold, silver and jewels he had taken were often quite valuable, and he had invested the money from his newfound wealth into real estate. After the war, the value of real estate skyrocketed and John Marks became financially set for life. Greta never asked where the initial money came from to fund such endeavors, nor did he volunteer it.

The drive along the Salzach River was quite calming after they left the city proper and got onto the winding country roads. The roads were quite dark, but John knew them by heart and took the turns faster than he should have, enjoying the feel of the car as it hugged the curves. More than once, Greta asked him to slow down, but John paid her no heed. She didn't drive, never did, and was a very cautious person who hated anything reckless, including speeding. Even after thirty years, she was still uncomfortable being a passenger in a speeding car.

The Marks were only a kilometer or so away from their home, a sprawling three-story house nestled in the foothills of the mountains when Greta saw a figure standing in the middle of the road ahead.

"Look out, John!" she screamed.

John noticed the figure and knew instinctively that he did not have time to stop. At the speed they were driving, he would surely kill the man who stood ahead in the road. Without thinking, he swerved the wheel sharply to the right, just missing the figure, and skidded off the road. As he passed the figure, John only got a quick glance but noticed the man's incredible size and that his features seemed hidden by shadows. The car spun out of control and slammed directly into a tree. Greta was fortunate that she was wearing her seatbelt so that the only injury she sustained was from the spray of shattered glass from the front windshield. John, on the other hand, never wore a belt, and this night was no exception. Upon impact, he shot like a projectile through the front windshield and landed roughly on a patch of grass between two trees.

Barely conscious, John tried to move and found that he couldn't. He had no sensation below his waist, and the pain he felt elsewhere was excruciating. He lifted his hand to his face and winced at the pain that the cuts and scratches of the windshield had inflicted on him.

"John Marks…" a voice called out to him, raw and abrasive, yet ethereal, as if carried on the wind. A thick, frosty mist swirled around the trees.

"Greta?" John called out weakly, his voice barely carrying. He waited and heard nothing. He could not see the car, nor could he move any closer to see if his wife was all right.

"John Marks…" the voice called out, closer, yet still with that dark, detached quality. John heard the words but could not tell where they were coming from. Was it his imagination or were there waves of darkness swirling around him? He felt a chill breeze caress him as the waves swept over his prone form, sending shafts of ice up his spine.

"Who are you?" John cried out as loud as his voice would allow him. "Show yourself."

He emerged from the shadows, as if poured from the inky darkness, a large, manlike being. Its skin was dark and rough and smelled like freshly dug soil. Its features were obscured by the shadows, but John noticed the faintly glowing markings on its arms and legs. It took a moment for him to register the markings as Hebrew.

"What do you want?" John asked faintly as he struggled to stay conscious.

"Retribution," the creature replied, its voice seemingly emanating from everywhere at once. It bent over to pick up John's shivering form, grasping him by the neck. John made gurgling sounds as the creature began crushing his windpipe. It eased John into a sitting position and John attempted to gasp breath into his ruined throat. The creature then pulled each arm from its socket and laid them across his lap. John howled in agony and passed out from the pain. It then placed a rough hand on each side of John's head and pushed together until it felt the skull split and the warm fluid cover its unfeeling hands.

The creature then stood up and walked over to the car, where Greta was trying to free herself from the jammed seatbelt. Hearing the figure approach, she cried "John?" before she looked up and screamed. Her screams did not last long as the creature tore her from the car and deftly ripped her in half. After placing the pieces of her body atop John's ruined remains, the creature walked back into the shadows to its master.

CHAPTER 7

Allen Hart awoke with a splitting headache and a dry, acrid taste in his mouth, as if he were having the mother of all hangovers. His still cloudy memory reached back, trying to remember where he was and what had happened. He felt a stiffness in his body and when he tried to rub some of the numbness from his aching muscles, he found that he couldn't move. Panic seized him and he forced his eyes open so he could get a fix on his surroundings. He couldn't move a muscle below the neck. He saw that he was sitting in a darkened auditorium, bound securely to a chair. By twisting his neck to either side, he could discern other people sitting in similar chairs, also bound securely. No one else appeared to be awake. Just to his right was his wife Judith, who was still unconscious. In the quiet of the room he heard her breathing, heavy and slow, as if she were in a very deep sleep.

Allen forced himself to think. He felt sluggish and groggy and realized that he'd been drugged. From the stiffness in his muscles, he estimated that he hadn't moved for a few days. The last thing he remembered was the man who had claimed to be from Fox talking about a new reality television show. Then the bastard had turned and shot them with some kind of tranquilizer. He remembered thinking as his world went gray how quickly the drug worked.

Allen wondered if this was part of the show. If so, he would sue the network for as much as he could get. In addition to it being illegal to kidnap people (*did I sign a waiver?*), it was potentially very dangerous. Of course, he really had not looked over the fine print of the contract. He grimaced when he thought about how the other lawyers at his firm would have analyzed the contract to death before signing. *I guess I'm not the world's sharpest lawyer*, he thought, and sighed. He knew he should have followed his dreams and become a baseball player, but he had let a girl get inside his head and he had dropped his scholarship for her. When she dumped him less than a year later for being a nobody, none of the schools who were once interested in him had any desire to rekindle their offers. "Non-committal" was what they said, and instead of trying to prove them wrong, he simply acquiesced and gave up on the game entirely. Thankfully, he was blessed with enough intelligence and by hard work had managed to get accepted to a small law school, eventually graduating with honors and passing the Bar with ease. He even managed to get hired by a mid-sized law firm.

Life hadn't been easy, though. He knew his wife put up with his anti-social issues, and as a result, they found themselves with a dwindling group of friends. His work was frustrating as well, and the promotion to partner always seemed just a bit out of reach. He silently wished that he were financially comfortable enough to quit the rat race.

Allen heard a low groan coming from somewhere to his right. He wished he could see, but the restraints were too tight. He noted that the room was so dark that even though he could see his wife asleep beside him, she seemed to melt into the darkness as if she were an intimate part of it. "Hello?" Allen called out to the person waking in the darkness to his right. He got a muffled reply, as if the person were still quite sedated and fighting his way back to consciousness. He cursed silently, realizing that it could be awhile before the person next to him was alert enough to communicate.

Suddenly a bright yellow-white circle appeared directly in front of Allen. The circle expanded out to an elliptical shape and stretched outward, eventually expanding to the full extent of his peripheral vision. Allen squinted, trying to shield his eyes from the bright light. With dawning awareness, he realized he was sitting in front of a giant screen, curved to fill the front half of a room, similar to the ones he'd seen at Omni theatres. From all around him came a low humming. The sound seemed to emanate from the floor, walls and ceiling. The humming grew louder and Allen felt the vibration coursing through his body. The humming increased in intensity until every bone in his body seemed to be in synch to the same rhythmic pulsing. Everything around him was humming and vibrating and Allen screamed as the sound sent waves of pain through his body. The decibels kept rising at a steady state until, abruptly, everything stopped and the only sound that could be heard throughout the room was myriad voices screaming in unison. Soon the screaming died away and the room was silent once again.

On the screen, the image of a young man appeared. His image reached from floor to ceiling and by Allen's best guess was at least fifty feet high. The image had surprising depth, almost as if he were watching a hologram. But holograms were years away, Allen thought, weren't they? The holographic head seemed to stare out over the room, as if the image were an actual person there in the room with them.

"I hope that you all are well rested," the voice boomed, broadcast in surround sound, the tone menacing. "My name is Ryan and as many of you have likely surmised, you were brought here for a purpose. I want to set the record straight before I explain the reason you are all here together. I do not work for Fox, this is not a reality show and you have no choice in whether or not you participate. This is a contest of sorts, and the winner or winners get the most cherished of prizes. But I will get to that shortly. Please keep watching as I tell you a tale of tragedy and sorrow."

Pictures flashed on the screen of a smiling man and a beautiful young woman. All the photos were black and white. Some were a bit out of focus or grainy, but they clearly showed two very happy people. In the background, classical music began to filter through, slowly building in volume and crescendo. *Wagner*, Hart thought, and though the tune was familiar, he couldn't place it. He knew he had unconventional taste in music, preferring rap metal, and though he'd never admit it to his co-workers, he had an extensive collection of CDs in that genre.

"These are my great-grandparents," Ryan said harshly, his voice booming over the entire auditorium. "My great-grandfather was a quiet man who used to box semi-professionally. He eventually retired and became a successful importer and exporter." As Ryan spoke, still photographs of his great-grandfather flashed across the screen, accompanied by the thundering sounds of the classical piece. "My great-grandfather was a kind-hearted soul, well-liked in his community, and completely devoted to his family which he valued above life itself. His wife, my great-grandmother, was not only beautiful, but brilliant as well." The images on the screen switched to that of a fair-haired, smiling woman. As the still photographs flashed across the screen, Ryan continued. "My great-grandmother was a rare personality. She taught physics, a field almost exclusively dominated by men, at the University of Hanover, in Germany." With this, Ryan paused and then went on. "Like my great-grandfather, she loved her family and put them above all else."

The images switched over to still black and white photographs of three children. The eldest daughter was in her late teens and was clearly on her way to becoming a classic beauty. The youngest son resembled his father, fair-haired and solid, and though still young, he appeared to have his father's poise and confidence. The third child had dark hair and pale skin, was in his mid-teens, and always seemed to look away from the camera, clearly uncomfortable with having his picture taken. Allen Hart froze as he noticed the striking resemblance between the brooding youth and Ryan's holographic image.

"My grandfather," Ryan continued, affirming Allen's suspicion, "was the teenager you see before you. He was also the only surviving member of his family." The pictures disappeared and the screen went blank. From the top of the screen, red began streaming down. A single photo of Ryan's grandfather filled the screen, his head angled forward, the spray of blood, brains and bits of skull clearly visible. Behind him was a soldier's arm holding his gun to the back of Ryan's great-grandfather's head. The image was blurred between the muzzle of the gun and the back of his head. "This is how my great-grandfather died. Cut down in the prime of his life by a Nazi's bullet. His only crime was being born Jewish. He got off lucky. He died quickly and did not live to see what was done to his cherished family."

The screen filled with eight photos of Ryan's great-grandmother and great aunt being savagely raped and then murdered by the three soldiers. Although slightly blurred and in black and white, the horror of the scene was clearly apparent.

Allen Hart heard low sobbing and looked over at his wife, tied securely in her chair, her head down, trying to avoid the images before them. "What the hell do you want from us?" Hart screamed at the screen. "What have we done to deserve this?"

Ryan continued. "I'll get to that. Even before they raped and murdered my great-grandmother and great-aunt, they fired through the wall to where my great-uncle was hiding with his camera. They killed him, too. He was just a child, a little boy with his whole life ahead of him, a life that promised laughter, love and promise, yet they gunned him down like a criminal. How do I know this? My grandfather had gone to save his brother and saw him gunned down in cold blood. He took his camera, stayed long enough to take these pictures you see here, and fled the country."

Hart yelled back, "Answer me, damn it, what does this have to do with us?"

The screen went blank and then Ryan's face appeared again and zoomed forward until it seemed to fill the entire room. "Do you really want to know, Hart? Do you?" he shouted back. "Your ancestors were the ones who murdered my family. Every one of you here is either descended from those animals who nearly wiped my gene pool from the face of the Earth, or married to one who is. And," Ryan continued, regaining his composure, "you are the last living descendants of those soldiers. My grandfather spent his whole life tracking down his family's killers, eliminating them and their offspring one by one. Now you are the last."

"So what are we here for then?" a voice asked from the back. "If you were simply going to kill us, we'd be dead by now."

"You are very astute, Mrs. Martin. It's almost a shame you married into the wrong bloodline. Every one of you has my family's blood on their hands. I could easily kill you all. But," Ryan paused, "I will be more humane and offer you all the chance to survive, a luxury that was never afforded to my own family. Beneath this house is a maze. The maze is several square miles in size. There is one way in and one way out. To win the big prize, your very lives, you merely need to reach the end of the maze and leave. But the maze is full of traps, secrets and something else, something so horrible you really don't want to know what it is. So, there you have it. The ultimate in reality competitions, except this is real and those who lose will die. Anyone have any questions?"

"I have one, you miserable prick, why don't you untie me and come down here where I can see you face-to-face?" a rough voice from the back called out.

"Folks," Ryan addressed the crowd, "that was Paul Kaufmann. He is the head of one of the largest chapters of white supremacists in the Northeast. He is a racist killer who has no compunctions about taking human lives, as his ancestors did before him. Kind of makes one proud to be the same species, doesn't it?"

Kaufmann strained against his bonds and cursed up at the screen. "When I get out of this, I will track you down and kill you. It's a fucking shame Hitler never finished what he started."

"Will you shut up!" Derek Martin hissed. "Are you trying to get us all killed?"

"Want to make something of it? I'll break your fucking neck."

"Enough," Ryan bellowed. "You are here together and can work together or work alone. It is your choice. Now pay attention to the floor in front of the seats."

In the ground, a door slid back, exposing a black pit. "Behold, the maze," Ryan exclaimed. "You will have two minutes to enter it. After that, I will pump Zyklon-B gas into the room until there can be no doubt that whoever remains will die a very painful death. For those of you who don't believe me, Zyklon-B was the gas they used to gas prisoners in the showers of concentration camps. It's very deadly and works rather quickly."

The restraints on each seat slid back and across the room people slowly stood up and began rubbing their arms and legs. Paul Kaufmann ran to the walls and began frantically looking for a door. "There must be a goddamn door here somewhere," he cursed. "How the fuck could they get us in here?" As he searched along the walls, a vent opened up and a thick gas began pumping into the room.

"If I were you, I'd pay attention to the gas being pumped into the room and consider entering the maze," Ryan's voice said from speakers overhead. "Stay here and you will succumb to the gas and die. The choice is yours."

"What should we do?" a young, petite blonde woman in her twenties asked aloud. She ran her hand through her long hair. "It doesn't really seem fair, does it? If we refuse to play, we'll choke to death here. If we play along and enter the maze, who knows what horrors may be waiting for us?" She began to weep, her face reddening and her body trembling slightly. "I don't want to die...especially for something I didn't even do. How is that fair?" She covered her face with her hands and turned her back to the others, sobbing. Another woman, shorter and a bit heavyset, with graying hair and thick glasses, walked over to her and put her arms around the crying woman.

"It will be alright," she whispered, calmly and soothingly. "We'll work together and find a way out of this." She smiled, stepped back a pace and placed her hands on the young woman's shoulders. "My name is Suzanne, but all my friends call me Suze."

"Hi, Suze," the woman replied, sniffling, "my name is Kerry. I usually don't break down like this. But I just felt like we were being judged and that we were going to die horribly for the sins of others we never even knew."

"So, Kerry," Suze remarked as she put her arm over Kerry's shoulder, "since time is rapidly running out for us, let's enter the maze and show him that we won't go gentle into that good night." Around her Suze saw the others, all except that Kaufmann character, who was frantically searching for a way out of the room, nod their assent and move towards the yawning abyss that stood before them in the center. She saw that there were no stairs. Rather, the hole was a roughly five-foot circle in diameter that opened up into the inky darkness of the pit.

"How deep do you think it is?" asked a teenage boy Allen Hart assumed to be the son of the man who had told Kaufmann to shut up.

"No idea," Suze replied, "but we are pretty much out of time." With that she walked to the edge of the pit. "See you on the other side," she exclaimed and stepped into the darkness, followed shortly by everyone in the room except for Kaufmann, who frantically clawed at the walls, screaming curses and racial epithets, all the while vowing revenge.

Chapter 8

Paul Kaufmann was starting to have trouble breathing. The gas felt like a blazing fire in his lungs, causing him to cough violently. His sputum was already beginning to contain more than trace amounts of blood. He knew that he didn't have a lot of time left. He traced his fingers quickly over each surface, looking for either a crack or seam in the wall which could indicate an egress from the hell in which he was trapped. Perhaps even the slightest breeze would give away the position of an opening. He was pissed and when he got pissed like this, someone usually ended up dead. What infuriated him even more was the way all the others walked into their situation like so many sheep. Clearly, they were nothing but bleeding heart liberals, and to Paul Kaufmann that made them as low on the humanity scale as the mongrel races themselves.

Fuck them, Kaufmann thought as he coughed again, spraying blood explosively over the floor. *I don't have to work with them, and I certainly don't care if any of them ever sees daylight again.* He staggered over to the pit and fell through, tumbling through the darkness until he landed hard on the cold concrete floor of the maze. He stood up and looked up toward the opening of the pit. It loomed perhaps eight feet above him.

Not too shabby, he thought, *that opening is attainable. A back door, so to speak, if the other way out proves to be unreliable.* Just as Kaufmann was planning his alternate escape route, the opening to the pit slid closed, plunging him into total darkness. "Goddamn motherfucker," he hissed under his breath then coughed wetly. The cold realization that he might have stayed too long above looking for a way out hit him hard. *If I'm already a dead man walking,* he thought, *then I will make damn sure that I take several others out with me.*

Kaufmann heard voices off in the distance and reasoned that the others must have gone off together. He didn't want anything to do with them. To be honest, if they all died in this maze, the world would be a better place for it. But, he reasoned, they could serve a purpose. If the maze was as fraught with dangers as that crazy bastard said it was, it would be wise move to follow the others, let them trip the traps, and then follow through afterward, completely unscathed. He grinned and repressed the urge to laugh. *This,* he thought, *is how the superior Aryan mind works.* With that in mind, he headed off into the darkness towards the voices.

*　　*　　*

Allen Hart looked around at their surroundings. The torches on the walls were easily lit and offered a dimly illuminated view of the maze. Following their rushed entrance through the hole in the floor into the maze, they had fumbled around in the total darkness until Suze had brushed against a torch hanging from the far wall. Thankfully, this young guy, Eric, had a lighter, and was able to easily light the torch. With the first torch lit, they were able to discern three others further down the wall. With four lit torches, they took stock of their surroundings. The maze began where they had dropped down from the house and stretched off down a long, dark, cobweb-filled corridor. The light from the torches cast long, flickering shadows that stretched and reached into the gloom ahead.

"Are we all here?" an older man who introduced himself as Rudolf Marks asked. He stood approximately six foot two inches, with a lean, almost lanky frame. He had closely cut gray hair and wore thin wire-framed glasses. He then introduced his wife, Annie, a sweet, quiet woman who stood at five feet five inches with a slim build and shoulder-length brown hair. Even though she admitted to being the same age as her husband, she easily could have passed for ten years younger. Rudolf then introduced his son, Eric, who nodded casually to the group when introduced. Eric was in his late twenties, tall like his father, but more muscular. He kept his light blond hair shaved to a quarter-inch buzz cut. Allen noted the broad gap in age between the Marks and their son, and thinking like a lawyer, he filed it away at the back of his mind for later retrieval.

"I think so," replied Kerry, "all except for that jerk. What was his name?"

"Kaufmann," Carl Martin added quickly. "Paul Kaufmann. Hopefully the gas got to him up in the house."

"And why is that?" Eric Marks asked, walking over to Carl. Even though Eric had nearly a decade on Carl, Carl had at least fifty pounds of muscle on the smaller Eric.

"Because that racist prick was going to get us all killed," Carl spat, his face reddening.

Eric snorted, "Dude, we're already dead. You just haven't realized it yet."

"Eric," his father snapped as he grabbed his son by the collar, "enough of this. We need to work together if we have any hope of getting out of this in one piece." He looked towards the others, avoiding Carl's gaze. "I'm sorry," he said quietly with his head bowed.

The older woman, who had earlier comforted Kerry, spoke up. "My name is Suze Greenberg. This may seem a bit of irony, but I never even met my genetic parents. I was given up for adoption when I was a child and was taken in and raised by a Jewish family. And unless our friend Ryan upstairs is wrong, I would say that I am likely related to one of you. Sure is one hell of a way to finally meet family."

Kerry came to Suze's side and put a comforting arm around her shoulder. She was an attractive blonde with fine, delicate features, pale blue eyes and a petite, waif-like frame. "I'm Kerry Ramirez. My family grew up in Argentina but after my grandparents died in 1962, my mother took me to the States, remarried and she and her new husband, Hector Ramirez, raised me. My mother passed away suddenly nearly ten years ago in a freak accident. In retrospect, it seems as if there has always been the specter of Death hanging over our family. Now at least I know who and why."

"Same here," Judith Hart added, her eyes welling with tears. "It seems like there was always someone close to us who died suddenly. In this context, it all makes sense." She looked at her husband, Allen, and then at the others. "We are all that's left of the extended families of the three men who murdered Ryan's family. That's it, eleven of us, and that is counting that Kaufmann fellow, and Lord knows if even he's alive."

Allen walked over to his wife and gently wiped the tears from her eyes. "Come on, group," he called out, "we'll never leave this place if we stand here feeling sorry for ourselves. The corridor only goes one way from here. Let's work towards getting out of here in one piece." With that said, Allen began walking down the hallway, closely followed by his wife, brushing aside the spider webs and stirring up a cloud from the thick carpeting of accumulated dust.

The group followed Allen and his wife down the darkened corridor. The light from the torches cast menacing shadows across the cobweb-covered walls and dusty floor. The air was cool and slightly damp, with a musty, earthy odor reminiscent of a crypt. After walking for perhaps fifteen minutes, the corridor took a sharp turn and doubled back in the same direction from which they had just come. They continued down the new corridor, noting that the air got damper and colder.

Derek Martin spoke, looking around. "Is it just me, or are we going downwards, somehow?"

"I think you're right," Rudolf replied, "although the descent is very subtle. It almost seems as if this maze needs to be down deep so it would be below any of the town's water or sewage systems."

"That's assuming we're anywhere near any town, Dad," Eric replied.

The group walked to the end of the corridor that like the previous one ended abruptly and then turned back in the direction it had led.

"Jesus Christ," Eric spat, "how long does this thing keep snaking around?"

"Eric, be patient," Rudolf replied, putting a hand on his son's shoulder. Eric promptly shook it off. "According to that Ryan character, there are miles of maze down here. Let's just try to keep our spirits up and make it out of here in one piece, alright?"

"Asshole. Maybe Ryan wasn't all wrong in trying to wipe our genetic history from the face of the earth."

"Eric," Annie cried out, her face reddening, "you apologize to your father this minute."

"Not a shot. If he's too stupid to be angry at this mess we're stuck in, he deserves all of our contempt." With that, Eric walked to the back of the group and sullenly followed the others. Rudolf, looking deflated, put his arm around the shoulder of his wife, who was quietly crying. The others looked at Eric with disgust, shocked into uncomfortable silence. They continued down the dark, musty corridor for another fifteen minutes before the corridor ended and they came to an old, rotten oak door. Allen grasped the handle and swung open the door, surprised at how easily it opened. The creak of the hinge echoed down the length of the hallway.

"Oh my God," Kerry whispered, her hands up in front of her mouth, "look inside." Everyone stared in stunned silence. "Look at this room, at how it's laid out. It's the sleeping quarters from a concentration camp!"

Chapter 9

Ryan Carson stared at the screen and watched, with growing unease, the prisoners in his maze. No, he corrected himself, his grandfather's maze. At first, hearing his grandfather's tale of how the soldiers had brutally killed and tortured his family enraged Ryan. He remembered the pain and longing in his grandfather's watery eyes but also how his grandfather seemed to have come to grips with the past as well. He played his part for the captives but knew it was only because the alternative was worse. To lose control of the *golem* would be catastrophic. Michael had explained that if the *golem*'s purpose were not satisfied before the death of its master, it would be free to exist and destroy with no one to rein it in. It couldn't be stopped by guns or fire or any conventional weapon. It had a task to do and then it could go back to the soil from which it was created.

He decided that self-preservation had also helped influence his actions. He sensed that his grandfather's assistant, Jason, was clearly a very dangerous man who, if necessary, would not hesitate to kill Ryan if the mood struck him. Jason had an agenda here. He was more than willing to perpetuate this insanity. It was clear that Michael didn't trust him. At some point he surely had but something over the years had broken that trust. He explained all this to Ryan in the days before he sent the two men out to bring back the prisoners. He also performed the ritual to transfer control of the creature to Ryan. He was concerned that his weakness of health and spirit might make the transfer unstable, but there was no other hope. If all went according to plan, the *golem* would complete its final task and Ryan would then perform the ritual to end its existence. The deaths of the prisoners would be a tragedy, but such a small group was better than tens or hundreds of thousands of innocent lives.

Ryan wondered where Jason was at the moment. He was never very far and looked in on Grandfather several times a day. Either way, he always seemed to be watching. Ryan supposed there was a reason he was having these misgivings, even though it all initially seemed to make so much sense. With a sigh, Ryan resigned himself to watch the prisoners, knowing that if things got out of control, he would have to take matters into his own hands, and face whatever consequences arose.

*　*　*

Paul Kaufmann kept to the shadows as he followed the others down the winding corridor of the maze. He saw that there was already in-fighting amongst the group. He also noted that the young man, Eric Marks, was angry and clearly an outlier in their little group. Someone like Eric could potentially become a valuable ally and would bear further scrutiny. The others eventually came to a door and entered and Kaufmann approached silently, remaining outside yet still in the shadows. He was able to discern voices on the other side of the door, and although the words were too muffled to make sense, he could tell that the others were still there. *I'll just wait them out*, thought Kaufmann, as he coughed and spat bloody phlegm to the dusty ground, *and then I'll follow them to my freedom.*

*　*　*

Kerry Ramirez walked around the room, examining the layout. She noticed the rows of bunk style beds, made from rough wood, the tiny areas of shelving for the few items that the camp prisoners would be allowed to have, and not much else. Even the walls and ceiling of the room were made of rotting old wood covered in grime and mold. From the ceiling hung a cracked, bare light bulb that looked about as ancient as the wood used to build the room. There were only the very basic essentials to support life.

The room itself was a perfect square, with doors on each of the four walls. Excluding the door they had just entered through, there were three exits. The wooden doors were flush with the walls. The gap between the walls and doors was negligible and far too narrow to even hope to get anything wedged between to force the doors open. There were no handles on any of the doors, which were made of featureless timbers. The only thing that made them discernible from the walls was the thin frame around each door and that the grain of wood was vertical on the doors and horizontal on the walls. Beside each door was a hole in the wall roughly the size of a large man's fist.

Suze walked over to Kerry, who was looking around the room in fascination. "What makes you so sure that this room represents the sleeping quarters from a concentration camp?"

"I hate to say this, Suze, but this room is either the best damn copy of a concentration camp's sleeping quarters, or it is the actual thing."

"But how do you know?"

Kerry licked her lips and walked over to one of the walls. "I did my Master's thesis on atrocities committed during World War II. I visited the camps open to the public and read every document published on the Nazi use of the death camps. I scanned through thousands of photographs and read more transcripts of conversations with guards and survivors than I can even remember. Do you see this?" she asked, gesturing to a series of scratches on one of the bedposts.

"Yes. What is so important about that?"

"Each scratch," Kerry continued, "represented another day survived in their hellish lives as prisoners in such places as Auschwitz, Buchenwald, Sobibor, and others. From what I can guess, based on the vast wealth and personal investment of our captor, this room was brought here piece by piece and is very likely authentic."

"So what do you make of those holes in the wall, then?" asked Annie.

"To be honest, I don't know. Those look like they were added here, upon the construction of this room."

Judith walked over to Kerry. "Why do you think Ryan's grandfather went to the time and effort to bring this grim reminder of the Holocaust?"

"Perhaps to remind us why we are here," Kerry speculated.

"Or," Derek added, "perhaps to remind us that our future is as hopeless as the former inhabitants of this room. Either way, the sooner we press on, the better. Those holes in the wall must have something to do with opening the doors. I doubt a maze would be created to trap us before we even barely get started." He walked over to the door directly to the left from the one they had entered and stood before the hole, which was midway up the wall and to the right of the door. Derek peered into the hole and turned to the others. "It's too dark to see anything. Let me reach in there instead."

Ellen rushed over and grabbed her husband's arm. "Wait! What the hell do you think you're doing?"

Derek looked at his wife and grinned. "Surely you don't think I was going to put my hand in there without some precaution." He took off his sports coat and put it down on the ground. He placed his foot on one of the sleeves and grasped the coat by the collar. He then pulled until the sleeve ripped off from the body of the coat. Taking the detached sleeve, he placed his hand and arm in up to the elbow. He then folded the sleeve over to give an additional thickness. "Here goes nothing," Derek said to his wife with a grimace as he plunged his arm into the hole. "There's something in here," he shouted, "and it's alive and moving."

"Pull your hand out, Derek!" Ellen yelled, grasping his free arm.

"Hold on, there is a lever in here." Derek reached in a bit further and with a grunt pulled his arm back with an audible click. To his left, the door swung open and outwards a few inches. "Success," Derek said and pulled his arm free of the hole. Clinging to his sleeve were hundreds of insects, grubs, maggots, a few black widow and other venomous spiders and scorpions. Kerry let out a shriek as Derek hurriedly shook off the coat sleeve and began stamping the creatures into a yellowish-green pulp. "Jesus, if I wasn't wearing my coat I would have been bit and stung enough to have killed me several times over."

"We really are playing for keeps here, people," Suze remarked, "so we really should watch our steps from now on very carefully. Clearly the wrong move could be our last."

"Agreed," Rudolf added. "So we have one door of three open. We have options. We could all stick together and take this door to see where it leads, we could open the other two and see what happens or we could split up and take all three, and if one way seems to work, we could backtrack and regroup. This way, we'd cover a lot more ground, and a lot quicker. Remember, Ryan said there are miles of maze down here. Assuming that Ryan was telling the truth, and so far we have no reason to assume that he wasn't, that means that we can expect a huge maze fraught with danger."

"I really don't know about splitting up, Rudolf," Annie said. "Sometimes there is safety in numbers."

"If we don't split up, we may be trapped down here for a very long time. One mile in a straight line is a walk, but one square mile of twisting passages that may lead to dead ends and traps in the dark could take us weeks. We have no food or water. Assuming we survive the traps, we still run the risk of death by starvation or dehydration."

"I agree with Rudolf," Allen added. "As much as it is preferable to stay together, we need to find our way out of here. If we can't return to help the others, we can always escape and bring help back."

"Then let's vote on it," Ellen stated. "All for staying together, raise your hand." Annie, Derek, Ellen and Kerry raised their hands, while Carl, Suze, Allen, Judith, Rudolf and Eric kept theirs down and looked around at the others. "Alright, the votes have it. The majority feels that we should split up, so I guess we will. Who wants to get the next door?"

"This is bullshit," Eric growled, "are you people clueless? This is the basis of every horror film ever made. People split up and people die. Maybe you all don't care about living, but I sure as hell do."

"Eric," Rudolf snapped. Eric looked away and went to sit on a bunk across the room.

"I'll get it," Carl replied. He walked over to where his father's coat lay on the floor. He shook off the last few insect carcasses and wrapped the coat around his arm. He then walked to the door to the immediate right of the one his father had opened. Directly to the right of the door, at the height of where the door handle should be, was another hole in the wall. Without another thought, he plunged his hand into the hole. "I got it," Carl exclaimed as the door popped open a few inches. And then he screamed. He pulled his arm out, and attached to it were four tiny snakes. "I got bit," he screamed, "get them off me."

Derek ran over and helped his son free his arm from the coat. Then he and Rudolf stomped on the snakes, crushing their skulls. Carl's wrist and lower forearm were swelling and beginning to redden.

"Who's got a knife?" Ellen yelled, looking around wildly.

"I do," Eric replied, holding up a Swiss army knife.

Ellen grabbed the knife from his outstretched hand and yelled to the others to stay back. She rushed over to her son, who was sitting down, hunched over.

"I can't breathe, Ma." Carl whispered, his eyes welling with tears. "It's getting harder to breathe."

Ellen took the knife and kneeled by her son. "Eric, I need your lighter as well." Eric handed Ellen the lighter and she set the knife blade over the flame for a few minutes. "Derek, some help here." She rubbed her son's forehead. "This will hurt, Carl, but we have no choice. Derek, when I make the cut, I need you to suck the venom out as hard and as fast as you can. Got it?"

Derek nodded as Ellen cut a deep "x" in Carl's lower arm. Carl howled in pain. She then cut another "x" in his wrist.

"Now, goddamn it!" she screamed at Derek. Then they both began to suck out the venom and spit it on the ground. After fifteen minutes of sucking and spitting, Ellen spat once more and said to Derek, "I think we got it, at least enough to save his life. The rest will be up to Carl as his system fights it." She looked down at her son, who was a little gray and shivering. "How do you feel, son?"

"A bit better, Mom. It still hurts to breathe and it hurts like shit, but it's not getting any worse. But I feel so cold."

"That is the toxin we weren't able to get to that is now in your bloodstream. We got most of it, so hopefully, this discomfort will pass.

Another few minutes and it would have been too late. Right now, I need you to rest. Derek, help me get him over to one of the cots." Derek helped Ellen move Carl to a cot and lie down. Rudolf offered his jacket as a blanket.

Suze came over to Ellen. "That was amazing. Where did you learn to do that?"

"Before I met Derek, I did a six-month residency in Africa. We had more than our share of snakebites. Of course, we had actual medical equipment there and somewhat sterile conditions. Right now, though, that seems very long ago and very far away. These days, my medical work is mostly tending to sick children in my pediatric practice. How about you, Suze? What do you do for a living?"

"Nothing as glamorous as medicine," Suze replied, smiling. "I teach literature at a small community college. But I like to think that what I do matters to some people and that in some way I enrich the lives I get to touch."

"Of course it does, Suze," Ellen added. "Some of my professors have had tremendous impact on my life. I'm going to see if I can make Carl more comfortable. Think you can convince one of the others to try door number three?"

"I'll go one better, Ellen, I'll take care of the door myself. Now that I know that we have a doctor in our little group, I feel a hell of a lot more confidant that we'll all get out of this mess in one piece."

"Hey, Suze," Derek called out, tossing his jacket over to her. "Catch. It's been though insects and spiders and snakes. One more use can't hurt."

Suze grinned. "Thanks. I'll try to return it in one piece." She wrapped her arm in the sleeve and then doubled up by using the side. She winked at Kerry, who was watching her intently. "No use taking any chances." She closed her eyes and plunged her hand deep into the hole of the third door. "It's alright. It's just water."

"Just hurry, okay?" Kerry pleaded.

Suze reached around and pulled the lever, which opened the door a few inches. She pulled her arm free of the hole and looked down at the coat, which was smoking and dissolving before her eyes.

"Drop the coat, Suze," Ellen screamed, "it's acid!"

Suze dropped the coat and began wiping her arm on the dusty ground.

"I don't think any got through to my skin. Thank God I doubled up the coat. If I hadn't, I'm sure that there would be considerable damage to my hand and arm right now." She looked over to the Martins, who were sitting with their son on the cot. "How is Carl doing?"

"A little better, Suze," Ellen said, forcing a smile. "He should be ready to move in a few hours. If others want to head out now, we'll stay behind with Carl and catch up."

Annie walked over to Ellen and put a reassuring hand on her shoulder. "Hopefully I speak for all of us when I say that we could all use some time to rest and regroup, and that we can decide when and where we go when we are all ready."

Kerry came over and sat down next to Carl. She took a Kleenex from her pocket and began wiping his brow. She looked over to Ellen and Derek. "Why don't you guys get some rest? I'm too stressed to sleep. I'll watch Carl for a few hours."

"Much appreciated, Kerry," Derek replied, "It's been a long day so far, and Lord knows what we have in store for us. But no matter what is thrown at us, we will get through it if we work together." He paused. "All of us."

Kerry nodded, and as much as she hoped that Derek was right, she felt the worst was still ahead of them.

CHAPTER 10

In a darkened hidden alcove deep in the bowels of the maze, the *golem* stood unmoving, waiting for the signal which would set it free from its invisible bonds, free to carry out its orders and silence the white noise which had burned in its skull since it was given its directives.

Suddenly a jolt of agony rushed through the *golem*'s body, like a surge of electricity. The runes inscribed on its body began to glow faintly and pulsed with a rhythmic regularity. The creature opened its eyes and with great effort began stretching out muscles that had been dormant for years. It extended each arm, slowly rotating it. It took a tentative step, and then another, and slowly made its way across the floor towards the doorway.

It felt the presence of others, others who had to be destroyed by virtue of blood passed down from the three who were part of the original directives. These were the last of the families of the original three. Of that, the creature was certain. In the dim recesses of its mind, there existed a basal sentience, driven largely by need for survival. And the creature knew, although it had no basis to substantiate this knowledge that, once these last few were destroyed, its pain would subside and it would no longer be bound to its creator; it could return to dreamless sleep. Freedom was closer than it had ever been, and the freedom from pain was what drove it on.

It sensed that the others were in its domain, and although they were not all together, they were slowly making their way towards the hidden lair. As if it were a moth drawn to a distant flame, the *golem* slowly began walking. Each step was slow and arduous, and the creature focused its full attention on the task. After nearly an hour, it had barely moved fifteen feet, but it inched forward to its destiny. With each step, the task of walking became a little bit easier. Time had no meaning to the creature. It did not age, nor decay. Its memories began with its creation and would survive until its destruction, and whether the time between was a decade or a millennium, made no difference. The creature was an ancient primal force, bound by the name of God to its creator. Of course, it sensed a change in the control of the Creator. Something similar, yet different, and the pull to perform its designated task was not as strong, and this enraged the creature because if it could not complete what it was created to do, the blinding pain in its skull would grow until nothing remained but primal rage. It had limited sentience and awareness, but virtually no sense of the self. It could think, but only within the strict limitations of its original instructions. It had no ability for independent thought. The *golem* felt only primal emotions like anger or sadness. It existed for one purpose, and one purpose alone, and that was to destroy every living relative of the original three until their very gene pool was wiped clean. It sensed that its mission was drawing to a close, and thus it moved forward in its single-minded purpose towards the unsuspecting descendants, one slow step at a time.

CHAPTER 11

Boca Raton, Florida

Jeremy Balducci closed his smart phone and cursed. This was the fifth time in the last three days that he had tried to reach Kerry and had gotten her voice mail. It wasn't like her to simply disappear without letting anyone know where she was going. It was bad enough that she had stood him up on Saturday evening for their dinner date, but when he tried to reach her at home, he got her answering machine, and when he called her work he got a cryptic message from a coworker in her department that she had not shown up either Monday or Tuesday. Even worse, she did not respond to any of his calls or texts to her cell. He even checked to see if she had any recent activity on Facebook and found none. No, he thought, something was not right.

Jeremy had a bad feeling about this. He knew that his relationship with Kerry was ending, and to be honest, the dinner date she had missed on Saturday was almost certainly the one where she would dump him. However, never in the three years that he had known her had she acted so irresponsibly as to simply disappear without telling a soul. He knew that she had no family, and being such a private person had very few friends. If she were to simply vanish, there would not be many people to notice. Of course, Jeremy did not fall in that category. He was quite simply head over heels in love with Kerry. He had tried everything in his power to make her love him back, but the chemistry simply wasn't there, and he was beginning to think that they would never truly progress beyond being very good friends.

Jeremy knew that he wasn't the most dynamic man in Boca Raton. He was a professor of forensic psychology at a small local college. His last published paper had been years ago and it seemed as if he was destined for nothing more than teaching. At thirty-five, his best years were likely behind him. He was, quite simply, average. In a crowd, he always managed to blend in. In fact, he was so average that he was often mistaken for other people. He had few friends, and he had realized several years back that he would never have what would be considered a thriving social life. When he met Kerry, it seemed to bring out something extra in him, to make him want to be a better man.

One of the things Jeremy admired most about Kerry was her organizational skill. She had such brains and skills that, had she so desired, she could have been a head of industry, tops in any chosen profession. Instead she chose to teach world history and within eight years had risen to become chair of the history department. She had two books published and a third was under review with her publisher. Jeremy always knew she would have impact wherever she chose to be, and in the three years he had known her, he still found himself in awe of her uncanny ability to assess and resolve any conflict she encountered.

Jeremy decided that if Kerry were fine, she would have called him by now. It just wasn't her style to simply cut him off. The fact that she had not shown up at work for two days made him believe she was in some kind of trouble.

He drove over to her apartment and using his set of keys checked her mailbox. Her mail clearly hadn't been picked up in days. Not since Saturday. He ran up the stairs to her third-floor apartment and let himself in. Her cat, Socrates, ran towards him, mewling loudly as it curled about Jeremy's legs.

The cat is starving, Jeremy thought. *Kerry would never do this willingly. She loves that cat more than life itself.* He walked into her galley kitchen, opened two tins of Fancy Feast and scooped them into the cat's dish. The large grey Siamese ran over and began hungrily eating. Jeremy refilled its water dish and looked around the apartment. Everything appeared as it should be. There were plates in the sink, clearly left there for days. The air in the apartment seemed somewhat stale, as if the place had not used for a few days. The air conditioning was off and there was a damp heat to the air. Jeremy knew that Kerry hated to sweat and normally kept the place as cold as a meat locker. It wasn't like her to keep the air conditioning off long enough to let her apartment get so warm.

Jeremy walked into the bedroom and looked around. The bed was made, and all clothes were neatly put away. A copy of Del Toro and Hogan's *The Strain* lay bookmarked on her nightstand next to the bed. Jeremy knew that Kerry was reading that book the last time he'd seen her over a week ago, and that she never took more than a few days to finish any book.

He went to the bathroom and noticed that the shower was dry inside, as was the soap in the small ceramic dish by the sink.

Jeremy was about to give up when it hit him: the video recorder. Kerry taped her apartment using an x-10 mini-camera that sent the signal to her video recorder. She did this for two purposes. The first was to ensure that Socrates was fine during the day. The second was that ever since she had been robbed she wanted a visual record should it ever happen again. Jeremy turned on the television and rewound the eight-hour tape in the VCR. The first hour showed Kerry puttering about the living room, going back and forth between the kitchen, bedroom and living room a few times, before finally settling down on the living room couch with a cup of tea in front of the television. Socrates spent most of that time asleep curled up on her lap.

Midway through the tape, the doorbell rang. Kerry looked up at her watch and frowned. From the look on her face, she clearly wasn't expecting anyone. She got up and went to the door.

"Who's there?" she called out, looking through her peephole. The camera angle showed only her right side because the camera was positioned to show the doorway leading into the living room, with the kitchen and bedrooms being off to the back of the camera.

"Ms. Ramirez," the voice replied, muffled by the door, "I represent a new reality series from Fox television. You were chosen at random to be considered for the series. May we come in?"

"Do you have identification?"

"We do, Ms. Ramirez. Let me hold it up to the peephole."

Kerry leaned forward and squinted through the keyhole. She then stepped back, unlocked the door and swung it open. A man walked in and with his back to the camera shook Kerry's hand. "Pleased to meet you, Ms. Ramirez," the man said, "I'm James Rossi. Can we sit? I have a wonderful and exciting offer to tell you about."

Kerry gestured towards the living room. "Please, come in. Can I get you anything to drink, Mr. Rossi?"

"No, but thank you for offering." The man walked into the living room and sat down on the couch nearest to the door. His back was kept to the camera. From what Jeremy could see, the man had a lean and wiry frame, evidence of someone who kept to a strict daily exercise regimen. His hair was dark brown, cut a bit short, and appeared to be thinning at the back. Jeremy whispered to himself, hoping the man would turn around and reveal his face. "So tell me about the show, Mr. Rossi, and how does it involve me?" Kerry asked. Jeremy put his hand to the screen and traced the outline of her hair with his fingers.

"Well," the man continued, "we at Fox have designed the ultimate reality challenge, part treasure hunt, part survivalist game. We bring people to a secret locale and put them through a rigorous challenge, with the winner receiving a fifteen-million-dollar prize."

"What more can you tell me about the show?"

Mr. Rossi replied with a low chuckle, "That is part of the fun, Ms. Ramirez, because there is nothing more I can tell you. You see, we sign our contestants with the challenge unseen. All I can say is it won't be a picnic. But then again, for fifteen million, what would you expect?"

Kerry frowned. She bit her lower lip. *Don't do it*, Jeremy thought. Whenever Kerry bit her lower lip, she was uncomfortable. "It all sounds so intriguing, Mr. Rossi," Kerry replied with a sigh, "but I'm afraid I will have to pass. I am happy enough with my life the way it is and the lure for fifteen minutes of fame on a reality series just doesn't do it for me." She stood up and walked towards the door. "I appreciate the offer, Mr. Rossi. I wish you all the best with your show."

Jeremy watched as Mr. Rossi stood and walked to the door, again keeping his back to the camera. "Ms. Ramirez," he began, "you must have misunderstood me. I didn't ask if you would do the show." He slowly withdrew a tranquilizer gun from his pocket and aimed it at Kerry. "You have already been chosen," he finished as he fired a shot at Kerry, the dart striking her squarely in the chest. She took a step forward and then collapsed into his arms. He threw her over his shoulder and calmly left her apartment.

Jeremy was dumbfounded! Kerry had been abducted right there in front of him by a man who could hardly be recognized. The man never showed his face, had an average voice with no discernible accent or dialect and did not reveal who he was, except for the name he gave, Rossi. Jeremy deduced that the whole storyline about being from Fox was a ruse to gain access to Kerry's house. So, other than a partially glimpsed image and a voice on tape, there were virtually no clues as to who her abductor was. Thankfully, Jeremy knew someone who could possibly help him.

He realized that he should take the tape to the police. Of course, if he did, the investigation could drag on for months and Kerry could be dead by then. Besides, he realized that if he could somehow save Kerry himself, he'd be a hero in her eyes and that might rekindle a spark in their relationship. *Rekindle, my ass*, he thought. *If I can save her, she will certainly be indebted to me forever.* Jeremy grinned. He knew this wouldn't be easy, but he had faith in himself and his abilities. He grabbed the tape and headed for the door. At the door, he turned and went back for Socrates. *Mustn't forget the cat*, he thought. This was going to turn out just right.

CHAPTER 12

After a short rest, Derek Martin climbed off the wooden bunk, stretched and rubbed his stiff and aching back. He realized what strength the concentration camp prisoners must have needed, what sheer intestinal fortitude, to have been able to endure such miserable living conditions on minimal food rations with the fear of death hanging over them constantly with hope all but gone, yet were still expected to put in long days of forced labor. He swore to himself that if they made it out of this nightmare in one piece, he would do some form of reparation for the pain and suffering caused by his ancestors. He walked over to his wife, who was sitting by their son, gently wiping his brow.

"How is he?" Derek asked, trying hard to keep his voice from cracking.

Ellen motioned for her husband to step away from the cot. He followed, concerned by her expression. Derek looked at her inquisitively, the questions posed silently. Ellen forced a weak smile. All these years of marriage and they were truly open books to each other. She cleared her throat and finally found the words. "He's running a high fever. The small amounts of toxin in his system are apparently having a much more adverse reaction than I initially thought. I believe he can be treated, but only if we get him some proper medical attention. Realistically, we need to be very concerned, since the longer he stays down here in these cold, damp tunnels, the smaller the likelihood he will recover.

His youth and strength are helping to fight this, but even that can last so long."

Derek held his wife in his arms for a moment then, with grim determination, he stated, "Well then, what more do we need? Do we need an engraved invitation? We have three doors here and it's time we try to find our way out." He turned to the group. All were awake and looking as despondent as he felt. "Can I have your attention, please?" The others turned to look at him. "As you know, we have three doors available to us. Each one will lead us into the maze and to whatever dangers lie ahead. That madman Ryan who sent us into this maze said there were miles of tunnels down here. Our best bet for survival is to split up. I propose the following groups, and if anyone has any concerns, please speak up. Group one will be comprised of my wife Ellen, our son Carl and myself. We will take the first door we tried, the one with the insects in the hole. Group two will be Kerry, Suze and Eric, who will take the second door, the one with the snakes. And finally, group three will be Allen, Judith, Rudolf and Annie, and they will take the door with the acid. How does that sound?"

"Does Eric have to go with Kerry and Suze?" Annie asked. "Shouldn't he be with his family?"

"Actually, Annie, I thought of the division of groups for quite a while. If we keep Eric with you, we would likely need to have Allen and Judith with Suze and Kerry. By splitting up this way, we can have a better buddy system with the younger couple being available to help both you and Rudolf, if needed."

"Hold on a minute!" Rudolf bellowed. "We may be in our sixties, but we're sure as hell not helpless. I'd like to see you in twenty years, Derek. I'd wager you wouldn't be anywhere near the shape I'm in."

"Nor did I say you were," Derek replied, raising his hands in front of him in a calming gesture. "All I meant was that Suze and Kerry are two women and that a male presence might be needed, especially if that Kaufmann fellow decides to show his face. Allen and Judith would complement you and Annie that much better, that's all. Also, to your claim of how I'd look in twenty years, well, let's hope we all have twenty days. "

"Dad, don't worry. It's fine," Eric added, glancing over at Kerry. "I'd be glad to go along to protect Kerry."

Kerry grimaced and muttered under her breath, "Lucky us."

"All right then," Derek said, "let's do this." He turned to Ellen. "Is Carl ready to travel?"

Carl stood up and trembled somewhat as his legs regained their balance. He looked a little gray and had a thin sheen of sweat on his brow and neck. "Let's go, Dad. I can manage. I just want to go home."

And without another word, the Martins walked out through the door and into the dimly lit corridor beyond. The others watched them go, the light from their torch getting fainter and fainter as they moved further away. Eventually, they turned a corner and were completely out of sight.

Suze looked at Kerry. "Are you ready for this?"

Kerry swallowed hard and forced herself not to appear as scared as she felt. "I know we have no choice in the matter, Suze, but I can't help feeling like the worst is truly yet to come. I never thought that I'd be so scared of death but the fact is, I'm actually terrified and only the thought of maybe getting out of this hell is what will keep me moving on."

Eric walked over to Kerry, his hands loosely in his jeans pocket. "Don't worry, Kerry, I'll make sure that nothing happens to you while I'm around."

Kerry was about to offer her protests when Suze faced her, rolled her eyes and added, "Then let's go, team, and find our way out." With that, they walked out through the middle door.

"I guess that leaves just us," Judith remarked. "There really isn't anything left to say. We don't know what's out there, but as long as we stick together, we'll get through this. Come on, folks. First round is on me when we leave this place."

Shortly after the three groups left, the doors silently closed.

*　　*　　*

Paul Kaufmann snapped awake. The taste in his mouth was bitter and coppery, and he felt somewhat lightheaded. He looked at his watch but was unable to discern the time in the darkness around him. He cursed and carefully made his way down the fifty yards of corridor separating his hiding spot from the room the others were in. He put his ear to the door and listened closely. He did not hear voices or even any activity indicating that anyone was moving about. Of course, he reasoned, they might all be asleep. He was torn between going into the room immediately and risk being seen by the others or waiting a little longer. Waiting bore a new risk as it meant potentially losing the group and forcing him to fend entirely for himself.

He bent over and coughed violently, expelling viscous spittle on the dusty stone floor. His mouth tasted of blood and phlegm and although Kaufmann was no physician, he realized that the gas he had inhaled was messing with his lungs and slowly killing him. He needed a doctor or he'd be as good as dead. *Fuck those bleeding heart liberals*, he thought. *I'll kill them all if I have to.* He swung open the door and entered the room, ready for anything or anyone. Through the darkness, Kaufmann was able to discern what appeared to be bunk beds. He cautiously walked over and ran his fingertips over the wood. It was rough and cool, and slightly damp. He looked around the room and did not see any anyone.

The question, of course, was how long ago they had left. He felt along the bunk beds until he came to a wall. He continued to feel along the wall until he discovered a door. *They must have gone here*, he reasoned as he looked for the handle. After a short, tactile search, he realized there was no handle on the door. He ran his fingers over the door again, tracing its outline and feeling a cool breeze from beyond. He tried grasping at the door's edge but found that it wouldn't budge. He cursed and slammed his fist into the wood. *There has to be a damn handle*, he thought. The others had found it. No way in Hell could a bunch of bleeding heart liberals outthink a pure white American like himself.

He began running his hands around the outer edge of the door. Eventually, he felt a hole in the wood, roughly the height of where a handle would be. Kaufmann peered into the hole but saw nothing but inky blackness. He reasoned that there must be a lever or a latch and that if the others got out, so could he. He plunged his hand deep into the hole and screamed…

Chapter 13

Kerry, taking the lead, followed closely by Eric, with Suze in the rear, inched down the darkened hallway. The torch she carried emitted a small, orange-yellow circle of illumination, just enough to see a few feet in front and back of the group. The ceiling was high enough above them but revealed nothing save the inky gloom beyond their circle of flickering light. All along the walls and floor there was a faint luminescence, alternating between absolute darkness to barely manageable gloom.

After walking for what seemed like a good half hour they came to a three-way intersection. One corridor lay directly ahead of them, with the other two branching off to either side. From the point where all four corridors met, neither looked any more promising than the other.

Suze looked over at Kerry. "Do you have any thoughts?"

"Not really." Kerry shrugged and replied anxiously. "One pathway is just as likely to kill us as the next."

"So, if you had to pick, which one would you choose?"

"Does anyone want to hear what I think?" interjected Eric.

Suze looked at Kerry, winked and then turned back to Eric. "Sure, Eric, what do you think?"

"Since each one looks the same from here, I vote we go straight ahead. This maze is supposedly huge, right? I've always believed that the shortest distance between two points is a straight line. Besides, if we go straight, we are moving away from where we were. A turn either way seems to indicate that we move back towards where we started." Eric looked at Kerry, then Suze. "So what do you guys think?"

Kerry nodded and patted Eric on the back. "Good thinking. Works for me, bud. Come on, Suze, the road ahead awaits us."

Kerry led the way, and again Eric and Suze followed. After they crossed over into the corridor, a wall dropped down from the ceiling with a loud scraping sound, effectively blocking their way back.

"What the fuck!" Eric cursed as he whirled about. He ran back and began pushing the wall that sealed off the corridor. He felt along the edges, getting more frantic by the minute. "This isn't a door," he wailed, "this is a fucking wall. We are being herded along to our deaths. Don't you see? There is no free will. We're being led to a predetermined end."

"Eric, please just relax," Suze said calmly as she walked over to the young man. "We chose to come this way. Maybe it was a bad choice, maybe not. Either way, we need to keep our wits about us if we want to survive."

"Whatever, lady. As far as I'm concerned, we're already as good as toast. They're playing us like rats in a maze that doesn't end."

Kerry was about to interject, to suggest that they keep moving, when she heard it. A low sound, like a whisper, carried on the wind. "Do you guys hear that?"

Eric moved over to one of the walls, got down on his knees and put his ear to the wall. "It sounds like running water."

Suze, meanwhile, had gone to the wall across from the one where Eric was kneeling. She reached along the lower portion of the wall and then abruptly drew her hand back. "There's water coming out of a hole in the lower third of this wall. The hole is the size of a dinner plate. Guys, I think we need to get moving and fast!"

"Come on, Suze, there is no way that water could fill up this entire corridor."

"Eric, we don't know how far this corridor runs, or even if there are other places where the water is pouring out."

Kerry put her hand to the ground and noticed it becoming damp.

"Suze is right. I feel moisture on the ground. We need to move on. I think if we stay here much longer, we may find ourselves out of options."

The trio continued down the hallway, which went another ten yards and then veered sharply to the left, coming to an abrupt stop. Water was pouring out through several openings in the wall. The water was dank and stagnant and had a pungent stench that assailed their senses. Eric reached into one of the water streams and quickly withdrew it. He slowly brought his hand to his nose. Rubbing his fingers together, he grimaced. "This water seems to be lukewarm and it's kind of greasy. If I had to guess, this is sewer water pouring in on us."

Suze walked over to Eric, dipped a finger gingerly into the flowing water, and brought it to her nose. "I agree with Eric. This water smells of sewage. I'm sure it is filthy and unfit for human consumption. Frankly, it wouldn't surprise me if it was similar to water given to prisoners in the concentration camps. It might even contain human waste. Whatever you do, don't drink any of it."

"Thanks for the history lesson, Suze," Eric growled, "will there be a test later?" He paused. "Anyone have any ideas as to how we can get out of this?"

Kerry shone the torch at the back wall, trying to find some detail in the gloom. Through the flickering light, they were able to discern at least six holes in the wall, separated at equidistant points from each other, from which the filthy water poured. Beyond the holes, the wall was devoid of any other marking.

"This is the main source of the water," Kerry noted, "and it appears to be coming through as fast as physics will allow. This area will begin filling up fast. If we don't find a way out of this mess, and soon, we'll drown like rats. So come on, people, let's find that way out."

Eric stood leaning against the far wall, his arms across his chest. "Have you ever considered that there is no way out?" He spit a huge ball of phlegm and watched with mild amusement as it broke up on the inch-deep water. "Maybe we sprang a trap and we're already dead, but are just too dense to know it."

"I won't buy that," Suze cursed, "and as long as there is some air to breathe, I'm going to keep trying. Let's start at the beginning where we came in and search every square inch of these walls. We found the levers in the bunk room to open the doors. Something along those lines must be here, too. Are you with me, Kerry?" Kerry nodded and began walking down the corridor through the rapidly rising water to the point where they had first come in. "How about you, Eric?"

"I suppose," he replied sullenly. "Better to at least try than to just give up."

The three began scanning the wall that had closed in behind them. Eric held the torch and Suze and Kerry got down on their knees and felt around the wall, looking for a hidden lever or latch, or anything that would give them a way out.

They finished the first wall, then moved to the right, and began working on the next wall. The water kept rising, and by the time they had finished examining the second wall, it was up to their waists. The search was getting slower as the light from the torch did not illuminate the wall below the level of the greasy, murky water. Also, searching along the bottom of the wall involved holding one's breath and keeping the eyes open underwater. Within minutes, both Kerry and Suze needed to stop and rest, to catch their breath and to ease the burning in their eyes. Eric volunteered to take the next shift under the water and Kerry held the torch to give him what light was available. During this time, Suze searched the wall above the water line. By the time they had finished examining the corridor, the water level was up to Suze's chin, Kerry's collarbone, and Eric's armpits.

"You realize," Suze gasped, raising her chin somewhat to avoid getting a mouthful of water, "that at the rate this filthy water is pouring in here, we maybe have an hour before the water level reaches the ceiling. What's worse is within thirty minutes or even less, we'll all be treading water. Frankly, this doesn't look too good."

Eric looked over at Kerry, who stood there despondently. Her wet hair hung down in clumps, her eye shadow smudged around her eyes like a raccoon, and he couldn't help notice her stunning beauty which shone through, even in the worst moments. He realized that he'd never get a chance with her, and that they'd die here horribly. He gritted his teeth and vowed to keep fighting until he breathed his last. "Kerry, I have an idea. Can you swim over here with that light?" Eric swam to the back wall, where there were the six openings. The openings were all underwater but were still pumping in the stagnant water, rippling and swirling.

"Eric," Kerry gasped, "I'm standing on my tiptoes right now. There are maybe two to three feet between the water level and the ceiling. I need to keep this torch raised or we'll lose our light. The problem is I can't tread for much longer without using my arms. Suze has already started treading water. It's now or never, Eric. I figure I've got ten minutes worth of energy to hold the torch before I'll need what's left of my strength just to try to keep my head above water. Now or never. So go, goddamn it."

Eric dove under the water and opened his eyes. The filthy water stung his eyes instantly. He swam over to the wall and felt along the surface until he found one of the holes. He stuck his hand in the hole and felt along the rim. It felt smooth to the touch. He thrust his arm all the way in and found a lever in the back. Before he could pull it, he found he was in desperate need of air. He swam to the surface and took huge gulps of air.

"Any luck?" Kerry asked.

"I think so," Eric gasped, breathing in deeply. "I found a pulley of some kind in the back of one of the holes, but I ran out of air before I could pull it."

"Maybe it stops the water. Better yet, maybe it drains it out. But check the other holes, just in case. I'm sorry, but I can't hold this torch much longer."

Eric looked at Kerry, then up at the ceiling, which was less than a foot above the water level. And the last thing he saw before everything went black was the torch falling from her shaking hand into the filthy water's welcoming embrace.

CHAPTER 14

Allen Hart led the way down the corridor with his wife Judith by his side. Behind them, following closely, were Annie and Rudolf. The elder Marks couple held hands and walked slowly, almost hesitantly, as if each step were planned and analyzed. On several occasions, Allen and Judith had to either greatly reduce their pace or come to a full stop to ensure the Marks stayed within the circle of light emitted by the torch.

The air had cooled considerably, dropping to the frigid and chilly levels of a New England winter. The air was still and quite dry and stung the exposed faces of the foursome. The walls had changed from a gray, dusty stone to that of rotting wood rising to within a foot of the ceiling. The last foot between the wood and ceiling was barbed wire, wrapped in an odd, circular pattern. Where the walls had changed over to wood was right about the place the temperature had begun falling.

The couples had been walking for nearly two hours since they separated from the others. Through a series of twists and turns as they worked their way through the complexities of the maze, they all knew that if they tried to retrace their steps, they would be lost. The sound of low, guttural moans off in the distance caused them all to stop dead in their tracks. The sound carried through the twisting passageways and seemed to be coming from nowhere and everywhere at the same time.

Eventually, the passageway came to a door. The group gathered and considered their options.

"Here's how I see it," Allen remarked, "we can continue through the door that closes off this passageway, or we can backtrack about a mile or so to the last intersection and try another route."

"Really, Allen," Rudolf interjected, "as far as I can see, you're being a bit premature. So far this has not posed a threat beyond it being something new."

Annie stood there, looking flustered. "Remember the last time we had doors to deal with? There were traps on each door, and after we passed through, they closed behind us and we couldn't reopen them."

Rudolf went over to his wife, put an arm around her waist and gently stroked her hair. "That may be so, but we've seen that sometimes we need to face the worst if we expect to move on."

"I agree," Judith added, "because it seems that we are being guided through this maze and that while it appears as if there are numerous options, it feels more like a video game with a linear path. I doubt there is any free will in what we actually do. I believe that if we took another passageway, we'd only have to go through another test of our wills and that wherever we chose to go, we'd likely end up at the same place. In fact, I also believe that we will meet up with the others at some point later down the road."

"You may be right, honey." Allen turned to Rudolf and Annie. "So what's the verdict? Do we try the door or do we retrace our steps?"

"I'd rather we went back and tried another route," Annie said quietly, as if she knew her choice would not be a popular one.

"Annie," Rudolf replied, "do you really want to go back a good mile to try another passage? How could we be sure the choice we reject here isn't safer than something we may find on another route? I hate to disagree with you, dear, but I'd rather continue on the path we've chosen."

Annie looked imploringly at her husband, then at Allen and Judith. "Is that how you all feel?" Seeing the others nod their agreement, she walked up to the door with the others. "Fine, let's do this. Call me paranoid, but I have a bad feeling about this."

Allen checked the door. It was an ordinary wooden door, roughly four by seven feet. The wood on the door and frame was of the same material as the wood on the walls, and in the same state of decay. The handle was a rusted wrought iron and was chill to the touch. Allen gripped the handle and slowly opened the door. The group peered through the open doorway and saw another corridor.

"After all the worry," Judith noted, "it seems as if it was for nothing."

"Just don't get too confident here, honey," Allen cautioned as he walked to her side. "Our host is not going to make this easy for us to survive. We cannot drop our guard for even a minute." He put his hands loosely over his wife's shoulders and gave her a gentle, reassuring squeeze.

Allen led the way through the door, followed by Judith, Rudolf and Annie. Their torch cast warm, flickering light on the moldy wood. Their footsteps on the cold wood floor echoed and amplified in the narrow passageway. By the time they were fifty feet or so into the corridor, they heard a noise behind them.

"Stay here," Rudolf barked to the others and he turned and headed back down the passage. He came to the door that had led them to this corridor and noticed it was shut tight. Furthermore, he saw that on this side of the door there wasn't a handle or anything else they could use to reopen the door. He probed the wood and frame around the door, frantically searching for a way to open the door from this side. Frustrated, he returned to the group with the news.

"Well?" Annie asked as her husband rejoined the group.

"We have to move on," Rudolf replied grimly. "The door we came through is closed and cannot be opened from this side."

"I knew it." Judith stood with her arms akimbo. "We are being led to a predetermined destination. We should have never split up from the others. There is strength in numbers."

"Then that's what we'll do when we all meet up again. We'll stay together and face whatever is thrown at us as a group."

"*If* we meet up with the others, Annie," Rudolf added. "I think things will get a lot worse before they get better. Come on, then. Let's keep moving."

They walked on, moving slowly as the wooden passageway narrowed to the point where they were forced into walking in a single file. The temperature kept dropping until it was easily below freezing. They had to keep stopping to warm their hands over the flame of the torch. The mist from their breath seemed to hover before dissipating in the still air.

After another half hour of walking, the passageway opened up into a room, roughly fifteen by fifteen feet. Shackled against the walls on both sides were corpses that were little more than skeletons with tattered bits of decayed flesh hanging from the yellowed bones. Each corpse was clothed in the rotting remnants of a concentration camp prison uniform with a number lightly visible on the breast pocket. The shackles holding them up by their wrists and ankles were covered in a wet, greenish slime that was slowly pooling beneath each of the corpses. The floor was covered in a thick mat of dust that was crisscrossed with track marks. Across the room, located in the center of the far wall, was a passageway that led off into the distance. On either side of the passageway were piles of corpses, stacked at least four feet high with complete and partial bodies. These corpses were also clothed in the same rotting uniforms. The floor was covered with bones and various body parts in different stages of decay. The smell hit them at once, of rot and decay, causing them all to gag. Judith leaned over and forcefully vomited.

"Jesus Christ!" Allen muttered, his hand over his mouth, trying to reduce the stench, "this place smells like a slaughterhouse! We're dealing with a madman here! I suggest we move on, and quickly."

"Agreed," Annie added. The group hastily began walking from the room when a rustling noise came from one of the piles of corpses. They all froze in their tracks as a skeletal arm reached up from one of the piles and flexed its bony fingers. The arm was mostly bone, with gray decayed flesh loosely attached to it. They watched in horror as the rest of the corpse raised itself from the pile, bits of grayish flesh dropping from its frame. It extricated itself from the pile of bones, climbed down with surprising agility, and stood there in front of the group, effectively blocking their path. It glared at them, one eye yellowed and rheumy, the other an empty socket. Its visage was locked in a grinning rictus, as most of the flesh was missing from its mouth and from the right side of its face, showing the exposed hollow of its cheek. Through the remnants of the clothing, the grayish remains of flesh and tissue were seen clinging to the cracked yellow bones. It crunched its neck from side to side, the snap loud and sharp in the still cold air. Slowly it began to shamble forward, its grin widening.

Judith screamed and began to back up, trying to put distance between and the horror advancing on the group.

"It's not real, Judith," Allen yelled. "It can't be. It must be a machine of some kind. Either way, I'll distract it, and you three run like hell for the passageway."

"I'll stay and help," Rudolf offered. "You shouldn't have to handle this by yourself. Besides, the two of us stand a better chance of putting that thing down than just you alone." Allen was about to resist but realized that they didn't have time, especially when he noticed another corpse rising from the pile on the other side of the room. "Move it, ladies. Time to get going! Now!"

Allen positioned himself in front of one of the corpses, and Rudolf in front of the other, allowing room for Annie and Judith to pass through and get out of the room. The first corpse shambled over to Allen and with surprising speed swung its arm, raking its nails across Allen's cheek, creating five shallow furrows that welled up with blood. Allen howled in pain and stepped back. The corpse brought its fingers to its mouth and licked the blood from the razor-sharp nails with a long, black tongue that snaked out past the chipped, decayed mouth. It then advanced toward Allen, who was backed up against the wall.

The corpse nearest to Rudolf shambled over slowly and then lunged at him with unexpected speed, to which Rudolf responded by dropping to the ground and twisting away, causing the corpse to get in front of him. Rudolf rushed over to the corpse and kicked it in the lower left leg. He howled in pain from the jarring impact. The corpse fell forward and Rudolf took advantage of the situation. He stomped down on the creature's neck, severing the skull from the body. The thing stopped moving almost instantly. Rudolf ran over to help Allen, who was backed up against the wall as the corpse moved in for the kill.

Just as Rudolf was set to give the creature a kick and try to knock it over, it whirled around with blinding speed and thrust its fist hard into Rudolph's chest. It pulled its arm back with Rudolf's still-beating heart clutched tightly in its bony fingers. Steam rose from the freshly harvested organ and the blood pumped out in two short arcs before slowly stopping. Rudolf looked at it in shocked surprise, opened his mouth as if to say something then crumpled noiselessly to the ground. Almost at the same time, Allen grabbed the corpse's head in his hands and screamed his rage as he pulled it free from the body. The creature dropped, Rudolf's heart still clutched in its fist, and then was still.

Allen barely had time to register his shock at the loss of someone he'd already grown to care about and respect, when he noticed more corpses rising from the piles. Knowing full well that he couldn't fight several of these animated corpses at once and hope to survive, he turned and ran down the passageway towards where Annie and Judith would be waiting. The situation was beyond bad. The nightmare was just beginning!

Behind Allen, the corpses massed and began to follow, malevolence gleaming on their dead faces. The blood of the living was out there, and theirs for the taking.

CHAPTER 15

Stuttgart, Germany, 1980

Hans Krieger grinned, exposing yellowed teeth. He exhaled sharply, blowing thick cigarette smoke across the table into the face of the wiry American. The American coughed and looked down at his cards. He scratched a finger to the tip of his prominent nose and went back to studying his cards. Krieger recognized the man's tell and eagerly dropped some more money into the pot at the center of the table. The other three placed their cards down and folded. Krieger knew the men well. They often played cards here at the back of his club and could be counted on for their discretion. This American, on the other hand, was new, brought by Bernhardt as someone looking for a high-stakes game.

Krieger had lived most of his life by his wits. Following the war, with no discernible skills to speak of, he had turned to what he was best at… crime. Years of petty larceny, prostitution, drugs and murder followed and eventually, Krieger found himself one of the most feared men in Germany. Time had hardly mellowed him, and if anything had made him harder and meaner. He had developed his innate sense of self-preservation and had learned how to keep an eye out for trouble. He let his pale, watery eyes fall on the American and studied him intently. He felt that something was not right with the man but couldn't make rational sense of this feeling. He considered the fact that Bernhardt vouched for the man, and Bernhardt had been a regular for years. Still, instinct finally won, and Krieger decided to wrap up the game a bit early tonight.

He threw his last bet and called for the American to show his cards. The American threw down three jacks and looked up expectantly as Krieger put down the full house he held in his hand. The American's mouth went wide with surprise. Clearly he had expected to win and was speechless as Krieger drew the money towards himself. Then, without warning, the American stood up and pulled a gun on Krieger.

"You cheated, you fucking Kraut piece of shit," the American cursed, spittle flying from his thin lips. "Now just give me my money back and I won't spread your brains across the wall behind you. Better yet, I'll take your money as well."

The American reached across the table for the money, eyes focused on Krieger when Nicholas, one of the other players, casually walked behind him and put a bullet through the back of the American's skull. The man's forehead exploded outward, spraying the card table with skull, blood and clumps of brain matter. He then turned to Bernhardt, the small pistol still clutched tightly in his hand.

"I had no idea he'd pull this," Bernhardt stammered, "honest."

Nicholas glanced over at Krieger, who nodded briefly, then turned to Bernhardt and shot him through the heart. Bernhardt coughed and dropped to his knees, then fell face down onto the floor, his blood pooling around him.

Krieger went over to the American and riffled through his pockets. Pulling out the man's billfold, he examined the contents. The wallet was packed with more money than the normal poker player usually carried. He had an ID card from Interpol, identifying him as Simon Snelling. His other cards confirmed this, including an address in Surrey, UK.

"The fucker wasn't even American," Krieger muttered, "and if this was a sting, why did he lose it at the end?"

"You got me, Hans," Nicholas replied. "Maybe he was a dirty agent and was out for himself." He looked over at Heinrich, who was sitting quietly in the corner. "What about him?"

Krieger walked over to Heinrich and put his hands on the young man's shoulders. "We don't have any problem here, do we, Heinrich? After all these years that we've known each other, I can expect your discretion, right?"

Heinrich nodded and whispered, "Hans, you've known me for years. You can trust me with anything."

Krieger paused and then broke out in a huge grin. He patted Heinrich lightly on the cheek. "I know I can, Heinrich. You're way too bright a guy to try to fuck with me." He turned to Nicholas. "Get one of the girls to give Heinrich the night of his life, as my thanks for his silence." Nicholas left the back room and went out to the front bar. Loud, blaring music Krieger recognized as Zeppelin's "Black Dog" emerged from the nightclub and filled the back room. Minutes later, Nicholas re-emerged with a tall, buxom blonde, dressed provocatively in a sheer baby doll nightie.

"Anna," Krieger said authoritatively to the beautiful young woman, "please bring Heinrich upstairs and show him a good time." He took the bills from Snelling's wallet and handed them to Anna. Her eyes widened in surprise as she glanced at the small fortune in her hands and then back to Krieger and then at the two bodies lying prone on the floor. She then turned back again to Krieger.

She stuffed the bills in her bra and took Heinrich by the hand. "I will be happy to, Herr Krieger. It will be my pleasure." With that she led Heinrich from the room.

Nicholas watched her go and then turned to Krieger. "How come you let her see the bodies?"

"Because," Krieger grinned, "she would never betray me. She's been working for me for over a decade, ever since I found her living on the streets as a teenager. She owes me her life and she knows that what I give, I can take away. Now, please take care of the mess in here. I've had a long night and I want to go home."

Krieger left the bar and wandered into the darkened streets. The roads were narrow in this part of town and poorly lit. It had just rained and the cobblestone streets glistened with moisture. Krieger had a flat not far from the club. He owned a larger home in Heidelberg as well, but he liked being in the heart of the city. It made him feel alive and close to the action.

As he turned the corner of his street, the wind whipped the night air, blowing leaves around his ankles. A figure stepped out of the alley just ahead of him, his features well-hidden by the shadows. Krieger noted that the man was inhumanly tall and stood easily at eight feet, with a broad frame.

"Hans..." came the voice, dry and leathery, as if carried on the wind.

Krieger stopped. The figure stayed hidden in the shadows. Something on its person seemed to glow, ever so faintly. "Who are you?"

"Hans...Krieger," the voice called to him commandingly.

Krieger's mind worked at a furious pace. He wondered if this was part of the sting that prick Snelling might have orchestrated. He rationalized that any attempt to arrest him for one of the many crimes he had committed over his life would not be done in such as clandestine manner. Using that logic, he decided that the man up ahead was not law enforcement. Whether he was friend or foe though was still undecided. His gut told him that being here, alone on a darkened street with this man, was a very bad idea.

The figure began walking towards him, keeping to the shadows. The wind whipped around Krieger in a rising crescendo of howls and moans.

Fuck this, Krieger thought. *I'm going back to the club, but I'll be damned if I run.* He turned and began walking briskly back to the nightclub, a mere four blocks away. Walking quickly, Krieger heard the footsteps behind him, clearly closing the distance between them. He knew that he'd never make it to the club, so he turned and ran. He arrived at the back entrance, tried the door and found it locked. He cursed himself for being so paranoid that he had installed a solid steel door that automatically locked when closed. He fumbled in his pockets for his keys, which fell to the ground as he pulled them from his pocket. He didn't even get a chance to reach down for them when a set of powerful hands grabbed him around the throat and lifted him a good foot off the ground. The figure smelled of freshly tilled earth and although he was right in front of Krieger, his victim had a hard time making out his features. The swirling mists seemed to envelop the stranger, whose body had glowing characters written on it. Krieger tried to get a better look but could not move his head enough to see what they were.

The creature lifted him higher and Krieger felt his windpipe being slowly crushed under the strength of its grip. He looked into its eyes and noticed that though they had a slight glow to them, they were blank and unstaring, as if they had been placed on the head for sake of appearance, rather than function.

"What do you want?" Krieger croaked, struggling to breathe.

"Retribution..." the creature rasped and then, with one fluid movement, slammed Krieger into the steel door with such force that he was driven clean through to his waist. Krieger's ruined form lay half in the door and half out, his front half slumped forward, dripping blood onto the tiles of the back room. The *golem* grabbed Krieger by the legs and pulled him back out into the street. It tore off his limbs and spread his entrails out before his torso. It then hooked two thick digits into his eye sockets and pushed forward until the eyes burst over its fingers. The *golem* took one final look at Hans Krieger's mangled corpse and then turned and walked off into the darkness.

CHAPTER 16

Derek kept his arm around his son's shoulders as they walked down the dark, musty corridor. His wife Ellen, walked by their side, casting nervous glances at their son. She did note that Carl was showing some improvement from the poisoning and that his strength was returning, but she wouldn't be satisfied until she got him to a proper doctor. Chalk it up to the resilience of youth, she decided. The color was slowly returning to his face, and Ellen suspected that proper rest, food and medical attention were what he needed at a minimum, and in order to get that they needed to escape from this maze and get help. She whispered a silent prayer to God to protect them in their time of need and to give them all strength. She knew that they were good, honest people and that she was sure that her goodness and faith would see them through this nightmare.

Ellen looked ahead as they slowly walked in silence. The passageway was now more like a tunnel, the walls becoming rounded and the surfaces of the floor, walls and ceiling composed of hard-packed dirt. She wondered about where they were being held. Were they even in the United States? She assumed that they must be, because it would have been a lot more difficult getting all the people with whom they were trapped out of the country without detection. Of course, even if they were in the States, who knew how far from civilization they were and whether they would die from exposure to cold if they escaped? Ellen shivered when she realized that their fate was looking grim and that they would likely die here in this maze, a mystery to family, friends and coworkers.

Derek looked over at his wife and saw her wipe a tear from her eyes. He didn't have to ask to know what she was thinking. Twenty years of marriage, through good times and bad, and he knew her better than she often knew herself. He silently swore to himself that he would get his family out of this and that if anything happened to any of them, there would be hell to pay.

They kept walking, with Carl leaning heavily on his father for support. More than once, Carl would trip and sprawl forward, ending face down in the damp earth. Derek knew that his son needed rest, but he also knew that down in this damp, cold dungeon, his son's condition would surely only worsen. They urgently needed to get him medical attention. He was quite proud of how his son was handling things through sheer will and determination. In fact, Carl had not even uttered a single word of complaint the entire time.

Soon they came to the end of the tunnel, where the walls widened out and two new tunnels branched off. One went down a well-lit stone passageway that turned sharply to the left after about fifty feet while the other stretched out and expanded into a cave-like chamber. There were wooden stools surrounding a small, wooden table. On top of the table was a series of covered dishes. Derek's hope arose somewhat, praying that their captors had at least seen fit to feed them. They chose the path into the small cave and headed towards the table. He helped Carl over to a stool and let his son lean on him as he sat down. When Carl hit the seat, the stool sank down into the ground and a loud rumbling filled the air.

"Dad," Carl asked apprehensively, "what was that?"

"I don't know. Just be prepared to move if we have to."

"There," Ellen noted, pointing to the tunnel from which they had just emerged, "look."

The three of them stared as the roof of the tunnel came crashing down, tons of dirt and rocks closing off the mouth, effectively sealing them in the small cave.

"Oh my God!" Ellen cried. "What will we do now? How will we get out?"

Derek looked around the cave. The farthest points were obscured in shadows. No noticeable way out was evident. "There has to be another way out. Surely we didn't walk all this way for nothing. Carl, you rest up, and your mother and I will search this cave. If there is a way out, we'll find it."

"Dad," Carl called out, "let's at least see what's under these dishes. Some food would be a huge plus at this point. The way I feel, if it isn't moving, I'll eat it. And perhaps even if it is."

"Sure, Carl," Derek replied, "but let me lift the covers off, okay. And please, both of you step back." Both Carl and Ellen slowly backed away from the table as Derek lifted the cover of the first dish. On the plate were several bricks of different cheeses, piled quite high. Each subsequent plate held the same thing, brick after brick of cheese. Some were moldy but others looked as if they might actually be edible. He called his wife and son over. "What do you think?"

Ellen looked over the cheese. She wrinkled her nose and looked back at Derek. "Most of it has gone bad, but if we cut away the edges, there may be something salvageable in the middle."

Ellen began cutting away at the cheese, using her nails as a makeshift knife. She scraped away nearly two thirds of the first brick and stopped. She looked it over and tossed it to her husband. "This looks fine."

Derek grimaced and took a bite. "Well, it tastes fine too. Glad to be the guinea pig for the rest of us." He tossed the brick to Carl, who took a bite as well. Carl then brought the brick to his mother, who gladly accepted. She took a bite then paused.

"Do you hear that?" she asked.

"What is it, honey?" Derek replied.

"I hear a scratching noise," Ellen replied, pointing to the far side of the cave.

"I hear it, too," Carl added.

The scratching grew louder, followed by another sound that sent a chill up Derek's spine. "Shit," he cursed, grabbing one of the tarnished silver plate covers. He tossed it to his wife. "Here, take this." He turned and grabbed another plate cover and deftly tossed it to his son before grabbing one himself.

"What is it, Dad?" Carl asked, sensing his father's fear.

"That," Derek replied, pointing to the back of the cave, as a wave of the largest rats he had ever seen came running towards them. They were the size of medium cats, easily twenty pounds each. Their fur was gray-ish-black and they had long, pointed snouts boasting sharp, yellowed teeth. Derek estimated that there must be close to a hundred of them, and by the way they ran at them, they surely were on the attack.

"Derek!" Ellen screamed. "What should we do?"

"Use the plate covers as both shield and weapon. Slide your hand through the grip on the top and keep it fastened securely. When the rats get close, swing as hard as you can and crush the little bastards. Keep do-ing it until they're all dead."

"There are too many of them, Derek," Ellen yelled, "we'll never get them all."

"Mom's right, Dad," Carl added.

"I know," Derek added hastily, "but we don't have to get them all. All we need to do is clear a path to the hole the rats came from. Look closely. The tide of rats seems to have slowed down. That must mean that they are all here with us." Derek grunted as he swung hard and sent a huge rat slamming into a side wall with a wet, slapping sound.

"I get it, Dad," Carl added as he swung back and forth, crushing two of the rats with his powerful swings. "If the rats came through the hole, there must be a way out through there as well."

Ellen swung fiercely and knocked two rats down off her legs. A third rat bit her sharply on her calf. She screamed in agony and smacked the tray cover into the rat, crushing it into her thigh. It fell back in a bloody pulp, its blood mingling with hers, running down her leg.

Carl moved ahead of his mother, swinging fiercely back and forth, and sent the chattering creatures flying. The howls of the rats as they died merged with the screams of the Martins as they fought for their lives. They forged ahead, in back to back formation, crossing the room slowly, getting multiple bites in the process and laying waste to scores of the deadly creatures. The blood of the disposed rats splattered over them and blended with their own blood, which flowed profusely from the many bites and lacerations they had endured. More than once, they had to pause to wipe the blood from their eyes.

"Dad," Carl cried out, "I don't think I've got anything left. There's just too many of them." He grunted and swung again at two more rats, sending them flying in a spray of blood and fur.

"Come on, Carl," Ellen yelled back, "we're almost there. We need to stick together. I will not allow any of my family to not make it out of this hellhole."

"You heard your mother," Derek shouted to his son. "You can't quit, do you understand? Now let's kick some ass. We've taken out more than three quarters of these filthy creatures. We can do this. The hole in the wall is within reach. Don't let me down."

With a grunt of determination, Carl put his head down and tore through the wave of rats with renewed vigor. For every three they killed, at least one got through and bit, scratched or tore at their exposed flesh. Finally, close to an hour later, they stood by the hole in the wall, the crushed and battered corpses of rats piled high on both sides.

"Well," Derek said, his breath rising and falling rapidly, as exhaustion took over, "let's go and get the hell out of here." He leaned forward and crawled into the hole. He turned and called back to his family, "It runs for a while and then it appears to open up a ways ahead. Follow me, guys."

Derek crawled forward, followed by Carl and then his wife, limping through the twisted tunnel until they finally emerged into a cavernous room. The room glowed faintly with light green phosphorescence from the lichen that lined the walls. Throughout the chamber were large mounds of moldy earth, each one being slightly obscured by shadows.

"What the hell are those things?" Carl asked.

"Not sure, son," Derek replied as he ventured closer to the nearest mound. He raised his hand to his mouth, trying to filter the indescribable smell that emanated from the earthy pile. When he was nearly at the mound, he noticed it begin to tremble, barely noticeable at first, and then with renewed vigor as it appeared to come to life. It began to edge towards him slowly, almost hesitantly, and then emitted a roar which echoed across the cavern. As it emerged from the shadows, Derek felt his bowels loosen as he saw the largest rat he'd ever seen in his life. It stood nearly three feet high and was over six feet long, with eyes that blazed a ferocious red in the dim light. Its teeth were long, yellowed daggers which glistened with fetid saliva. It roared once more and then advanced upon the Martins.

CHAPTER 17

Paul Kaufmann pulled his hand back from the hole and stared at his ruined flesh. His skin smoked as the acid ate away at the tissue beneath. Though the pain was intense, he threw his head back and roared with laughter. He knew that the way things were going, he'd be dead long before he found the others. Here he was, a leader of the Northeast Chapter of the Aryan Nation, and he was doomed to die alone in the dark in a maze below the earth like the vermin he had sworn to eradicate.

Kaufmann peeled off a strip from his shirt and wiped down the skin of his hand, or, more precisely, what was left of it. He could see wisps of smoke still rising from patches of his ruined flesh. In some places the skin was merely red, in others the flesh was dissolved down to the bone. He was barely able to move his hand, let alone flex his fingers.

Kaufmann cursed, coughed a bright red globule of phlegm to the ground and then sat down on one of the bunks. He realized that the others had all made it out. Therefore, they had done one of three things. They either all went down one passageway together, which was a stupid option, since, although there was strength in numbers, it cut their chances of escape by a third. The second option was better since it meant they had split up in two larger enough groups for safety, thus having two routes covered. He coughed again and shook his head. These liberals were way too smart not to cover all their options. If he were them, he'd opt to split into three groups and increase their chances of escape. Whoever found their way out would then be able to send help back for the others. He grinned and then spit some bloody sputum to the dusty floor. Of course, he realized, there was always the possibility even if they truly did get out of the maze that their captors could be waiting for them, making this entire ordeal pointless. That's what he would do if the situation were reversed, he thought, give them a glimmer of hope, then tear it away and crush their spirits before he crushed their lives.

Assuming that the others chose the smart option, it meant that, no matter which route he chose, he'd run into some of them. Not like he had any preference. They were all a bunch of bleeding-heart liberals who would rather breed with members of a mongrel race than keep a pure society. So, he mused, whoever he caught up with would feel every ounce of the pain this ordeal has caused him, and then they would pay a steep price indeed: their very lives.

He took off his shirt and wrapped it around his other hand. He knew one of the holes led to a powerful acid. The other two were unknown quantities. The question was, continue with the one that he knew contained acid, or try for something that could be better. Kaufmann was always one to seek the best odds and quickly decided to try his luck with another door. He doubted any would be worse than the acid. He decided to risk the door to the left of the one that had led into the room. Making sure his shirt was tightly wrapped around his good hand, he plunged it into the hole.

Kaufmann felt things moving around his hand, but the shirt seemed to offer him enough protection. He eventually found the lever and pulled, causing the door to open, exposing the corridor beyond.

Bingo, Kaufmann thought, *party time*. He pulled his hand free from the hole and saw the writhing mass of roaches, millipedes and even a scorpion and back widow spider attached to his shirt. He quickly threw the shirt to the ground and stomped at it until everything was mashed to a thick, yellowish paste. Grinning, he put the shirt back on, oblivious to the sticky mess. He spit a thick crimson glob to the ground and walked through the door.

Kaufmann had walked maybe a dozen steps down the corridor when he doubled over and began coughing violently. He spat up a spray of blood and mucus and couldn't stop hacking for ten minutes. When it was over, he fell to his knees, his eyes tearing up and his limbs shaking. He knew that the gas had damaged him even more severely than he initially imagined. Thoughts of revenge seemed trivial compared to his imminent death. Making it out of this maze and getting to a hospital was his only hope, and no matter how bleak the odds, he knew he would have to try. He didn't want to die like this. He had way too much to do. His dream of cleansing America would never happen unless he guided the masses with his philosophy. As Kaufmann was ruminating on his chances for survival, the door closed behind him with a resounding thump. Kaufmann looked up and noticed there were no handles or levers on this side. He had only one direction to follow, so follow it he would, and when he found the liberal fools he would use them to escape this underground tomb and help him get to a doctor. But revenge would be coming. Of that, Kaufmann was certain.

He got to his feet and began walking as quickly as he could. The light from the torch made flickering shadows on the walls. After a while, the concrete walls became rougher, and noticeably rounder and more dirt-like. Eventually, it was like walking in a large dirt-packed wormhole. The rich smell of earth made Kaufmann think of a freshly dug grave, a smell he was quite familiar with. He knew he had done his share of ridding the world of blacks and Hispanics who made the mistake of passing through his neck of the woods, but the smell of the grave never failed to give him chills. Kaufmann knew he was on the right path because he saw footprints on the ground indicating that a few people had recently come this way.

Kaufmann kept walking until the tunnel came to an abrupt halt. The way through was blocked by debris. The footprints led right to the wall.

"Shit," Kaufmann cursed, "I don't fucking believe it."

He bent down, planted the torch in the ground, and began digging with his good hand. Someone had come through here, of that he was certain, and there was no way back. Therefore, if the only way out was to dig, then dig he would, and as God was his witness, he would get through and then people were going to die.

CHAPTER 18

Ryan didn't like how things were progressing. He pushed back from the monitors with disgust. How had he allowed Grandfather to rationalize this insanity? Sure, he was facing a nowhere existence and had done some bad things in his life, but nothing of this magnitude. He didn't care about an unstoppable monster. That was too grand a scale for him. He was a man of the people and this was simply wrong. He had never been a party to murder before and frankly it didn't sit too well with him. He looked back at the monitors to all the innocent people trapped in that maze and knew that the likelihood that any of them would ever get by the traps was remote. Then if they were fortunate enough to survive the traps, they still had the *golem* to contend with, and it would not stop until everyone it was targeted to kill was dead. He suppressed a shiver as he thought of that aberration lying in wait in the heart of the maze. None of these people deserved to die, except maybe that Kaufmann fellow, and especially not at the hands of a creature like the *golem*. He thought of the grisly end that Rudolf Marks had met, and that steeled his resolve.

Again, he wondered how many years his grandfather had had to study those arcane books to learn how to reanimate those corpses. All those years of hatred and the study of the black arts had surely corrupted his grandfather's soul. Sure, Grandfather seemed to have repented, but most men usually turned to God or some higher power when facing the end of their own mortality. Until recently, Ryan had never thought of concepts like Heaven or Hell, or even notions like God or the Devil, but after seeing what was loose in the maze, he began to re-evaluate his own beliefs. To brutally destroy these people for the sins of their ancestors was not only unjust, but it made him and his grandfather no worse than the butchers who had destroyed grandfather's family. He felt sickened by this madness and the fact that he had been so easily seduced into being an active participant.

Ryan knew that he had to speak to his grandfather. He created the *golem*. Perhaps there was a way to stop it without jeopardizing any more lives. He wondered again what role Jason played in this madness. Hell, he hadn't even seen the butler since the first night and wondered what had happened to the man. In fact, aside from himself, the house was empty except for Grandfather and Jason.

No sooner had he left the control room and entered the den than Jason appeared, as silent and quick as a serpent lying in wait. Gauging from his steely eyes, Ryan felt that this was actually quite an apt comparison. Ryan realized that Jason was keeping an eye on him, trying to determine where his loyalties lay and whether he could be trusted. Men like Jason were very cautious. They had to be, because either they learned to be cautious, or they did not live long.

His grandfather had hinted that he had known Jason for many years, but he had never revealed how they met or what brought Jason into his grandfather's employ. That was a mystery that Ryan would resolve. For now, he had to try and keep Jason's trust, all the while trying to find some way to right the atrocity unfolding in the bowels of the earth below their feet.

"Jason," Ryan stammered and then slowed to a calmer, more even tone, "how are you doing?"

Jason glided up to Ryan's side and threw an arm over his shoulder. "How's our little group doing down there in our own version of reality television?" He smiled wide, exposing his teeth, chilling Ryan's blood and making him wonder how safe he truly was here at his grandfather's mansion in northern Maine. He knew that this man could kill him and dispose of his body, and his grandfather would be none the wiser. Jason was clearly in Michael's employ, but Ryan sensed his relationship with the old man was a lot more complex than it appeared to be. Thanks to Grandfather, he certainly knew more about Jason than Jason was aware of. That was his one ace in the hole. It was something he knew that he needed to hold close to the vest in case things took a turn for the worse.

"Things seem to be moving as we planned. The group below has one less active member," Ryan remarked, forming a small grimace that he hoped was convincing enough to fool Jason. Sociopaths, he knew, were often very bright, and Ryan felt the less he said, the better his credibility would be. "I thought I'd take a break and go see Grandfather. I know he isn't well, but frankly, I haven't seen him since we got back from our little trip."

"I don't think that's a good idea, Ryan. Your grandfather is resting and needs to preserve his strength. He really would like to see our little challenge to the end. I really think you should go back to monitoring our guests, and when your grandfather is up to it, I'll coordinate with both of you to get some good quality time together. How's that sound?"

Coordinate? Ryan shivered. There was something Jason was not telling him. He needed to speak to his grandfather and would have to manage it without Jason's knowledge.

"I suppose that's okay, Jason. Before I head back to watching the monitors, though, I think I'll head downstairs to grab a quick bite to eat."

Jason patted Ryan on the back. "I think I'll join you. I could use a bite myself."

Ryan forced himself to smile as the other man gently guided him downstairs to the kitchen. His best course of action, he realized, was to do as Jason expected and gain his trust. His time would come, because no matter how things played out, Jason could not watch him all the time. He had to sleep, for one. Someone had to run Grandfather's special errands when it involved procuring items that were not available to the standard shopper. His time would come, but in the meantime he had to play it cool.

*   *   *

Ryan's break came earlier than he expected. Around midnight, he heard footsteps outside the door to his room. Being a light sleeper, Ryan was wakened instantly and held his breath as he listened intently. The footsteps stopped outside the door and Ryan waited anxiously. Then he heard the handle being turned and the door to his room swung slowly inward. He closed his eyes and forced himself to breathe slowly and deeply as if he were sound asleep. He heard light breathing as the figure stood there, watching him, studying him. Minutes later, he heard the figure turn and quietly walk out of the room, shutting the door softly behind him.

Ryan waited a few minutes and quietly climbed out of bed. He threw on a pair of jeans and slipped out of his room and into the hallway, careful not to make a sound. As he approached the staircase, he heard the front door closing. Ryan ran down the stairs and peered out the window, careful not to be seen. He saw Jason's car heading down the long driveway. Ryan knew that this was his chance to get to his grandfather.

He bounded up the stairs two at a time until he got to the top floor, where his grandfather's rooms were. Taking a deep breath, he tiptoed into the suite.

The outer room was used as a sitting room, with some couches and tables. The air was still and had a stale smell, as if it had not been used in a while. The room was dark and silent. At the far end of the room were two doors, which Ryan assumed led to the bedroom and master bath. Ryan quickly edged over to the door on the right, conscious of how loud his footsteps sounded on the rich hardwood floor.

Without knocking, he gently opened the door to his grandfather's bedroom and peered inside. He was able to discern the vague shape of the bed in the corner of the darkened room.

"Grandfather, are you awake?" Ryan called tentatively. There came no response. Worried, he made his way towards the bed. Upon closer inspection, he noted that the bed was actually a hospital bed. There was a bag with some fluid next to it with a protruding tube attached to the prone figure lying on the bed. The room smelled rank and somewhat sickly sweet, with a faint hint of antiseptic. With his heart hammering in his chest, Ryan leaned over the bed and put his hand to his grandfather's forehead. The skin was cool and felt stiff and waxy to the touch. It didn't take long to register with Ryan that his grandfather was barely clinging to life. And though he was certainly not a doctor, he knew that his grandfather would likely be dead before the morning.

Michael Carson suddenly lifted his arm and gripped Ryan by the wrist. His hand was ice cold and his grip was like a vice. His eyes grew wide and sparkled with clarity as he pulled his grandson close. "Ryan, I have something to say to you, and my strength is fading, so please listen closely. Jason is not who he seems. I have to tell you what I know about him before I die so you can better protect yourself.

"When I first met him, it was through a business acquaintance of mine who had used Jason for some work that fell outside the lines of the law. I realized creating the *golem* would require a man who had a certain skill in getting things done. He even helped me procure the bones of my family and the soil where they were buried to build the creature. Then he helped me bypass customs all over the world with the creature in a hidden hold on a privately chartered yacht so we could bring it wherever it was needed. We spent years traveling around the world tracking down all those who killed my family and their kin. Many years later, he gave me the idea to build the maze and eliminate their last surviving descendants. Again, he procured all the materials needed for the maze as well as getting men to build it. When all was done, I turned a blind eye while he disposed of the workers."

"But why, Grandfather?" Ryan asked.

"Listen, Ryan. I've been consumed by hate for so long that I allowed myself to believe what I was doing was justified. We spent years of tracking down the three men who killed my family and their descendants. The more innocent lives we took, the more it began to sicken me. I knew we were wrong but dared not say anything to Jason. I couldn't look at myself in a mirror. By the time the maze was done and I had time to think about what I was doing, I realized that I couldn't go through with it any longer. I'd had it with death and killing and wanted to stop. I told this to Jason and he threatened to not only expose me to the police, which at this point I suppose I could have lived with, but he also promised that while I languished in jail, he would destroy everyone I knew and loved in this world."

"Wait a minute," Ryan interjected. "How could Jason have been with you that long? He looks to be at most forty years old."

"Ryan, where do you think I learned how to create most of the arcane traps in the maze? Jason taught them to me from ancient books and grimoires. I suspect that his appearance is being manipulated by the same arcane lore that has helped animate the things in the maze."

"And did Jason create the *golem* too?"

"No, Ryan. That was my doing. Don't forget, the *golem* is from our heritage, not Jason's."

"What should I do, Grandfather?"

"Jason has been acting strangely as of late, Ryan. I suspect that he was waiting to get the last descendants into the maze and then allow me to perish, or hasten the process. That way, there would be no one left to control the *golem*. I suspect he has ulterior motives here, but alas, I just don't know what they are."

Ryan scratched his head and thought for a moment. "Does Jason know that you performed a ceremony down in the tunnels below the house transferring the *golem* to my control?"

"I doubt it. He has no access to the tunnels or the control center. That being said, once I die you might be in very grave danger as I doubt Jason will want to keep any loose ends lying around. You must leave tonight while Jason is out. Take one of the cars in the garage and go. It's for your own good."

Ryan put his hand to his grandfather's cheek. "We need to get you out of here."

Michael waved his hand in a dismissive gesture. "And go where, Ryan? I am dying. I'll be lucky to see tomorrow's sunrise. Ryan, please fix things and right the wrong we have caused to these poor people. But please watch your back. Do not underestimate Jason. He is much more dangerous than he seems. Always remember that, no matter what, I love you and am proud of the man you've become. Please go now, Ryan. Jason will be back soon and I don't want him to know that we've spoken. Goodbye,

Grandson." He closed his eyes and sighed deeply, trying to mitigate the effort of speaking.

Ryan hugged his grandfather and felt the tears fall. "I love you, too, Grandfather. I'll set things right."

Ryan felt sick. Clearly Jason has been pulling the strings here for years now. What the older man's motives were Ryan could only guess, but he knew that he wanted no part of any of it. That meant that somewhere down the road he would be made expendable and removed from the equation. *To hell with this*, Ryan declared, *I'm getting out now. I can always send for the police when I am far, far away.*

Ryan left his grandfather's suite and headed downstairs. He knew he had to pack what was his and wipe all trace that he was ever at the house to avoid any implications in any past and future murders in the maze. He also knew that Jason was due back from wherever he had gone and he didn't want to be anywhere nearby when he returned.

He rushed down the hallway and entered his room, only to find Jason sitting calmly on his bed.

"Hello, Ryan," Jason hissed through clenched teeth. "I see that you decided to pay a visit to your grandfather upstairs."

"Why didn't you tell me that he was about to die?"

"You didn't need to know. Your grandfather was getting soft in his later years, especially now that death was imminent, and was having second thoughts about what we were doing here. To me, that is unacceptable. People like them murdered my family for no reason, Ryan. These people are paying the price by proxy." Jason pulled a gun from his coat pocket and motioned for Ryan to sit in a Queen Anne chair in the corner of the room.

"Jason," Ryan begged, "we don't have to do this. These people really don't know who we are. We can let them go and go our separate ways."

Jason stood up and slowly walked over to Ryan. He put his face inches from Ryan's and said so quietly that Ryan had to strain to hear, "They need to pay for their crimes. They are all guilty and they all must die."

Ryan felt his blood boil and despite his intense fear of the man standing in front of him, he found enough voice to speak back, "Grandfather wants this travesty stopped."

Jason paused, then screamed so loudly that Ryan thought he was going to kill him immediately. "I know that, you stupid punk. Why do you think I had to hasten his impending demise? He could have lived for months more, but I made sure he would go much sooner, before he changed his mind. I need that *golem* for my own revenge, and without its creator, it will continue to kill even after the victims are dead." His eyes bulged and his lower lip trembled, damp with spittle.

"You won't be able to control it, you fucking idiot," Ryan yelled.

"You won't be around long enough to worry about it."

Ryan's eyes went wide and before common sense could stop his actions, he reached back and threw the hardest punch he had ever thrown in his life, connecting squarely with Jason's chin, sending the man sprawling back and causing him to hit his head on the wardrobe next to the bed. He dropped to the floor and was still.

Ryan went over and felt for a pulse. Jason was quite alive. *He may be out cold*, Ryan reasoned, *but he won't be for long. Shit!* This complicated things. Jason would hunt him down until he found and killed him. There was nowhere safe he could go without spending the rest of his life looking over his shoulder. Ryan knew that he had to kill the man, and he had to do it before Jason woke up.

Before Ryan could make his mind up on the action he should take, Jason stirred and moaned in pain. Ryan knew that he would be up soon and that he had to move immediately. He grabbed Jason's gun from the floor and fired a shot, grazing a shallow furrow in Jason's chest. Blood welled up from the wound, yet Jason still managed to get himself to a sitting position. He smiled maliciously and taunted Ryan. "That all you got, kid? If you plan on using a gun, make sure you aim." Ryan turned and ran from the room.

I shot him and it grazed across his chest, he thought, *which must hurt like a son of a bitch, and yet he sat up easily as if it was nothing.*

Ryan realized that the only safe place was below the house in the maze. Jason did not have access to the control room or the maze and he would need a proper palm and retinal scan to get in. And if by some chance Jason managed to bypass the defenses, he didn't know the maze's layouts or the location of the traps. This caused Ryan to reason that if Jason were to follow him in there, he might not make it out alive, thus ridding the world of a yet another dangerous sociopath. Meanwhile, Ryan decided he owed it to the people trapped below to help them escape.

His choice made, Ryan ran for the control room for the maze's traps, picked up a chair and threw it at the monitors, shattering the glass and making all the screens go blank. Now Jason would not be able to track where Ryan went. Ryan then headed downstairs to the maintenance entrance to the maze, hoping that Jason didn't know this way in. It would give him a solid head start since it would deposit him in the maze ahead of the group. Ryan had another ace in the hole. He had eidetic memory and reasoned that it would help him find his way to the end of the maze, whereas Jason would have to blunder his way through the maze and traps like anyone else. He also doubted that Jason knew where the maze ended, since he assumed that no one would survive it or the *golem*. If he wanted Ryan, and logic dictated that he did, he had to go in to the maze after him.

CHAPTER 19

When he was twelve years old, Eric Marks had gone away to camp and very nearly drowned. It was a private camp that all the children from his family's neighborhood went to every summer. Eric had begged his parents for months to send him, not knowing that they were overextended with a mortgage, private school, a country club and a host of other expenses so that they could keep up with the other families in their upscale neighborhood in suburban Chicago.

Camp was everything that Eric had heard it would be. He had his friends from the neighborhood, and he had met several other kids that he knew would be amongst his friends for years to come. He had even managed to get his first ever girlfriend, Lucy Norman, and by mid-summer had managed to get his first kiss behind the boathouse after lights out.

One night, towards the end of the summer, he met up with Lucy around midnight, well after lights out, and after the counselors had snuck off for their own private party. They met by the boathouse and took out a canoe. The plan was to row to the other side of the lake and watch the stars. Of course, they both wanted to be alone, but were more comfortable not admitting that they looked forward to stealing a few kisses. Eric was always a confident boy but around Lucy he felt shy and uncertain and even a little jittery, but it was a feeling that seemed to suit him.

They pushed the canoe out from the dock and climbed in, Lucy at the head of the canoe, and Eric at the back so he could row. It was a perfect night, the sky clear and the moon full and bright, its reflection mirrored on the calm surface of the lake. The air was warm with only the slightest breeze. Lucy remarked that it was a very romantic night, to which Eric blushed and shyly looked away.

As they rowed out onto the lake, the clouds slowly and imperceptibly moved across the sky until the moon was completely covered. The air also seemed to be getting cooler. Lucy shivered and gazed at the darkening sky. She leaned over and imploringly asked Eric to head back to camp. Eric also was feeling uneasy at how much darker it had become and how much cooler the air felt, but he certainly was not going to admit it, especially to a girl like Lucy. How she saw him was very important and he did not want her seeing him as weak.

Eric assured her that there was nothing to worry about and that it would be fun to sit by the lake on the other side. Lucy shivered and sat in silence. Eric rowed on for a while longer, his mind focused on how he would soon have Lucy in his arms. He barely noticed the rapidly dropping temperature. All of a sudden, in the middle of the lake, the canoe came to a dead stop.

"What's wrong, Eric?" Lucy asked, her eyes wide with fear.

"I don't know, Luce. It feels like we're stuck on something." Eric took his oar and began prodding under the canoe, but couldn't seem to feel anything. He looked up at Lucy and shrugged, trying to look nonchalant and not let her know how scared he really was.

"Eric, I really want to go back. Please." She looked over at him and he noted her eyes were rimmed with tears. "It's cold and dark and I just want to go back."

Eric knew he had to do something. He was only twelve, but he knew how important it was to save face. "Okay, Luce," he said while taking his t-shirt off, "hold on to my legs while I lean out and try to dislodge us from whatever we're stuck on."

"Be careful, okay?"

Eric winked at her and leaned over the edge. Through the gloom and murk of the water, he thought he saw a faint luminescent glow beneath the canoe. He jabbed the oar under the canoe and felt it strike something solid. "What the fu…" Eric began when he was wrenched over the side of the canoe into the water.

"Eric!" Lucy shrieked and leaned over the edge of the canoe. She saw him being dragged under the canoe by his oar. Thinking fast, she grabbed his ankle and pulled back with all her might. At first, she felt an incredible resistance and then it relaxed and she managed to pull Eric back. She helped him climb back on board and he flopped to the bottom of the canoe, gasping.

"There's something down there," he whispered while trying to get his breath back. "It was holding the canoe."

Lucy looked at him with a mixture of fear and uncertainty. She grabbed the spare paddle and began paddling towards the shore. To her delight, the canoe moved fluidly through the still water. They had gone perhaps ten feet when the bottom of the canoe near Lucy cracked and broke off. It happened so quickly that Eric didn't have time to react. One second, Lucy was frantically paddling towards shore, the next she was gone, dragged under the murky depths.

Eric dove into the chilly, dark water in a desperate attempt to save her. He knew even as he dove that she was gone. After perhaps twenty minutes of fruitless searching, repeatedly diving and rising for air, he began to swim towards shore. He was nearly at the beach when he stopped to look back. In the distance, beneath the water level, he noticed the same green luminescence rapidly approaching him. He frantically made it to the beach and ran out of the water screaming like all of Hell was on his heels, drawing a crowd from all the different bunks at the camp.

He was sent home the next day, partly for breaking curfew, which had resulted in Lucy Norman's drowning, and partly to insulate the other campers, because Eric Marks had sworn that a glowing giant of a man-like creature had dragged Lucy to her death and was after him as well. Even after being cleared by a police investigation and after years of therapy and countless hours of hypnosis had finally buried that traumatic event, he had never again gone near any body of water.

*   *   *

Eric awoke abruptly, with the memory of that day at camp, repressed for so many years, rushing back in a torrential flood. He was lying face down in a shallow puddle of filthy water on a muddy floor. His nostrils were assailed by the damp smell of human waste and decay and the salty tang of the sea. He managed a few short coughs and expelled some of the brackish fluid from his lungs. Using his trembling arms to raise himself, he managed to get to a kneeling position and then weakly to his feet. He looked around, his panic building, as he realized that he was alone, the inky darkness so nearly complete that he could hardly see. Other than a faint luminescent sheen on the walls and floor that dimly outlined his surroundings, he could not see anyone else. He noticed how eerily quiet it was in the still gloom. Aside from sounds of dripping water off in the distance, it was quiet as a grave. He called out to Suze and Kerry but got no response from either of them. Either they were lying dead somewhere in the darkness or had somehow managed to get out. He couldn't believe that they would leave him to die here by himself in the dark. Of course, he reasoned, in darkness this complete, they would never find him unless they tripped over him. He felt the cold grip of panic seize him and he had to fight back the feeling. He needed a cool head now more than ever, and regressing to the trauma incurred by his twelve-year-old self would not help him stay alive.

He remembered his last waking thought before the water level had overtaken him and the world went black was that they were all going to drown. He recalled with crystal clarity that Kerry had dropped her torch, plunging them into total darkness as the water rose up. Now here he was alive and alone, feeling like shit, with every childhood fear tormenting him. He also wondered what had happened to the water. How could a tunnel fill so rapidly and then empty out even quicker? It didn't take that long for a man to drown, so he suspected the water must have filled to the ceiling then drained right away. Nothing else made sense. More puzzling was why the tunnel had emptied of water to spare his life. Were his captors playing with him? These questions gnawed at him, pushing him to walk slowly onward. He had no sense of direction, but anything was preferable to lying in the muck and waiting for death. His experience at camp had forged one facet of Eric's personality. It made him a survivor, and this present nightmare was no different from any other adversity he had faced in his life. He would confront it and he would win.

Eric slowly began walking, using the faint light to guide him down the passageway. With each step, his shoes stuck in the damp muck and tried to pull him back down to the fetid earth. Moving was slow and deliberate and Eric found himself getting increasingly more frustrated. His fingertips soon reached the wall and he felt the reassuring cold and damp texture of the stone. Keeping his left arm extended so that his fingertips kept contact with the wall, Eric picked up his pace and then tripped over something, sending him sprawling and landing face down in the mud. He groped forward in the darkness until he felt the shape with his hands. He quickly realized that the shape in front of him was human, most likely that of Kerry, based on the slim figure that felt so good to the touch.

"Kerry?" Eric whispered as he gently shook the prone figure. There was no movement or any indication of consciousness, but her body was warm, even lying in the cold, damp mud, so he knew that she must still be alive. Of course, he was only assuming that the figure lying unconscious in front of him was indeed Kerry. He began to wonder if, instead, this was another trap.

Eric lifted the figure, threw her over his shoulder in a modified fireman's carry and again used his hands to feel along the length of the wall. After what seemed like endless walking in the stygian darkness, he saw a faint glow off in the distance. Eric prayed that this was the way out.

As he moved down the corridor, the light at the end increased in intensity to the point where he felt he could see well enough not to use the wall as a guide. He also knew that he had to rest. Carrying someone for as long as he had, especially after not eating for a full day and then nearly drowning, was clearly taking its toll and he was feeling the burden. He wanted to rest but decided to keep going until he reached the light.

At the end of the corridor, there was a steel door and beyond that a room which emanated a warm and inviting light. Eric stopped and paused for a moment. When the corridor had filled with water, they had been at a dead end. True, he did see levers in the wall as the water level was rising, but he had lost consciousness before he could pull the levers and see what effect it would have. He doubted that Kerry could have done anything since he had seen her drop the torch at the last minute. As for Suze, she had slipped under the water before them and had never reappeared. Somehow, the maniac running this freak show had opened another corridor from the one that had them trapped and had drained out all the water, sparing their lives only to play with them later on. Eric realized that their captor could have them killed at any time but preferred to toy with them, giving them glimmers of hope, only to take it away on a whim.

Carrying the woman over his right shoulder, Eric walked into the bright room with his left hand up to shield his eyes from the glare. The room was a perfect ten-foot square, with solid steel walls, floor and ceiling. As he was adjusting to his new surroundings, the door behind him rapidly shut with a barely audible hiss. The door itself seemed to blend in with the wall, leaving only the faintest hint of a seam.

Eric gently put down the person he was carrying on the steel floor and to his relief saw that it was indeed Kerry. She still did not wake, even with vigorous shaking. He tried CPR on her, as well, also to no avail. She was out cold. He felt for a pulse and found it to be strong. Her breathing seemed normal as well. For now, the best he could do was try and keep her warm and safe as he worked on a way out of the maze.

Against the far wall, he noticed a series of buttons. Each one was numbered from one through four. Aside from that, the room was completely featureless, suggesting neither a way in nor a way out.

Taking a deep breath, Eric pushed the first button and watched as a panel slid open, revealing a computer monitor. On the screen, the following appeared:

```
Congratulations on making it this far. You will
be given a chance to earn a reward. Please turn
around and note the floor behind you.
```

Eric did as told and noticed a five-foot square hole appear in the center of the floor as the floor panel slid seamlessly under the existing edge. A ladder led down to the bottom. Eric turned to look back at the screen, where there were now more instructions:

At the bottom of the pit is a button. In order
to get the reward, you must push the button.
This is not as simple as it appears.

As you must have noticed, there are four buttons just below this monitor, which includes
the button you pushed to trigger the operation
of this room. Each button serves a purpose.
One button will give you a reward and spare
your life, but do note that the other three are
not so kind. The other buttons represent three
extremely torturous deaths for one of you. You
must make your selection from one of the four
remaining buttons below the monitor, then climb
down into the pit and press the button down
there to activate your selection. Pushing the
button will either mean instant death for the
person who does so, in effect sacrificing himself so that the others could live, or give you
all a free pass to the next phase of the maze.

Doing nothing is not an option. You have only
five minutes to choose because, after that, a
lethal gas will be pumped into the room from
vents on the ceiling. Death from this gas is
fast, but not without pain, internal bleeding
and eventual breakdown of all motor activities
in the body. The gas does not discriminate and
will kill everyone. So there you have it: one

```
option gives certain death for all involved,
simply for doing nothing, and the other op-
tion gives life for potentially everyone if the
right button is chosen. Now you ask…what is the
reward mentioned earlier? Why, that is simple.
The reward is to live a bit longer and allow
you to cling to every precious moment of life
you have left. The clock has now begun.
```

Eric looked at the monitor with horror as the number 5:00 appeared and began counting down the seconds. With Kerry unconscious, he didn't even have the option. The way things looked, they both would almost certainly die. At best, he had a twenty-five percent chance of survival. He felt numbness creep up his spine as he realized that the next few minutes might actually be his last. He slumped down against the wall, put his head in his hands and tried to focus. As long as he had a one-in-four chance of survival, he wouldn't give up.

CHAPTER 20

Jeremy sat in the passenger seat of Nick's Hummer H2 and marveled at how well it plowed through the unrelenting storm. The snow, sleet and wind had not stopped since they hit New England's outermost fringes, and more than once Jeremy wondered if they were doing the right thing.

Nick glanced over at Jeremy, who seemed lost in thought. When Jeremy had come to him with the story about his missing girlfriend, Nick had thought his childhood pal was once again showing the familiar patterns of being a first-class loser. Only upon further digging had he found out some very interesting tidbits. Nick Lord was a journalist, and a damn fine one if he did say so himself. He prided himself on his ability to uncover leads and flesh out a story. His hacker skills were superior to anyone he knew and he always bragged that there wasn't a website he couldn't get into. After years toiling away at the paper on low-level stories and fluff pieces, this looked to be the break he was waiting for.

At first, when Jeremy had called him with his outlandish tale of Kerry's abduction, Nick was skeptical. After all, why would an armed man come in and kidnap someone like Kerry? She had no money and did not hold a powerful or influential job. Essentially, she was nobody who mattered, so why kidnap her? That alone got Nick's gears turning, and before long he had the identity of the man in the video Jeremy had brought over. Of course, that had led to more unanswered questions. In addition, the video showed another man entering Kerry's apartment to help the kidnapper carry her out the door.

The kidnapper was a riddle. Nick had to search from database to database, but each search yielded no results. The other man was found easily enough and identified as a hard luck loser from Boston, with a small rap sheet. Petty stuff, but by digging into his past, Nick came across the break he needed. It was only by chance that Nick had stumbled across the image of the man who bore a striking resemblance to the profile of the kidnapper standing behind Michael Carson at a charity event. Several calls later he confirmed that the man was Carson's personal assistant, Jason Froemmer. The fact that it was pretty apparent he was seen in the video with Carson's grandson kidnapping Kerry was reason enough to follow up on this lead. Unfortunately, the trail ended there. Jason Froemmer did not exist on any database and no matter how deep he hacked, Nick was unable to get any closer to this enigma of a man. He had no social security number, no driver's license, no passport or any other valid sources of identification. With no other leads to work on, Nick delved into Michael Carson's history.

Carson's history was spotty at best, which was remarkable for someone so successful. He was rumored to be worth billions yet rarely was seen in public, a behavior that fueled the rumor mills. The one bit of truth to all the rumors was that he had not been seen in over a decade. Well, thought Nick with a wry smile, tonight would change all that.

The Hummer crested a short hill and through the blowing snow the mansion came into view. Nick looked over at Jeremy and then back at the house. Gothic was the term that immediately came to mind. Here, nestled in the outer reaches of Maine, set deep in the woods, amidst a raging winter storm, the house was an imposing monolith that watched over the unforgiving landscape.

"What do you think we'll find there?" Jeremy asked, his voice a hushed whisper.

"Probably a lot of ghosts," Nick grinned, his levity masking his real concerns. *Probably we'll find a lot of death. A house like this has to have its secrets from the world. One does not build an isolated house like this unless one wants to hide from the world.* Nick shuddered and subconsciously turned the heat up a little higher.

Jeremy pointed to a window on the second floor where, just moments earlier, he had seen a shadow move behind the partially drawn curtain. "Looks like someone knows we're here."

"So what, Jeremy? It's not like we're doing anything wrong. Look, we have our cover story. We are two reporters who want to do a feature piece on Michael Carson for *Fortune* magazine." With that, Nick pulled a photo ID from his jacket pocket showing him to be a senior editor from *Fortune*. "Best that money can buy," he grinned. "But don't worry, Jeremy, I got you one as well. You can't pretend to be a top photographer without one."

Nick steered the Hummer up the long, circular drive, amazed at how little accumulation of snow and ice there was. "Could it be that this entire driveway is heated? The cost to do this would be incredible."

"Look at this house, Nick, and tell me that the owner ever has to worry about what anything costs." Nick nodded his silent agreement, keeping his eyes to the windows. *They almost seem to be watching us, as if the place is alive.*

Both men climbed out of the Hummer. Jeremy hugged himself against the blistering wind and cold while Nick went to the back to unload the photographic equipment. He took half and handed it to Jeremy, then grabbed the rest and shut the back. "Come, Jeremy," he intoned in his best Sherlock Holmes, "the game is afoot." He then walked up the long stairs without a backward glance. Jeremy broke into a short run to catch up. As soon as they reached the landing, well-sheltered from the storm around them, the front door swung open and both men stood face to face with Jason Froemmer.

Jason smiled at the men, his lupine grin wide and menacing. "To what do I owe the pleasure of a visit on a night such as this?"

"We were sent here by the editor-in-chief at *Fortune* magazine to do a piece on the ten richest men in America," Nick replied smoothly. "We tried to call but were unable to get through. The purpose of the piece is to show how one can amass an incredible fortune even though they might have come from humble beginnings, as did Mr. Carson."

"I'm sorry," Jason continued to grin, "but you've come all this way for nothing. Mr. Carson does not grant interviews. You should have continued calling. It would have saved you both the trip." With that, he turned and started to close the door.

"Wait!" Nick cried out. "What about Kerry Ramirez? We know that she was taken here."

Jason turned around slowly. "And who is this Kerry Ramirez?"

"You play your innocence well," Jeremy spat out, "but I've seen the tape from Kerry's security camera. You were on it. You and Ryan Carson were seen abducting Kerry. We're here to get her back." Nick looked over at his friend, silently cursing his impetuousness. Their best chance was to play it cool, not put all their cards on the table at once.

Jason shrugged and gestured for them to enter the house. Nick and Jeremy pushed past him into a well-lit foyer that opened into the most opulent sitting room that Jeremy had ever seen.

"I'm surprised I didn't notice the camera. She must have hidden it well. Such initiative and cunning will take her far…below." Jason's eyes shone with dark malevolence. "What is your angle, young man?" he asked. "Who is this woman to you?"

"She's my girlfriend," Jeremy answered, "and I mean to get her back. My name is Jeremy Balducci."

"And who is this with you, Mr. Balducci?"

"Nick Lord," Nick replied. "I am a reporter and we know you, Mr. Froemmer, so cut the crap and show us where Kerry is. And don't even think of trying anything. We left detailed messages with our families as to where we were going."

"As you wish." Jason walked past them and went to a door at the far side of the room. "She's in there."

Jeremy ran past, quickly followed by Nick. He opened the door and peered in. Nick turned to Jason. "What kind of game are you playing, the room is…"

Nick never finished his sentence as the shot from Jason's gun blew off the top of his head. Nick's body stood there, motionless, then swayed to the side and collapsed in front of a terror-stricken Jeremy, who fell to his knees. "Please God, don't kill me."

"I've got something better in mind for you. Seeing as how you miss your precious Ms. Ramirez so much, I've decided that you shall join her." Jason grabbed Jeremy by the collar and pulled him to his feet. Jeremy remarked at the man's incredible strength. Jason dragged him through a series of rooms and then down two flights of stairs to a massive wooden door. He threw Jeremy to the ground as he fished through his pockets for a key. With the door open, he grabbed Jeremy once more by the collar and dragged him into the room. Jeremy saw it was a giant theatre. The air was bitter and caused him to cough almost as soon as he was dragged into the room. He noticed that Jason seemed unaffected by the poor air quality.

In the center of the room, Jeremy noticed that he was being dragged towards a circular opening in the floor.

"Where are you taking me?" Jeremy demanded.

"Why, to your beloved, of course, down in the maze. You may opt to call it Hell." With that, Jason pushed Jeremy through the aperture in the floor and smiled widely. Yet one more problem solved. All that remained was dealing with Ryan and the old man. Jason wanted to savor the pain he would inflict on Ryan. Nobody crossed him and lived. *Ryan is a dead man*, he thought, *he just doesn't know it yet. As of now, he has outlived his usefulness, and the old man as well.* Things were coming together quite nicely.

Chapter 21

She also wondered what had happened to Kerry and Eric. She woke up alone in the dark and while not completely dried off, she wasn't drenched either, which indicated that she had been out awhile. She didn't like being alone in the dark and much of this distaste stemmed from an incident that when she was a thirteen-year-old growing up in Long Island.

Suze Greenberg remembered how, as a shy, awkward, and unfortunately stocky and completely unappealing girl, she had somehow come under the malevolent gaze of the school bully, Joey Donato. Joey was a fat, greasy kid with bad acne who was as nasty as he was ugly. All kids made it a rule to keep away from him because, once he set his sights on you, he would terrorize you until you broke. Joey's reputation preceded him since he had been thrown out of his last few schools and had moved from foster home to foster home. Rumor was it he had even killed a cat by forcing a lit firecracker down its throat.

The day that Suze was walking home from school when Joey pulled up behind her with his two toadies would herald the start of the worst ordeal in her life that even to this day, caused her to see a therapist.

"Hey, guys," Donato had said in a sing-song kind of way, "look who we have here. Suze Greenberg, Long Island's answer to the Goodyear Blimp. Hey, Goodyear, whattaya say?"

Suze kept walking and did not look back. She knew that making eye contact would only encourage him. Unfortunately, she was still close to a mile from home and on foot, while Joey and his goons were all riding their Schwinns. She knew she could never outrun them. At best, she could keep walking and pray that she ran into someone she knew.

"Hey, Goodyear, what's your hurry? Off to float over a game?" Joey kept taunting her and began circling her on his bike. Suze kept her head down, trying to avoid eye contact and doing her best to choke back tears.

"Look at me, guys," Joey chanted, "the way I'm circling her you'd think that Fatty Goodyear here had her own gravity." The other boys roared with laughter. This sent Suze over the edge, triggering a heavy flow of tears. Not wanting to give Joey Donato any satisfaction at seeing her suffer, she broke into a run. Half a mile or so to her house and being overweight were not good odds, but she knew she couldn't take any more of his abuse.

"The bitch is on the run, guys!" Joey yelled. "Get her." Joey took off after Suze, followed by his two pals, Mark and Nicky, who were making whooping sounds. Joey pulled up in front of Suze and clumsily jumped off his bike. He fell forward, landing palms down. Suze veered sharply to the right and headed for the woods. Joey got up and headed after her with Mark and Nicky rapidly gaining ground.

Suze knew the woods were a bad idea because she would be all alone, but there was no way that she would outrun Joey and his buddies on their bikes. At least the woods were the great equalizer in that they had to go on foot, and Suze knew the woods quite well, having spent many a lonely hour lost in their calming solitude. She darted between the trees and dodged under low-hanging branches, and soon she saw that she had evaded Joey and his goons. She stopped to catch her breath and in the distance heard the boys frantically searching for her. Feeling cornered, Suze scrambled up the nearest tree, intending to hide in the upper branches amongst the leaves until they left.

She watched as Joey and his goons tramped through the woods, not caring how much noise they made. They knew they had her and were taking their time about it.

"Goodyear," Joey chanted, "we all know that there's no way out except past us. Behind you is the quarry and we're blocking the route back to the road. Make it easier on yourself and come out from wherever you're hiding. If you make me wait, I swear you'll be sorry."

Suze tried to keep her tears in check. She swore she would never let Joey see that he had gotten to her.

"Goodyear…Goodyear. Where are you? I just want to talk about your sister."

Suze flinched at the mention of her sister. She had gone to play outside one day and been found in these very same woods, torn to shreds. Suze was the one who found her. The grim memory of her sister Katie, lying there on her back on a bed of leaves and branches, with her legs askew and her panties down around her ankles, always made Suze cry. The sight of her internal organs ripped out through the gaping aperture in her stomach was enough to traumatize Suze for years. In addition, her eyes had been ripped out and shoved down her throat and her arms had been pulled free from their sockets and left several feet from the body, clasped together as if in silent prayer. The media had hounded Suze mercilessly for months, asking if they had any enemies or even if there could be a connection, since she and her sister had been adopted by the same family a decade earlier.

"Goodyear," Joey continued his taunts, "I raped your sister. And she liked it!"

"Drop dead, you fat piece of shit. Katie was repulsed by the sight of your fat, greasy face!" Suze screamed, the tears streaming down her cheeks. She then froze, realizing her mistake. Now Joey Donato and his goons knew where she was hiding. "She's up there!" Mark yelled out, pointing up so Joey and Nicky could see.

Joey and his pals began scouring the ground for good-sized rocks and started hurling them upwards in Suze's direction. Many of them sailed past, getting dangerously close.

"Stop it, you bastards!" Suze shrieked, trying to scramble higher up, deeper into the branches' protective cover.

"You're toast, Goodyear," Joey taunted and hauled back with a rock the size of a baseball. This time, his aim struck Suze in the back of the skull. Suze felt a momentary burst of pain, then a bright light, before everything went dark. She lost her grip and plummeted down to the ground to a waiting Joey Donato and his two buddies.

Suze woke up bound naked to a scratchy, wooden floor, tied securely by her hands and feet. She was unable to move, and could not see even an inch in front of her face. She was also gagged with a bitter-tasting rag and unable to make a sound. Her other senses were working, however. The place where she was tied had a moldy, ripe scent as if something had recently died in the vicinity. The air was cool and caused the fine hairs on her body to stand up. The silence surrounding her was suffocating, except for the chattering of insects from somewhere nearby. Her head throbbed from where the rock had struck her, and she had aches from all over her body from the fall. She also felt a wet stickiness between her legs and prayed that it was only blood.

Suze began to panic, even though she knew it wouldn't help. Those bastards had done something horrible to her and left her there to rot. She tried to scream again, to no avail. She kept struggling against the ropes that held her securely and after a while gave up and cried herself to sleep.

When she awoke, she saw that there were thin cracks of light filtering through the wooden roof overhead, making the darkness somehow less threatening. She still couldn't see anything of her surroundings, but the thin slivers of light gave her some degree of comfort.

Suze felt numbness in her extremities. Unable to hold in her natural bodily functions had caused her to soil herself, which cooled and dried all over her skin. Day turned to night and Suze began losing track of time. She was thirsty and hungry. Her thoughts floated between lucidity and madness. In her lucid moments, she wondered about her parents and whether they were as scared as she was. She kept reminding herself that, no matter what, they would find her. The worst thing of all, though, was the darkness that night brought. Helpless and immobile, she felt the insects and small woodland animals crawl over her bare skin and often enough take small bites. She made noises in her throat until her voice was hoarse, and then sobbed until sleep took her away.

Eventually, Suze was found. After three miserable days where she alternated between prayers for salvation and prayers for death, she was discovered by a young boy walking his Labrador in the woods and happened by chance to pass by the shack and hear her crying inside. Terrified, he ran home to tell his parents, who knew of the missing girl and promptly notified the police. What followed was an investigation and it was discovered that the three boys had raped Suze repeatedly while she was unconscious. All three boys, being fifteen at the time, were sent to a juvenile detention center.

Three years later, the nightmares were still as fresh in her mind as the days of her ordeal. Suze became withdrawn and sullen and distanced herself from all her friends, preferring to be solitary. Even more noticeable was how she refused to date and seemed to go out of her way to avoid men.

The day that Joey and his friends were released from juvenile correction Suze had a complete breakdown and tried to commit suicide. Three years later, she was still suffering and her tormentors were free to move on with their whole lives ahead of them. It was then that something broke within her.

She watched the boys from a distance and got to know their habits. She also did a lot of reading as she plotted revenge. She got her chance with Mark and Nicky by cutting the brake lines on Mark's Jeep one Saturday evening while they were in a local bar. It didn't take much for the combination of alcohol, speed and no brakes to end their useless lives. Alcohol and excessive speed was blamed. No one even considered that their deaths were anything but accidental.

Getting revenge on Joey was a bit more difficult. His former foster family had money and had arranged for a small trust for Joey when he turned eighteen, and for the most part since his buddies' deaths, he had kept to himself in his apartment. Suze set up a surveillance camera outside his window and watched and waited, until she eventually saw her opportunity arise. Joey was still a bully at heart and she knew that she would be able to use that to her advantage. Joey needed to live by intimidating others. That fear was his driving force. Anything else would make him less a man in his eyes. What she saw him do in the privacy of his own living room, and what she got on tape, would be his downfall.

Suze carefully typed the letter and explained in detail what she had seen and that if he wanted the tape back, he would have to meet her that night by the same shack in the woods. She did not sign her name. She didn't have to.

Suze waited by the shack, hidden in the shadows, anticipating her revenge. Soon Joey showed up, warily looking about. Being this close to him made her want to vomit. If anything, his three years in juvenile detention had not done him any favors. His long, greasy hair was tied back in a ponytail. He was significantly heavier than the chunky fifteen-year-old who had ruined her life. The one thing that was the same was the cold malevolence in his eyes.

"You there, bitch?" he growled. "I know it's you who's behind this. Now give me the tape before I make you really sorry."

From behind Joey, a battery-powered television turned on. Suze, still hidden in the shadows, pushed another button and the tape started. It showed Joey, all two hundred and fifty pounds of him, in a very compromising position with another young man.

"Turn it off, bitch." Joey screamed. "I don't know how you got that on tape, but you won't ever get a chance to show it to anyone. What I did to you three years ago will seem like a picnic after I'm done with you."

Suze pushed another button and inside the shack a recorder with her voice called out, "You want the tape, you miserable bastard, then pretend to be a man and come get it."

Joey screamed and ran straight into the cabin towards the sound of her voice. Stepping out of the shadows, Suze rushed over and jammed the cabin door closed behind him. She then placed a large padlock on the new lock she had put on the cabin earlier that day.

Joey realized that he'd been tricked and ran to the door. His eyes bulged out as he stared at her through a hole in the wood. In slow, laborious breaths, he cursed her and threatened her and insisted she let him out.

"So what's the deal, Joey, do you prefer boys?"

"I like girls," Joey said quickly, almost as if to convince himself.

"Do you?" Suze screamed. "What you did to me three years ago sounds more like a scared little boy trying to look like a man in front of his friends. But maybe I'll give you a chance."

"How?"

"Take off all your clothes and push them through this small hole in the door and maybe I'll let you out." Suze smiled.

"I don't trust you," Joey muttered.

"Trust is all you have left, Joey. Of course, I can leave you here to rot like you did to me."

Joey quickly stripped down and began shoving his clothes through the small hole in the wood. When done, he stood there naked, arms crossed across his chest. Suze looked through the hole in the door at the rolls of fat on his pasty belly, the thick pimples on his chest, and his thin chicken legs. She had to fight back equal urges to laugh and be sick at the same time.

"What are you going to do?" Joey demanded. "I did what you wanted. Now let me out."

Suze reached to her pants pocket and took out a small gun, aimed through the hole in the door, and shot Joey in his thigh. "You chased me, you hurt me, raped me and left me for dead," Suze raged. "Did you think I'd forget? Did you?"

Joey was crying and trying to staunch the flow of blood. "Please," he begged, "let me out of here!"

Suze walked around the cabin and came back with a red metal can. She began splashing the cabin with fluid. When the can was empty, she bent over to grab matches from her purse. The first one failed to light, but the second roared to life and she tossed it on the shack's roof, which quickly set it ablaze. "Joey, what you did to me was unforgivable." She sat down in front of the shack and lit a cigarette. "So I'll need to do something equally unforgivable to you. Of course, you won't have years of torment thinking about how your life was ruined. I'll let you watch me sitting here enjoying this smoke be the last thing you see."

Suze lit a cigarette and smoked it silently as she watched the shack burn. Joey's screams filled the air, first as pleas for help, then as threats. After several minutes, the screams stopped and there was only the crackling of the wood as the fire raged. Suze poured another can of gasoline on the fire and it raged even hotter. She then wiped the television down to be free of prints, popped out the tape and wiped it down as well. She then threw both into the blazing fire and watched them burn. When the fire was done, there was nothing left of the cabin and not much more than that left of Joey. Suze smiled and walked away; her work was done.

The police eventually did question her in Joey's death, but Suze had had lots of time to set up an alibi, and eventually the investigation turned to a search for a killer who didn't exist.

*   *   *

The memory rocked Suze back to her present situation. There had been so much hatred and pain in her life, and yet, as an adult, she had learned to harness it to help her become a stronger person. She knew why the dark terrified her, and she knew about revenge. She wasn't proud of the fact that she took three lives, but they were bad people, she reasoned, and the world was likely better off with the three of them dead.

Suze kept walking, slowly, with her hands outstretched until her fingertips brushed the wall. Using the wall as guidance, she kept walking. After perhaps half an hour of walking in pure darkness, she saw a small glow off in the distance. Suze picked up her pace and as she walked the glow began to take on the form of a man.

Suze paused to look at the figure in the distance, outlined by a faint luminescence. Something held her back from calling out to the stranger. She wasn't sure why the man filled her with dread, but she relied on her instincts a lot and they were sending out loud warning signals. Off in the distance, the stranger had apparently noticed her since he began walking towards where she stood.

Suze heard her name whispered in the still darkness of the maze and felt a chill. She felt the temperature drop suddenly. Her name was whispered again and it seemed to be coming from everywhere at once. Whoever this man was, he knew her name and it filled her with dread. Every fiber of her being screamed that if she stayed where she was, she would die.

Turning blindly into the darkness, Suze ran from the stranger, hearing his voice whispering promises of death and retribution trailing along behind her.

CHAPTER 22

Allen ran up the corridor and came to a stop where Judith and Annie were waiting. He leaned forward, hands on his knees as he fought to regain his breath. He spat a thick wad of phlegm to the ground and wiped the perspiration from his brow.

Annie looked past Allen, then directly at him. Her eyes grew wide, the realization that her husband had not come back with Allen suddenly hitting home. Allen merely lowered his head, avoiding Annie's direct gaze. "I'm so sorry," he half whispered, "it all happened so fast."

"What happened, Allen?" Annie asked, her voice shaking and fearful. "Where is my husband?"

"It just happened so fast," Allen repeated, looking away.

Annie burst into tears and started pounding her fists on Allen's chest before collapsing in his arms, whimpering like a child. She shuddered and tried to speak, but barely managed to utter an audible sound.

"He died saving me, Annie," Allen added and put a reassuring arm around her shoulders, "and, if I could, I would switch places with him right now. But I can't. It happened too fast for either of us to expect it. Right now, though, we just don't have the time. Those creatures are coming. Lots of them, and we can't fight that many. We have to run… now."

Annie looked up at Allen, then at Judith, through red-rimmed eyes.

"You go ahead. I don't want to live without Rudolf. Besides, I'm a lot older than you and will only slow you down."

"We are not leaving without you, Annie," Judith said, grabbing her by both shoulders. "You have a son who needs you. Rudolf would not have wanted you to give up. Besides, if you don't come, then we won't either and our deaths will be on your conscience."

"Damn you, Judith," Annie cried while wiping the tears away. She allowed them to take her by the arms and lead her further down into the maze.

The three ran as fast as Annie was able. The light from the torch cast flickering shadows across the dusty walls of the maze. Judith could see the concern in Allen's face. She knew that Annie was holding them back and that it wouldn't be long before the corpses caught up with them. When they did, then what? It was either flee or die. If they stopped, they would be forced to fight for their lives. But how many could they manage before they were killed? Their best hope was to find a door or other barrier to put between the corpses and them. If not, then distance was the next best alternative.

They kept running, with Allen helping a struggling Annie along. She had fallen twice and had to be helped back to her feet, each time protesting and insisting they leave her behind. The moans and the howls from the corpses were also getting closer, clearly indicating that they were closing the gap. Eventually, the corridor came to a dead end. The wall was broad and made of what appeared to be reddish-brown clay that looked like dried blood under the light from the torch. Set in the wall were five man-sized holes. Above the holes was a sign carved into the surface of the wall that read:

Here are five tunnels.
Three will get you that much closer to the freedom you seek, but beware of the other two because the only thing they offer is the sweet release of death.
Be warned that once a tunnel is entered, there is no way back, so go forward and choose your destiny wisely.

Allen walked over to the wall and peered into the first hole. He inserted the torch, hoping it would cast enough light to help in their decision. All he was able to see was the opening to a tunnel with a smooth, glassy surface; it seemed to drop beyond the light from the torch. Allen knew that it would be easy to slide down, but there would be no way in hell any of them could ever hope to climb back up. Each successive hole was the same. They were blind slides into the darkness that led to some unknown fate. Nothing about any of the slides seemed to differentiate it from any of the others.

"What do we do, Allen?" Judith wailed. She kept glancing back over her shoulder, expecting the corpses to show up at any second.

"There's a riddle here, somewhere, Judith," Allen replied while pacing back and forth in front of the wall. "The problem is that we have only a few minutes before the walking dead arrive. We need to decide. Do we go together or take our chances separately?" He looked around urgently.

Judith walked over and put an arm around her husband. "I vote to stay together. Who knows if the tunnels all end up in the same place? At least there are three good tunnels, right? Assuming that logic, the odds are with us."

"I agree," Annie added. "Besides, if we go it alone, we don't stand a chance. There is strength in numbers. So," she said, gesturing to the holes, "which one?"

The cries from the approaching dead were getting louder and more distinct. They all knew that they did not have much time left.

"Which one should we pick, Allen?" Annie shrieked. "We don't have time for indecision."

"Damn it, Annie," Allen growled, "I don't believe that this is a random choice. There is a pattern to this. If we're smart, we can succeed."

Annie looked over at Allen and Judith, then back down the dark corridor and screamed. The dead were approaching fast and they looked ready to kill. "No time, folks. I made our choice for us," she called and ran over to the last hole on the wall, looked back and dove through head-first.

"Allen?" Judith looked imploringly at her husband.

"Go. Follow her now. We're out of options."

Judith ran over to the hole, closely followed by Allen. He helped her through and scrambled into the hole. He was mostly through when he felt something grab hold of his leg, followed by a searing pain. He didn't have time to think and pulled himself fully into the hole. There was some resistance on his calf and he felt a burning sensation shoot down to his ankle. Then the resistance gave way and he plunged down the tunnel.

Allen slid down the smooth surface for what seemed like an eternity, plunging downwards and picking up speed before he felt himself going upwards and then coming to a rest at a plateau. Ahead of him he was able to discern the faint outline of his wife in the dark.

"Allen," Judith called back tentatively, "is that you?"

Allen crawled forward and put a reassuring hand on his wife's leg. He winced in pain as another jolt tore up his leg. "It's me, honey. I caught my leg on something and it hurts like nobody's business."

"What happened?"

"I honestly don't know, but the pain is unbelievable. Hold on a second." Allen reached back and felt down his leg. His hand grazed over the curved, rough surface of a rounded rough object which had its jaws clamped tightly to his lower calf. He recoiled in horror as he realized that the object holding fast to his calf was the rotted skull of one of the walking dead. Allen remembered that these things died, or at least stopped moving, when the head was removed. He realized he had been bitten by one of them and the head must have been wrenched from its shoulders as he fell down the tunnel. He grunted and tried to pull the skull free, but it was held firmly with its teeth embedded in the thick muscle of his calf. With each pull, a searing burst of pain slammed up his leg. He also felt the warm wetness of his blood freely flowing around the wound.

"Honey, what's wrong?" Judith called back fearfully.

"I was bitten," Allen grunted through clenched teeth.

"What do you mean?" Judith asked, a growing knot of ice forming in the pit of her stomach.

"One of the corpses must have grabbed me as I was going through the hole. It bit me. As I fell through the hole I managed to somehow rip its head right off. Now the damned head is stuck on my leg and won't come off."

"Can you break it?"

"The tunnel is too narrow," Allen remarked, wincing at the pain, "and besides, I have nothing to use as leverage to break the damn thing." More worrisome, he thought, was whether he would get infected from the bite. *Will I become like them?*

"Judith," Annie called back, "is everything okay with Allen?"

Allen crawled past Judith and came up to Annie. He noticed that the smooth surface of the tunnel had given way to a thick, rough clay surface. Up ahead on every surface was barbed wire as far as the light from the torch would show. He looked back at his wife and the smooth tunnel behind her and knew that they could not go back. Even assuming that they managed to crawl up the shiny, smooth surface, there was still the horde of the dead to contend with. And ahead of them, they had razor-sharp barbed wire.

"Let me go first, Annie," Allen said as he squeezed by her in the tunnel. "We'll take this slow, but as I see it, we have no other options. Either we go forwards and get cut to rat shit, or we stay here and die of starvation." He grimaced, got to his hands and knees and began advancing through the tunnel. He looked back and grinned weakly at Annie. "I wonder if this was one of the three good tunnels."

Allen began inching forward and stopped at the periphery of the barbed wire. He reached over with his right hand, gave a sharp tug to his left sleeve and kept pulling until he heard the fabric tear at the seams. He kept pulling until it ripped entirely from the body of the shirt.

"What are you doing, Allen?" Judith called out.

"I'm creating some insurance." He lifted the torn shirtsleeve and by the light of the torch wrapped it around his right hand several times until it gave him a thick protective layer. He then tore at the right sleeve until it ripped as well, and he proceeded to wrap it around his left hand. "I'd advise you both to do the same. Try to minimize contact with the points of the barbed wire, okay?" He then lifted the torch with his left hand and advanced slowly forward.

The first few feet were the worst. The barbed wire scratched his face, back, hands and knees. Each movement that he made slashed across some part of his body and he felt as if he were bleeding from everywhere at once. The pain was excruciating, with some movements embedding the barbed wire into his flesh and tearing pieces of his body out as he advanced. He heard the screams from his wife and Annie a few feet behind him, and it helped steel his resolve to try to ensure that they all escaped this hellish maze.

After crawling for another half hour, Allen was exhausted. Blood was flowing copiously from fresh wounds on his forehead, mingling with sweat and dripping, burning drops into his eyes, blurring his vision. With a shaky hand, he raised the torch and pointed it forwards. The light still showed barbed wire until the periphery of its light. He looked back and saw the mix of pain and exhaustion in his wife's and Annie's faces. They were also bleeding from multiple wounds and their bodies were crossed with countless slashes.

Allen turned back to the task at hand and pushed forward, nearly oblivious to the pain. He was too numb. He could barely see, his vision blurred from blood and tears. Eventually, he put his hand forward and felt nothing beneath it. He wiped his hands across his eyes, using the tattered remnants of his sleeve to wipe away the excess blood. He was dimly able to see that he had reached the end of the tunnel and that the hole opened into a room beyond.

Through sheer force of will, Allen pulled himself forward and through the hole. He dropped three feet to the ground and lay gasping in a heap on the floor. Although his legs were trembling and he wasn't sure they would support his weight, he pulled himself to his feet and raised the torch to the hole in the wall leading to the tunnel. About fifteen feet back he saw the forms of his wife and Annie.

"Judith," Allen rasped in a voice that had nothing left, "I'm through. We made it." There was no response from either of the two women. "Judith," Allen tried again, his raw voice raised in panic.

"She's not moving, Allen," came Judith's pained reply.

Allen looked down at his bleeding arms and hands and then tore another section off his shirt. Even though he could barely make a fist, he managed to rip enough fabric off to shield his hand for one more foray into the barbed wire. But first he had the matter of getting the skull off his leg.

Allen held the torch so he could see his lower leg with better clarity. The sight made his blood run cold. A skull with sections of flesh still attached was clamped down on his lower calf. One socket was an empty hollow and the other held a rotting eye hanging limply from nerve and muscle tissue. Patches of yellowed flesh still clung around the mouth, pulled back to expose cracked and grey teeth. Trailing behind the skull was over a foot of spinal column, which still twitched. Allen drove the base of the torch repeatedly into the skull until it shattered, loosened its grip and fell lifelessly to the ground.

Allen crouched down and looked at his leg. The skull had done its work. A thick chunk of his calf was exposed, the muscle ragged. White-grey viscous pus oozed around the open wound and there were greyish green tendrils extending out beneath the skin from the source of the wound. Allen had never seen an infection spread so quickly, but had little doubt the leg was infected. At best, he'd lose the leg when they escaped this nightmare. *If we escape, what will happen to me?* He forced the thoughts from his head. Tearing another section of his shirt, he wrapped it around the gaping wound to staunch the flow of blood. He hoped that the infection was not spreading to his bloodstream.

Facing the tunnel, Allen hoisted himself up and began dragging his protesting body back over the barbed wire to where his wife and Annie were. It took some time and the pain was barely tolerable, but he made it over.

"She's not responding, Allen," Judith whimpered, tears welling up in her eyes.

Allen reached a bloody, trembling hand to Annie and felt her neck for a pulse. "She's still breathing, although it is quite weak. Come on, Judith, help me get her out of here."

With Judith at the rear, and Allen at the front, they slowly lifted and pulled Annie towards the end of the tunnel. Sheer exhaustion and the cramped space in the tunnel with the barbed wire all around made for slow progress. Judith said a silent prayer that Annie was not conscious. She didn't want to think what additional damage she and Allen were doing to her as they dragged her prone body over the razor-sharp wires.

Eventually, they managed to get out of the tunnel and lower Annie to the floor. Allen then gently helped Judith get undressed and he tended to her wounds as best he could by pressing down on all bleeding gashes with a clean section of his shirt. He looked at his wife of over two decades and felt his heart break. Her face was scratched in crisscross patterns, but at least her eyes seemed untouched. She had deep gashes over thirty percent of her body. Her long and shapely legs, which had once caused men to stop and turn, were in bad shape, with sections of skin hanging down in loose strips with the flesh exposed. At least, Allen reasoned, he had stopped the bleeding, and barring infection, she would escape with only scars and bad memories. He helped her dress then suggested she get some rest to preserve her strength.

Sobbing silently, Judith lay down next to Annie, hugging her protectively in an attempt to give strength by body heat to the older woman. Annie barely stirred, and her breathing was shallow and labored.

Once Allen was sure his wife was asleep, he picked up the torch and decided to explore. On the wall where they had escaped from the barbed wire were two other holes, likely from the other "safe" tunnels. Allen had to force himself not to laugh. *Imagine that*, he thought, *we actually picked one of the good tunnels.* He wondered what nightmares the bad tunnels held, if this was considered a safe bet. *Good choice, Annie*, he thought, nodding to the unconscious woman who he doubted would live through the next few hours.

Allen walked around the periphery of the room, which was perhaps a ten-foot square. The air was colder here and he saw the condensation from his breath even in the dim light cast by the torch. Tendrils of thick darkness seemed to wrap itself around the torch's flickering light, pushing back the dim glow.

The room itself looked to be a natural cave, the walls made entirely of rock. Lichen covered them in sporadic groupings. Stalagmites hung down from the rocky ceiling. At the far end of the room, next to a small, dark pool was another hole large enough to crawl through.

Allen approached the hole and crouched down next to the dark pool of water. He dipped a finger in the cold water and brought it to his lips. He quickly spat it out, since it was stagnant and foul. He cursed silently. Couldn't the bastards even give them a fair chance to survive? With no food or water, they would eventually be too weak to continue and would simply starve to death with no one to mourn their passing. He then got on his knees and with the torch in front of him crawled through the hole to the corridor beyond. He stood and thrust the torch forward and saw a narrow stone passageway extending for the next several feet. He began walking, cautiously, down the narrow corridor. Soon he came to a pit that extended across the entire corridor, which he estimated to be a good five feet wide. Looking down with the light from the torch, Allen saw many razor sharp spikes protruding from the floor of the pit. He knew they would have to try jumping it and in their condition it was certain Annie would not be able to make it across. In their weakened state, he had his doubts about himself and Judith as well. Allen just sank to his knees and felt the despair well up. They were never escaping this hellish ordeal. They would never feel the warm rays of the sun on their faces again.

Allen was sure that all was lost. As he turned to return to his wife and Annie, a blood-curdling howl like that of a wolf echoed through the still air of the maze.

Chapter 23

The giant rat shook the mossy earth from its fur and cast a hungry glace towards the Martins. Its fur was mottled brown and black, with patches missing as if stricken by some form of mange. It roared its displeasure at being roused from its slumber, and now being awake its first thought was to find food. The Martins would do for a start.

"Get behind me," Derek yelled, "while I engage this thing, I want you both to run past me and escape through the corridor on the far end of the cave."

"We're not leaving you, Dad," Carl screamed. "If we leave you, you'll die. You can't fight that thing by yourself."

"Derek," Ellen pleaded, casting furtive glances towards the advancing rat, "we'll deal with this as a family."

"Damn you, Ellen, there's no reason we all have to die."

Derek didn't get much more of a chance to argue since the giant rat was on him, throwing him hard to the ground. It sank its yellowed fangs in his thigh and he howled in pain. Blood streamed from the bite and down his leg. Carl reacted without thinking and leaped onto the rat's back, hoisting his serving dish high overhead. He sent it crashing down again and again on the rat's head until he saw the fur darken with the rat's blood.

The rat roared in pain and rage and buckled, throwing Carl off its back. It turned to confront Derek and attempted another bite. This time, Derek was ready and got his arm up in enough time to protect his neck. The rat sank its teeth deep into Derek's forearm and pulled back, its muzzle and teeth soaked red with blood.

Ellen ran to her husband's aid and slammed the serving tray down on the rat's skull. Its edge plunged deep into one of the beast's eyes and sent a shower of gelatinous humor over her arms and clothes, causing her to pull back with disgust.

Carl, meanwhile, got up and slammed his tray again and again onto the rat's head, each swing increasing in strength and intensity. Ellen joined in and together they kept raining blows down on the creature's head. Soon, the rat lay still. Carl kept slamming the tray down, harder and harder, screaming curses as the tears streamed down his face. Ellen put a reassuring arm around her son's shoulders until he stopped his assault on the rat and slumped down to his knees, sobbing violently and completely spent.

Ellen ran over to her husband, who lay prone, to tend to his wounds. She gasped as she saw the exposed bone on his arm.

"It looks worse than it is," Derek weakly tried to say, but his words came out slurred. Ellen could see the pooled blood around her husband and knew he had lost a dangerous amount of blood. She ripped a section of his shirt and wrapped it tightly around the wound on his leg and then did the same for his arm.

Derek tried to stand and managed two steps before his legs gave out and he fell forward to the ground. As he fell, he used his arm to shield his impact and pulled the homemade bandage free. It started bleeding all over again. Ellen helped Derek to a sitting position, stopped the bleeding and bandaged the arm once more.

"We have to wait until you have your strength back," Ellen said.

"We need to keep moving, dear. We don't have any food or water and will die here if we can't find a way out."

"Dad," Carl interjected, "you'll die here if you try to move right now. You lost a lot of blood. We can rest here a day. There's still some cheese left. We can have that for today while we rest. I could use some down time too."

Ellen held her hand to Derek's cheek. "Not one word, you got it?"

Derek mildly nodded his assent. He felt the world around him grow hazy as he slowly lost consciousness and fell into the icy embrace of memory.

Derek was back in his youth, on a camping trip with his father in Northern Maine. He remembered how perfect life seemed to be on that last day of the trip deep in woods. The sun was bright and hot overhead and had warmed them through the lush canopy of leaves on the thick copse of trees around them.

Derek and his father were sitting at the edge of a small lake fed by a turbulent river, fishing poles at the ready. They had both already caught enough fish for their dinner, but the setting was so idyllic they decided to keep fishing. Derek remembered how his father gave him his first beer, even though he was only twelve, and though he thought it tasted like crap, it was a bonding moment with his father he would never forget.

His father looked over his way and seemed to grow serious for a second, as if he were going to share a secret but was unsure how to begin. But the moment never came. Before he could say what seemed to be on his mind, the weather suddenly changed. Dark clouds rolled in and obliterated the sun, and the wind began to howl, whipping the leaves into a frenzy.

Derek looked over at his father, who had jumped to his feet, and was horrified to see a man who had never shown fear in his entire life suddenly look very afraid. At that moment, he seemed pale and very small.

"Dad, what is it?" Derek asked nervously.

His father swallowed and put both hands on his son's shoulders. "Derek," he paused, noting the thick, white mist that was rolling in, swirling frosty tendrils around them, "we need to leave right now."

Derek registered the fear in his father's eyes and grew afraid as well. He had always imagined his father as the strongest man in his world. Anything that could make his six-foot-two inch frame tremble like a child's was something to be taken very seriously.

"Dad? What's going on?"

"Derek, I know you never met your grandfather since he died before you were born. The thing is, he was murdered." Derek's eyes grew wide.

"What I am about to tell you may come as a shock, but it needs to be told. You're old enough to know our family's darkest secret. Now, hurry up and grab your coat. Don't worry about the gear. We have to leave right away. We'll talk as we go."

Derek started to protest. He couldn't understand why his father would willingly leave their tent, fishing gear and fish. Of course, the purplish-black sky with the frightening thunderhead clouds was one argument for leaving. The other was the frosty mist rolling in over the water and filling the gap through the trees, covering everything in an eerie white shroud.

"Now," Derek's father began, ushering his son hurriedly through the woods, back down the worn trail to where he knew their car was parked, and resisting the urge to run. As they walked, Derek's father kept glancing back. Eventually, he spoke. "Your grandfather did some horrible things in his youth. To begin with, he was a member of the Nazi Party in Germany and murdered many innocent people simply for having different religious beliefs."

Derek was speechless. He'd read about the Nazis in school and seen enough movies to know about the atrocities they had committed. Although he had never even met his grandfather, imagining anyone from his family as being part of that scene seemed completely unbelievable.

"So, as I was saying, something happened early on in the war," Derek's father continued, pausing to get through this without breaking down. "He and two other soldiers entered the home of a wealthy Jewish family in Hanover, Germany. They raped the mother and teenage daughter and then murdered the entire family. But someone got away. A teenage boy who saw everyone he loved brutally and violently taken from him. That teenager had photos of what happened and a burning need for revenge."

Derek was shocked. "How could your father know this, Dad?"

Derek's father sighed. "He got a letter from the boy, who apparently had tracked down all three soldiers over the years. The letter came shortly before he died telling him that he would suffer for the crimes he had committed. Along with the letter were copies of the photos implicating him in the rapes and murders of the family. Furthermore, he was told his entire family would suffer for his sins."

Derek shuddered, partially due to the horrific family secrets being revealed to him, and partially due to the plummeting temperature. "Did he try calling the police?"

"Derek," his father sighed again. "Have you been listening? My father was a war criminal. He committed atrocious acts that would have gotten him the death penalty. Someone sent him a letter saying they had proof that he had raped and murdered an entire family, along with incriminating photos. Would you go to the police? Yeah, they might try to help him, but he would have had to take accountability for his crimes."

"I guess not. Dad, what does my grandfather have to do with what is going on? What does this have to do with the sky going from blue to black and the temperature dropping like winter is coming? It looks like the storm of the century."

Derek's father stopped and turned to face his son. "Not a storm, son, something much worse. You see, grandfather had changed his name right after the war and went into hiding in Argentina. His wife left him shortly after and moved the family to the States. Your grandfather remarried and kept a low profile. We did keep in touch by letters and the occasional call. One day, he called me and relayed the story I just told you. He said that they had found him, but his voice was slurred and I wondered if he had been drinking. He told me that he was being hunted by supernatural means and that it was just a matter of time before they got him. He warned me to be careful and watch out for the signs. He mentioned that a cold, frosty mist and darkness will precede the death. He told me one more thing before he hung up."

"What was that, Dad?"

"He said, 'Beware the *golem*' and then he hung up. I never spoke to him again. Two days later, we got a phone call from a neighbor of his telling us that his house had been trashed and that he and his wife had been found brutally murdered. They were torn to shreds and could only be identified by their dental records."

Derek was about to further question his father when a man-like creature stepped out of the mist and grabbed his father by the collar of his shirt. Derek's eyes widened in horror as the creature, still partially hidden by the mist and shadows, squeezed his father's throat. Derek wanted to run but found his feet frozen in place by fear. He watched helplessly as his father flailed his arms, struggling to breathe. With a sickening crunch, followed by a wet, tearing noise, Derek's father's head was wrenched from his body.

Seeing his father decapitated before his eyes snapped Derek from his terror. He turned and ran as fast as he could through the darkened woods, tears streaming down his cheeks. He ran for what seemed like an eternity, fighting the stitch in his chest, trying to put as much distance between himself and the creature. He didn't know the woods and realized that he was lost. Between the icy mist and the darkness, he realized that he could be anywhere.

His foot caught on a rock, sticking out from the ground, which sent him sprawling forwards, down a hill and into the frigid waters of the river he assumed was the one he and his dad had been fishing in less than an hour earlier. Derek struggled to gain his equilibrium in the choppy water and was tossed mercilessly as he was buffeted downstream. As he lifted his head to get some air, he felt a sharp pain behind his right ear and then everything went black. The last sight he had before he was dragged under to blissful darkness was of a man-shaped figure at the water's edge, glowing faintly with a green phosphorescent light from odd markings on its body.

*   *   *

Derek snapped awake. He was bathed in a sticky sheen of sweat. He looked around at his wife and son, both casting nervous glances in his direction.

"Are you okay, honey?" his wife asked nervously.

Derek licked his lips, noting how dry his mouth felt. "It's here," he croaked. "Dear God, it's here."

"What is, dad?"

Derek took a deep breath and replied, "The *golem*. God help us. Our predicament just got much, much worse."

"What is this *golem*, and why would you possibly assume it's here?"

"Ellen," Derek hissed, "it has followed me my whole life. Somehow, whenever it was getting close, I would get this sensation in the pit of my stomach, like someone was plunging an icy dagger through me. I used to move around a lot when I was younger. It's why I changed jobs so frequently."

"Dad," Carl replied, "we haven't moved in well over a decade. I thought you said the creature was after you?"

"For some reason, after you were born it disappeared. I thought maybe it had been destroyed or something. I just know that I hadn't felt it. Now I know better. It was kept here in this maze, waiting for us all so it could finish the job."

"So, what makes you think it's here in this maze?"

"Because," Derek growled, "that icy feeling in the pit of my stomach is back. And by the intensity of it, the creature is very, very close by. I haven't felt it this strong since I was a boy, and believe me, it's here and it's after us. God help us, because unless we can find a way out, we won't live to see another day."

CHAPTER 24

Paul Kaufmann wanted to go home. This day was nothing short of hell and he was far too important a man to die in this miserable pit like a common rat. He chuckled as he considered his predicament. His right arm was a mess of ruined flesh up to the elbow, thanks to having been immersed in a powerful acid. The gas he had been exposed to in the house was eating him away from the inside, doing something to his lungs that made it hurt to breathe and forcing him to expel a bloody mass with every few breaths. He had spent the latter part of his life eradicating the vermin races from the States, and now he was doomed to die amongst them.

He had been digging with his good hand for several hours and his face was grimy with sweat and dirt. His tattered clothes were damp and felt glued to his aching body. Kaufmann's perseverance and blind determination were beginning to yield results. Because the earth that blocked his way out was so tightly packed, his makeshift tunnel was holding up quite well. Kaufmann had managed to dig through his body length and felt the earth loosen further as he went along, a sign that he was nearing the other side.

Two things happened simultaneously. Kaufmann punched his hand through to the other side just as the makeshift tunnel came crashing down on him. He thrashed about, twisting to give him room to breathe as he spat out a bloody mouthful of damp earth. Kaufmann tried to open his eyes but only managed to get gritty earth in, effectively cutting off his vision and making his eyes water. He exploded in a mix of rage and agony since he could not even reach up to wipe his eyes, his hands tightly held in place by the collapsed tunnel.

Kaufmann used his feet to gain a solid foothold on the packed earth behind him, and with all the strength he could muster, he began pushing himself forward inch by inch. With each push, he felt his muscles straining, threatening to give out. After a few more feet, he managed to get both of his arms, his head and shoulders through. From there it was easy to pull the rest of his body free of the tunnel. He collapsed in a heap, breathing in huge amounts of the damp, earthy air before bending over and coughing up several thick, bloody masses.

Kaufmann stood up and wiped the dirt from his eyes. They burned and when he opened them, they watered. Eventually, his sight came back and he tried to take stock of his surroundings. The room he was in was cavernous, that much he could tell since the lichen encrusted the walls and ceiling gave off a faint fluorescent glow. He had lost his torch in the collapse of the tunnel and it made no sense to even bother trying to retrieve it since the fire had gone out and he had neither matches nor lighter, having lost those as well.

To his left, Kaufmann noticed a faint glow in a rectangular outline. *Could this be a doorway out of here?* he wondered. He decided to investigate. Using his good hand to feel his way along the walls, Kaufmann soon felt the earth beneath his fingers give way to cold stone, with just a hint of dampness. The closer he got to the light, the more convinced he became that it was framing a doorway.

Kaufmann moved to where he assumed the door would be and saw that the outline of light did come from behind an opening. That left him two options: he could try to find some way to open the door or he could turn around and explore the dark, musty cave. He reasoned that he would rather deal with a problem in the light than be ambushed in the dark.

Feeling around the perimeter where the light shone through, Kaufmann felt a gentle breeze from beyond. There were no hinges on either side to show how the door would open. He began running his hand on the door itself and felt a smooth metal plate where a handle would have been. Without hesitation, he pushed down on the metal plate and felt it sink into the stone door.

The door slid back, exposing a brightly lit tunnel. Kaufmann turned to look at the cave behind him, now that the glow from the tunnel was able to afford some light to the rest of his surroundings. The cave was larger than he had thought. Far off to his right he saw a wooden table and some wooden stools. There were plates scattered around the table with what looked like cheeses spread across the table and floor. Even more noticeable were the countless pulped bodies of some of the largest rats he had ever seen.

This changed things. Kaufmann needed to think. Something had happened in the cave to kill that many of rats in such a violent manner. Either some of the others from his group had come this way and already dealt with the trap, or something worse lay in wait in the darkness ahead. On the other side of the coin, perhaps someone had been here, he reasoned, fought the rats, and then escaped out the well-lit tunnel adjacent to where he stood.

Kaufmann paced back and forth, debating his options. Either choice likely led to something worse. He had no illusions that anything in this death trap would be easy. *To hell with it*, he thought, *the choice is simple.* Either go forward through the darkness or follow a lit tunnel, both to unknown ends. He smiled grimly, turned and walked through the doorway into the tunnel. As soon as he stepped on the stone floor of the tunnel, the door behind him began closing.

A muffled, terrified scream broke through the still air and it took Kaufmann a moment to register that it had come from within the darkest recesses of the cave. By this point, the door was mostly shut, with too small an opening for Kaufmann to have any hope of going back. The door closed shut with a solid thump of stone upon stone. He looked at the door and noticed that on this side there was no handle, door plate or any other means of opening the door. Everything in this maze seemed designed to keep ushering people onwards towards some specific end, and Kaufmann was smart enough to realize that, while it appeared to be a maze, it really was more of a series of linear paths that interconnected.

Kaufmann coughed and violently spat out a thick and bloody viscous mass. He was feeling weak and lightheaded and knew his time was short. His main priority was getting out of this nightmare and getting medical help. Then he would come back with his army of followers and burn the mansion to the ground with all its inhabitants. Of course, he'd save something special for that Ryan character, the cause of his current miserable state.

Kaufmann looked around. To his left, the tunnel ended with a wall of earth and rocks, presumably the same thing that had blocked him on the way in. To his right, the well-lit tunnel extended for a while, then branched off sharply to the left. The tunnel was made of solid gray stone, carved fairly smooth on all surfaces. While well lit, there was no visible light source.

Since he had no other options, Kaufmann began walking down the tunnel until he came to the bend. He cautiously peered around the corner and saw that the tunnel extended maybe fifty feet and then turned sharply to the right. The tunnel was as featureless as the one he had just come from.

Kaufmann walked down this tunnel and peered around the next bend. Like the one he was in, the new tunnel extended another fifty feet then turned sharply to the left. The tunnel was also featureless, nothing but cold gray stone as far as the eye could see.

Kaufmann was getting frustrated. What was the purpose of this tunnel? Perhaps it was to lull people into a false sense of security so they would let their guard down. Or perhaps, he reasoned, it was a maintenance tunnel for whoever had built this place, to make sure all the traps were in working order. After all, someone had to keep this funhouse of death functioning.

Kaufmann continued walking and came to where the tunnel turned. He peered around the bend and saw that, perhaps a hundred feet down, the tunnel came to an abrupt end. On the far wall was a round man-sized opening that led off into darkness. The tunnel walls were crisscrossed with grooves that formed a grid down the length of the wall.

After coughing violently and spitting another bloody mess from his lungs, Kaufmann took a tentative step into the new tunnel. After all the shit he'd been through, he wanted to be damn sure he was being careful. When he was halfway down the tunnel, he heard hissing and grinding from behind him. Kaufmann quickly turned around in time to see a wall closing behind him, effectively sealing him in the tunnel. What was worse was the crisscrossed pattern on the walls started to glow a bright red until, finally, lasers shot out between the walls, forming a mesh-like barrier, and they began moving down the wall in his direction.

It only took a moment to realize that the lasers would cut him to ribbons if he stayed where he was, so Kaufmann turned and ran for the far end of the wall and the round opening as fast as his battered body could take him. *What the fuck do lasers have to do with the death camp motif?* he thought sourly. Unless this was a maintenance tunnel and these were security features.

He dared look back only once and noticed that the laser grid was getting closer. At the rate he was moving, he wouldn't make it to the hole in the wall. This grim realization spurred him on faster and when Kaufmann was a foot from the opening, he dove through headfirst without looking back.

The other side of the opening was a smooth and slick slide that seemed oiled to prevent someone from trying to climb back up. For what seemed like an eternity, Kaufmann slid faster and faster headfirst down into the darkness until he was finally forcefully expelled from the slide and sent crashing hard into a stone wall. There was a brief flash of intense pain and then Kaufmann's world faded out in a wall of red.

Kaufmann was brought back to his youth, to when he was nine years old and visiting an aunt in Boston. While his mother visited with his aunt in her stately old Dorchester home, he played outside. He noticed how the neighborhood seemed to be changing, moving from a once-affluent demographic to something else. He was too young to understand the nature of economic change, but he was old enough to see that the neighborhood was deteriorating. The once-beautiful mansions were being sold off and subdivided into lower income housing. His mother had pleaded with her sister to sell and move to a nicer, more upscale neighborhood like Weston or Newton, but she simply refused, arguing that this was her home and that she shouldn't be chased out of it.

After unsuccessfully searching for kids his own age to play with, Kaufmann decided to head inside and hang out with his mom and aunt. He walked into the house to hear sobbing coming from the living room. His aunt was on her knees with blood streaming from her nose and her eyes were wet with tears. His mother, who was by far his favorite person in the world, was kneeling next to her sister, comforting her. Three black men in their early twenties stood above the two women, each holding a gun.

"Give me the money, bitch," one of the men spat at Kaufmann's aunt. "I won't ask again."

"I swear," she replied tearfully, "I gave you all I have. I don't have any more."

"Just off the bitch," another of the men blurted out. He was twitchy and shaky and seemed like he wanted to explode.

"Mom?" Kaufmann asked in a barely audible whisper. What happened next came so quickly, yet always was replayed in slow motion in Kaufmann's mind.

"Run, Paul," Kaufmann's mother shrieked and pushed herself forward into one of the men. Kaufmann's aunt did the same, knocking the man in front of her off his feet. The third man responded by firing at Kaufmann's aunt, the bullet hitting her square in the right eye and punching through her brain and skull and out the other side in a shower of blood and bone. She made an odd gurgling sound and dropped to her knees, then pitched forward, face down. Kaufmann tried to run but found himself frozen in place, too terrified to move. His mother tried to reach him but was cut down by a spray of bullets as they punched into her back and into her lungs, heart and throat. She looked imploringly at her son as a thick red tear fell from her eye, and then she too died.

Kaufmann shrieked in agony and rage and turned to face the man who had killed his mother. All he could think of was killing the son of a bitch. His roar of anger was cut short as he heard the crack of the gun being fired, felt a sharp pain in his head, and then the world went dark.

He awoke in a hospital bed, a thick coating of gauze and bandages wrapped around his head. A pretty young Hispanic nurse stood by his bed. She looked at him compassionately and took his hand. "Welcome back, honey, you had us worried for a while."

Kaufmann pulled his hand back and screamed at the top of his lungs. "Get away from me, you bitch." He kept screaming until several other nurses ran in to see what the problem was. The young nurse left the room in tears, unaware of the reason for such rage in the young man.

The next day, he was sent to live with cousins in Oregon. There he found his anger grow into hatred and met others who shared in his beliefs. Over the years, he moved around the country spreading his hate through organizations that shared his beliefs and where his intelligence and sheer determination took him to the top. He had been planning a revolutionary operation in New England, where it had all begun, from his Vermont base when he was captured and thrown into the maze.

Kaufmann awoke to a dull throbbing in his skull. He reached up to his forehead with his good hand and felt the wound and the stickiness of the blood that was already coagulating. His vision was somewhat blurry and when he tried to move his head, he felt a surge of nausea well up quickly. He bent over and vomited.

He hated reliving that day from his youth when his whole world changed. He believed it was his destiny to cleanse the world of the mongrel races. It had just taken the loss of his beautiful mother to get him to see the light. Still, he agonized over his mother and aunt and wished that they had not been taken from him so abruptly. He saw the same terror each and every night he slept, wishing for a reprieve.

He leaned against the wall and used it to support himself while he got unsteadily to his feet. His vision was beginning to clear, although the blackness was nearly absolute with the exception of a faint fluorescence scattered haphazardly on the cavern walls. A faint sound in the distance caused him to turn. Far off, Kaufmann was able to discern the faint shape of a man, glowing slightly with an emerald green to the edges.

"What the fuck is that?" Kaufmann muttered. It seemed to be coming his way, almost as if it were gliding. The air around him seemed to grow colder and colder.

For the first time in his life since the day his mother was killed, Kaufmann felt his bowels loosen and he felt himself rooted in place, unable to move. He knew he should run, of course, but it was dark and he didn't know where to even run to. He was coughing some bloody phlegm when he felt a hand on his arm.

He snapped to his right and even though it was dark, he recognized the woman from the auditorium. He hadn't caught her name at the time. He saw that she was perhaps forty, a bit short and somewhat on the stocky side. She was gasping for air and seemed short of breath. "Come on," she said between shortened breaths, "we have to go."

"Who or what is that?" Kaufmann gestured towards the rapidly advancing man, who seemed to glow brighter as he got closer.

"Death," Suze replied. "It's the end for both of us if we don't get a move on."

Kaufmann looked at Suze and then at the mystery man and then growled, "Then move it, because I sure as hell don't want to die down here." Taking Kaufmann by his good arm, Suze led him off into the darkness away from the *golem*.

CHAPTER 25

Allen returned to where Judith sat with Annie. His wife looked so fragile by the flickering light of the torch. There were cuts on her face, arms and legs. He knew the pain she must be in, yet she had put that aside to help that sweet, elderly woman, Annie, who still was unconscious.

"How is she?" Allen asked.

"Not good," Judith replied, sighing softly, "she's lost a lot of blood. At her age, she needs medical help or she won't make it."

"We have another problem, Judith. Outside this room is a corridor with a pit that spans a good five feet across. Lining the bottom of the pit are sharpened spikes. Hell, at our age, after all we've been through, I worry about us being able to jump across. There is no way Annie could make the jump."

A look of horror crossed Judith's features. "I don't like where this is heading, Allen."

"What are our options, Judith?" Allen growled. "We can stay here and die of starvation and exposure or we can move on and try to survive. In case you forget, it's as cold as a meat locker in here. We need to stay warm and to do that we'll need to keep moving. Besides, we've all been hurt and are not functioning at our best right now. You are cut to ribbons and need stitches. My leg is almost certainly infected from that thing's bite. I just don't want to die like a rat in a maze."

Judith moved closer to her husband and took his hand in hers. "I hear what you're saying, Allen, but that goes against everything I hold dear. If we leave her here, Annie will die."

"Damn it, Judith," Allen spat out, "if we stay here, we will all die. Is that what you want?"

A shallow cough from behind them stopped them cold. Annie was awake and trying to force herself to a sitting position.

"Annie…" Judith began.

Annie held up her hand, and Allen noticed how badly it shook. "I want you both to go on. If you can get out, you can send back help. I heard what you said and there is no way I can get across a five-foot gap. Honestly, I can barely sit up, let alone walk. Managing a running jump would be impossible. And you're right, you know. If we stay here, we'll all die. I'd rather take a chance at being rescued than know I've caused you both to die alongside me."

"Annie, we can't."

Annie sighed, looked at Judith, and took her hands. "My husband died here. My life was tied to his. If I don't make it, I can say I've led a full life. You both have many years to go and so much more to live. Please, I don't want any more arguments. Also, I'm just so tired and honestly refuse to go another step. My mind is made up. You go and I'll stay."

"We'll get out, Judith, and send help," Allen said quietly, almost ashamed of his actions. His resolve still stood and he knew that to survive, they had to get out.

"Allen," Judith pleaded.

Annie hugged Judith close and said in a low voice, "I can't make it, Judith. I will not have your deaths on my conscience. Look, I'm not kidding anyone here. I have nothing left. I can barely walk. I cannot run and I certainly cannot jump across one foot, let alone five. I hurt and will not allow you both to die because of me. But I do have something for you." Annie reached around her neck and removed a small locket on a silver string. She opened the locket and showed Judith the picture inside. Judith saw that it was Annie and Rudolf, in black and white, back when they were much younger. "This picture was taken over forty years ago," Annie said solemnly, "shortly after I married Rudolf. I have kept it close to my heart ever since. Now you can do me one last favor. You can keep this and promise me that you will let the authorities know what happened here, and that good people died. And please, just remember me."

Judith hugged Annie close. "Please be strong, Annie, and please don't give up hope. We will get out, and we will send help back for you. I promise."

Judith wiped back her tears and went over to her husband. "Let's do this." She looked back at Annie sitting there looking so frail and small. "We will be back for you," Judith said, with as much conviction as she could muster, tears streaming down her cheeks. "I promise."

Allen led Judith through the hole in the wall to the corridor beyond. He held the torch high to give them enough light to see for ten feet in all directions. They began moving down the corridor until they came to the pit. Allen held the torch over the edge and Judith saw that the pit was deeper than ten feet, since she could not even see the bottom. Of course, the light did reflect cruelly from the many sharpened metal spikes rising from the pit floor. Across an open span of approximately five feet, the corridor continued.

"Now do you see what I meant?" Allen asked.

"Allen, how can we get across this? With all we've been through, I don't know if I can make the jump. Maybe we should just stay with Annie and hope that some of the others get away and send help."

Allen took her by her shoulders and saw the fear etched in her features. "Honey, I know this is a hard thing we are doing, but we have no choice. If we stay with Annie, we'll be dead within twenty-four hours. It's like a meat locker down here. If we don't keep moving, we will die. Annie knows this, Judith. She does not expect us to return with help."

Judith's eyes widened with horror. She opened her mouth to say something, but the words would not come. She cursed herself for being so naïve and then lowered her head. She knew that, for the rest of her life, she would remember condemning that sweet old woman to a grisly fate of freezing to death. "How do you want to do this, Allen?"

Allen looked at Judith, then at the pit. "I think of the two of us, I stand the better chance of making it across. Therefore, I'll carry the torch as I make the jump."

"Are you insane, Allen? You can't possibly make the jump carrying the torch, especially with your calf muscle torn."

"Listen to me," Allen shouted, "if I don't carry the torch, then we have to go the rest of the way in darkness. You can't do it. Look at you. You're a mess of wounds all over your body. I'm worried you won't make the jump on your own."

"I can throw it to you," Judith replied.

Allen shook his head. "If you don't throw it far enough, or I miss it, we run the risk that the fire goes out. We need this fire for light and for heat. This torch is our lifeline and I, for one, refuse to let it go."

Judith walked over to Allen and hugged him tightly. "Alright, go ahead and try this. I trust your judgment, Allen. Just be careful, okay?"

With a wink and a lopsided grin, Allen walked down the corridor until he was as far back from the pit as possible. He lowered the torch and held it tightly in his right hand. He felt his heart pounding in his chest like a jackhammer, and though it was freezing, he felt cold perspiration bead on his brow. Without another word, he put his head down and ran towards the pit, ignoring the shooting agony in his leg. At the edge, he jumped with every ounce of strength he could muster.

Allen easily cleared the expanse and fell forward. Not wishing to take any chances with his torch, he held his right arm high in the air and without both hands to brace himself he hit the ground hard, first with his chest and then with his chin.

Judith shrieked as she saw her husband fall and then breathed with relief when she realized he was safe. A bit more banged up, perhaps, but safe, nevertheless. Allen triumphantly held the torch up high from his position on his stomach. He got slowly to his feet and lowered the torch so it rested against the wall.

"Your turn, honey," Allen called out. "It's easier than it looks. I'll be here to catch you."

"If you let me fall, Allen, I'm leaving you," Judith said. Allen smiled. He knew that even under such extreme circumstances Judith managed to keep her dry sense of humor. She moved as far back as she could and psyched herself for the task. Putting her head down, she ran for the pit. Just before the edge, she stopped short.

"What's the matter?" Allen called out anxiously.

"I can't do it," Judith sobbed, "it's too far."

"Judith," Allen yelled back, "you can do this. Just run and jump. Don't even think about it. Just do it."

Judith walked back down the corridor and turned to face her husband, who stood there across the expanse of the pit. She bit down on her lower lip, wiped the tears from her eyes and then ran as fast as she could towards the pit. At the edge, she jumped with all the force she could muster. She barely cleared the five feet and landed at the edge. She frantically flailed her arms, trying to grasp onto something as she slid back into the pit towards the sharpened spikes. She shrieked in horror as she slid back, her nails digging grooves in the dusty, dried earth of the floor. Allen lunged forward, grabbed Judith by her wrists and pulled her back toward him. With a final tug, he managed to yank her free of the pit and they both fell backwards onto the ground, Judith landing hard on top of him.

"See," Allen rasped, "I told you it would be easy. Come on. Let's try to get out of this Hell hole."

* * *

Annie sat huddled in the corner, the freezing air sending icy waves through to her soul. She sat still, barely moving, not to conserve energy, but because she didn't have any strength left to move. She hadn't lied to Allen and Judith. Not one bit, in fact. She felt broken inside and hurt all over. Right now, she just wanted to sleep. Even though she could see the frosty plume with each exhalation of breath, she began to feel warm and drowsy.

She opened her eyes somewhat, and though she saw through a dull haze, she did notice a tall figure walking her way. The figure emanated warmth and Annie felt herself reaching out to him. Though still hazy, she felt that it was Rudolf coming back to be with her once more. She allowed herself to slip into his warm embrace and found herself young again.

Young and vibrant and in the arms of the man she loved. She felt him put his arms around her and she closed her eyes, welcoming his embrace and the chance to be back with her beloved.

The small cavern got colder still and frost formed on the walls and floor. In one corner, a small figure sat still, frost gently coating her features, making the skin seem to sparkle in the dim natural light of the cave. What was most distinctive was the single tear, frozen halfway down her face, and the smile, forever etched on her lips, as if she were frozen in a state of bliss.

Chapter 26

Eric felt the panic rising. Time was running out and he had no clue how to get out of his predicament. He rubbed his temples and grabbed two fistfuls of his short, spiky hair and bellowed in rage. He saw that there were less than two minutes left before some deadly gas flooded the room. He had a one-in-four chance of escape. No matter how scared he was, he had to push at least one of the buttons. If he did, he would at least guarantee Kerry's safety for this room and, he reasoned, provide a chance for himself as well. If he did nothing, they both would die painfully. Not the greatest of options.

Eric stood and walked to the monitor. He hated making decisions under duress, but he simply did not have the luxury to think about it any longer. He was too strong to just give up in life. He hadn't been raised that way and survived a tough adolescence to just give up.

Eric was so focused on making his choice that he did not hear the door slide open behind him.

"Eric, Stop!" Eric heard someone shout. Eric quickly turned and saw Ryan standing in the doorway, on the other side of the pit.

"You…" Eric growled and balled his hands into fists as he leaped across the pit and connected solidly with a haymaker to Ryan's jaw, sending him sprawling back into the wall. "I'll kill you!" Eric yelled as he rained down punch after punch. Ryan did not try to fight back. He simply kept his arms up to ward off the blows.

"Listen to me, Eric," Ryan gasped between punches, "we don't have time for this now. If you want to live, you'll listen to me." Eric seemed oblivious to Ryan's pleas and kept punching him. Ryan knew that they had practically no time left, so he fought back and connected squarely with Eric's jaw, knocking him back. "I said stop it!" he bellowed. "I'm here to get us all out of this mess, but I need your cooperation."

Eric rubbed his jaw and looked over at the clock. Forty seconds remained. "Spit it out."

"Get in the pit and when I yell 'now', push the button to activate it."

"Why should I get in the pit?" Eric yelled back. "How do I know you won't screw me over and push the wrong button?"

"You dumb bastard," Ryan said, lowering his voice slightly, "there is no right button. If you push any of the four, you would have been killed. I know every trap in this maze. To get out of here, you would need to push them all." Ryan glanced back to the clock. "Fifteen seconds, ace. What's it going to be?"

With a quick glance over to the ticking clock, Eric jumped down into the pit. "Push the button, and hurry."

Ryan ran over to the console and pushed buttons three, two, one and four in that order. "Done!" he screamed to Eric. "Push the activate button. Do it now!"

Without a second thought, Eric pushed the button. He felt it click into place, and then the bottom three-quarters of the wall slid back, exposing a small chamber behind the pit. Eric leaned in and saw that the wall moving back exposed a small, square room. On one wall there was a ladder heading up. Aside from that, the room was bare.

"Where does this ladder go to?" Eric called up to Ryan.

"Deeper into the maze," Ryan called back down.

Eric climbed out of the pit and stood before Ryan. "Why should you help us? In fact, why should we trust you? Give me one reason not to kill you right where you stand."

Ryan shoulders sagged a little. "I'll be brief because we don't have much time. The short and not so sweet of it is your relatives brutally murdered my relatives early in World War II. My grandfather was there and saw it happen. He escaped as a teenager and while escaping watched his girlfriend get killed. Then, years later, a shocking event became the final straw for him. His wife was brutally murdered. Something broke in him that day and he swore to get back at those who had hurt him the most. To him, that meant finding and killing the three soldiers who killed his family and all their living descendants. Anger and hatred filled his every waking hour until just before his death. My grandfather just died, but on his deathbed he admitted that he no longer wanted revenge. Facing his own mortality, he reasoned that carrying this hatred around for so many years was a mistake. He would have fixed things at the end if he could have."

"What stopped him?"

"The problem was that his assistant was blackmailing him and that if he stopped what he was doing, his assistant would kill his entire family. The other problem was the creature loose in the maze, the *golem*. My grandfather was far too weak to stop it and I simply don't know how. I'm working on a plan, though. And that is to get as many of you out of the maze and if possible seal the creature in here forever. That way, you will be safe and it won't be able to get you. But we need to act fast. Your life forces are driving it and it senses that the end to its purpose is close. You see, once that happens, it can finally sleep for good. "

"Look," Eric continued, "that is the most messed up excuse I have ever heard. I can understand your grandfather's pain, but these things were done to his family decades ago by men long dead. None of us that you forced into this mess had anything to do with it. Why should we have to die for relatives we never even met? And who the hell are you to act as judge, jury and executioner? You say some guy manipulated you into doing this? Well, that's not good enough. You now owe us and for everyone that dies in this maze. Their blood will be on your hands forever. Right now, though, you can go to hell. I simply don't care. I just want this to be over. I don't want to die here."

Ryan dropped to his knees, the tears welling up in his eyes. "Why do you think I came down to the maze? I couldn't allow people to die because I was afraid. I knew that I had to do what I could to rescue as many of you as possible. But it will do us no good. My grandfather's assistant, Jason, is a very dangerous man. I'm sure he's down in the maze looking for me. If he finds me, I'm dead. If I die, you lose your way out. The problem is, if he finds anyone else in the maze, he will simply kill them to ensure that everyone dies and there are no loose ends to connect him to this."

"Okay, I get it. This Jason guy is dangerous. We'll try to avoid him. Now tell me about this *golem*. What is it?"

"This creature is an unstoppable creation and will kill anyone who gets in its way. The ritual to create the beast involved having a pure soul. My grandfather's soul was not pure. It was riddled with pain and hatred, two powerful emotions that were transferred to the creature upon creation. With each passing day, the pain from these emotions built up in the creature, making it even more deadly an adversary. It feels pain and the only way to ease some of its pain is to take one of the lives it was tasked to destroy. It's an unstoppable killing machine. As I said, the only way to stop it is for you all to die because then its pain ends and it can cease to exist. But if I can get you all out and seal it in the maze, it will be trapped forever."

"Jesus," Eric grunted. "Let's get the hell out of here."

"Remember, the creature will live until every last member of the three soldiers' bloodlines are utterly destroyed. We cannot destroy it. At best, we can evade it while we try to escape the maze. I'll try to figure out a way to shut it down. If not, I will try to trap it in the maze. The reality is this: I can lead us out of the maze and try and trap the *golem* here, but if it escapes, it will hunt you and your families down for the rest of your lives. My atonement for my part in this tragedy will be to get you out and keep you all one step ahead of the creature. I will also do whatever it takes to try and stop it, even if it means sacrificing my own life."

"So let's do this." Eric looked down at Kerry. "What about her?"

"We'll have to carry her. But we have to move fast."

"Is the creature close?" Eric asked nervously.

"Oh yes," Ryan answered. "Before I entered the maze, I checked on the monitors we have that show the activity down here. It was closest to you and Kerry so it made you two the natural choice of who to try and save first. Like I said, it's in the maze and is drawn to all your life forces. The closer it gets to you, the stronger the pull."

Eric threw his arms up in exasperation, "So what chance do we stand?"

Ryan smiled and his eyes twinkled with malice. "Better than you think. I know the maze and have an eidetic memory. I also know how to deactivate or bypass many of the traps. The man I warned you about has no knowledge of any aspect of the maze and is unfamiliar with the traps. With any luck, he will fall victim to the maze and I'll be able to get as many of you out as possible without running into the *golem*."

Eric looked at Ryan and realized he stood a better chance taking him at his word than being left to his own devices in this death trap. "Okay, we'll go with you and we will get out of this hell. But, so help me, if you screw us over, I will see you dead. You got me?" He extended his hand, which Ryan shook.

"Fair enough," Ryan replied. "Now come on, we have a long way to go and there is one more piece to this puzzle you need to know."

"Shit. What else can there be?"

"The maze is a dynamic creation. My grandfather was a brilliant man. He would have to have been to design something like this. First off, he used different groups of contractors from different states and even different countries on the project. No one was ever privy to seeing more than a small fraction of the maze, which grandfather explained as the foundation for a new mansion. All contractors were paid in cash so there would be no records."

"I still don't understand why this maze is so different."

"Eric," Ryan continued, "this maze is built as a three-dimensional construction. It is not flat. There are rooms and tunnels that span several levels. Sometimes a room will take you up or down or even to both levels. Some rooms have dead ends, others have multiple egresses. In fact, the choices you made would determine where the maze took you. But the thing that is certain is that no matter what choices you make in the maze, they are the ones you must live with because all doors are one-way."

"Why were they designed that way?" Eric asked, growing increasingly more curious.

"Well," Ryan continued, "even though the maze was designed with enough traps and was non-linear in design, by having doors that only opened one way it ensured that all people in the maze would be directed towards the *golem*'s lair."

Eric looked puzzled. "What did you mean when you said that the maze was non-linear in design?"

Ryan sighed and continued. "The maze was designed so no one who went through the maze would ever be able to follow the same route should they do it again. The means to this end are movable walls and floors. Sensors indicate when no one is nearby and at random intervals walls move to form new corridors leading to different sections of the maze. Some sections of the floor move as well, revealing hidden staircases down to lower sections. Overall, there are a few square miles of maze beneath the mansion and beyond. And yet in all this chaos there is only one way out."

"Well," Eric demanded, "do you know how to get there?"

"I do. However, in order to get there we need to pass the *golem*'s lair."

A low groan from the other side of the room caused both men to turn. Kerry was getting herself into a sitting position. She looked from Eric to Ryan and said in a low and raspy voice, "Where are we? How did we get here?" And then she pointed to Ryan and asked with a bit more effort, "And what is he doing here?"

Eric walked over to Kerry and helped her to her feet. She wobbled slightly and looked unsteady. "He's going to help us get out of here. He promised to help. I think we need him if we want to get through this alive."

"Do we?" Kerry asked, disbelief in her voice.

"Yes," Ryan added, "we do. But don't get your hopes up just yet. We have a ways to go to get to the exit, and there are countless hurdles we will have to get by. Don't get me wrong. I'm your best hope of getting out of here, but it won't be a picnic."

"I don't care," Kerry wailed, "I just want to go home, so please get us out."

CHAPTER 27

Jeremy knew that he was in trouble. This Jason character was clearly insane. The way he had killed Nick was one indicator. The other was that he was taking him down into a dark series of tunnels where, apparently, Kerry and several others had been captured and left to die.

"I don't understand any of this," Jeremy said to Jason as they walked down the tunnel's corridor, ever conscious of the gun pointed at his back.

"Well, Jeremy," Jason replied, his features almost twisting as he broke into a wide grin, "what I am about to tell you will shock you senseless. You see, the likelihood that you live to see beyond the next twenty-four hours is very slim, so I may as well fill you in on some of what has been going on here."

Jeremy kept silent but angled his head in a gesture to let Jason know that he was listening.

"Basically," Jason said in a sinister whisper, "we kidnapped Kerry and a host of others and forced them down into this maze. The maze is full of deadly traps and more likely than not, each and every person here will die a horrible and painful death. Know why we're doing this, Jeremy?"

Jeremy paused, uncertain how his response would cause Jason to react. He forced himself to speak, because he knew that Jason was awaiting a response and that it was never a good idea to piss off a crazy man holding a gun to your back. "I don't know. Are you planning on blackmailing their families?"

Jason tossed his head back and laughed, exposing a mouth filled with very white teeth, surprisingly sharp, which looked almost lupine. Jeremy shuddered and tried not to let his nervousness show. "Thanks, Jeremy. I appreciated that. Naivete like that may even prolong your life. But then again it may not. Here's one to chill your bowels, boy," Jason said slowly and deliberately, looking straight at Jeremy as he did so.

"No, Jeremy," Jason continued, savoring the look of fear on Jeremy's face, "they are not here for blackmail. I have something far worse and far more final in mind for them."

Jeremy turned suddenly and threw himself at Jason, knocking the gun from his hands and making him lose his balance. The man may have terrified him, but there was something about the way he mentioned finality that had struck him hard. Jason was playing for keeps and he had to get far away from him as quickly as he could or he'd be killed himself and left to rot here in the dark in the tunnels below the house.

Jeremy used his momentum to rain down punch after punch on Jason, who just lay there, not even defending himself.

Jason grinned. "Are you through, boy?" he hissed. He caught Jeremy's next punch in mid-throw and held it there in a steel grip. Still holding Jeremy's fist in his hand, he slowly stood and twisted Jeremy's arm behind his back. Jeremy howled in pain as Jason twisted even further, threatening to pull the arm from its socket.

Jason then spun Jeremy around and moved his face inches from the young man's. Jeremy stared in terror as he sensed that Jason had been merely toying with him. He knew then and there that there was nothing he could do to escape.

"You get one freebie, Jeremy," Jason growled, his voice taking on a lower and darker tone. "You've just used it." He took Jeremy by the collar and threw him nearly ten feet down the hallway. He rushed over and scooped Jeremy back up. "That took no effort at all, so imagine what I could do if you really angered me. Know this. I am stronger and faster than you by a very, very wide margin. I could snuff out your petty life in the blink of an eye, but I may yet need you. So if you keep to your place, and do as I say, you may yet live to see your precious Kerry. Have I made myself clear?"

Jeremy nodded and then lowered his head. His body was screaming out in pain from being tossed like a child's toy, but he held it in. He was smart and a survivor, and if he stayed smart he would find a way to get through this as well.

"Good," Jason replied, almost purring. "Come then, young Jeremy, lead the way. We have a ways to go and a rough road ahead and I don't want to miss any of the fun."

They walked until they reached the end of the winding corridor and entered a room that waited at the end. Inside, Jeremy noticed the rows of bunk beds, the wood aged and almost grayish. The room even had a smell to it, like death and despair. Jeremy felt himself grow cold as he realized that this room was a representation of the bunks of a concentration camp. He had visited one while touring Germany many years ago as a college student. He was more horrified now than he had been that day so many years back.

"Is this…" Jeremy stammered, "is this a copy of the sleeping barracks from a concentration camp?"

Jason grinned. "Actually, Jeremy, it *is* the sleeping quarters of a concentration camp. The entire contents of this room come from Dachau, to be precise. The boards, the beds, every last piece was smuggled out of Germany and reconstructed exactly as it was."

"But why go to so much bother?"

"That is the million-dollar question." Jason spun his flashlight around the room. "All this was for the benefit of what was to befall those who entered the maze. The revenge was for Michael Carson's benefit. The fear, the hopelessness, the despair and every other emotion generated by the people trapped in here was for me. I wanted to see that the people felt hopeless and lost before their lives were taken."

Jason led Jeremy by the arm to the opposite wall. In the center was a dusty wooden door with a hole in the wall next to it. On the walls on either side were similar doors with similar holes. "What are they?" Jeremy asked.

"They are traps. If not dealt with correctly, they will kill you. I was here for the building of the maze and oversaw some of it. Now, while I do not have the memory that Ryan does, I do know enough to think our way through this maze. What I don't know...well, that's the reason you're still alive."

Jeremy felt the rage build within. "You miserable prick, you mean you're keeping me alive as a guinea pig for the traps?"

"Of course," Jason smiled and gestured to the door. "I may be a monster, but I am hardly stupid. Now, we need to open a door. Since I have no clue where Ryan may be or who he is with just yet, we'll take the middle one for shits and giggles. Now remember, I do not want you to die just yet. The maze is long and fraught with many threats, some unlike anything you could even hope to wrap your brain around. So I need you. Stay useful to me, and you may yet live to see the outside again. But fuck with me and I'll rip you open and feed from your still-beating heart. Got it?"

Jeremy nodded. "So, what should I do?"

"The answer should be obvious, Jeremy. Open the door. Put your hand in the hole, grab the lever and pull."

Jeremy reached for the hole then felt Jason's hand grip his forearm. His grip was like a steel vise, much, much stronger than Jeremy would have initially believed. "Don't be stupid, Jeremy," Jason hissed, "protect your hand and arm. Take off your jacket, bend the sleeve in half, and use that to cover your hand and arm. But do it quick, and don't hesitate. Understand?"

Jeremy nodded and went to the hole in the wall. He could feel Jason watching him intently like the way a wolf watches a sheep. It made him very afraid because it was clear that at any point Jason would snap and kill him on the spot. He quickly plunged his covered arm through the hole. He felt things moving on the outside of the jacket and felt the fear knot like a brick of ice in his stomach. *Just do it, Jeremy*, he thought; he found the lever and pulled, quickly extracting his hand from the hole as the door opened.

Jeremy wanted to scream but found he could not as he saw three tiny snakes coiled around his arm, their fangs attached to the thick winter coat but not penetrating the material. Jeremy threw the coat to the ground and watched as Jason dispatched the snakes with three rapid shots from his gun, each shot obliterating the snakes' heads.

Jason motioned for Jeremy to retrieve his jacket. Jeremy bent down, grabbed the jacket and shook free the dead bodies of the three snakes. He then headed through the open door to the hallway beyond, with Jason directly behind him.

Jason put his hand on Jeremy's shoulder and Jeremy fought the urge to recoil from his touch. It felt cold and reptilian and chilled him to the core. "You've done well for your first trap, quite well indeed. Who knows, Jeremy, I may let you live yet as my own personal assistant."

Even though everything in his being told him that he needed to risk escape and that he needed to run, it felt good to hear the words of encouragement. *Keep him happy and he keeps you alive. Who knows, there may come a point where you can escape from him. After all, even madmen have to sleep, right?*

Jason said, "Excellent. Now, here's something that will interest you. I have spent my life learning and perfecting the dark arts that have been lost to the general population for centuries. Call them magic, call them sorcery, call them whatever you like. Frankly, I do not care. I have read books that opened doorways man was never supposed to open. I have raised the dead and killed with a single touch. I taught Michael Carson the basics so he could populate the maze with an army of horrors and helped him procure materials so he could create the ultimate nightmare. He learned quickly and was such a brilliant student that this was a case where the pupil surpasses the teacher. But," Jason winked, "Michael bit off more than he could chew. He created a creature, now here in the maze, that is unstoppable by all except he who created it. And since its creator is now dead, a royal shitstorm has been unleashed in the maze. I now need to make sure that it all goes down as planned. After all, I've spent my life preparing for this experiment. I need this to work. The wild card here is that Carson's grandson is trying to stop the wheels that have already been set in motion. And now, with your help, I'm going to make sure things get back on track."

Chapter 28

Ellen helped Derek stand by placing his left arm over her shoulder and with Carl's help got him to his feet. She fought to hold back her tears as she saw the extent of his injuries. She knew that Derek must be in unbelievable pain but was being strong for her and Carl's sake. She wished she could ease his pain but knew that, at best, she should be strong for her family.

Derek gritted his teeth and fought back nausea and blinding pain that wracked his body. "Okay, guys. It just looks worse than it really is." Derek took a few tentative steps then nearly fell on Carl. Only sheer will kept him going. The creature was near and he would not allow it to get to his family, so pain or no pain, he was going to lead them out of the maze.

"Dad," Carl asked, "do you want me to try to find someone to help us?"

Derek rubbed his son's head, accidentally smearing some blood into his hair. "I appreciate the offer," he said through clenched teeth, "but if your mother and I stay here, the creature will find us and destroy us. No, it's best if we keep moving."

The Martins hobbled down the dark and dusty hallway. While they had no light source other than the faint luminescence on the walls, they seemed to be able to see where they were going. Ellen wondered about just that. Was there some ambient lighting to take them one step above impenetrable darkness, or were they simply adapting to their environment?

In the distance, they heard howls and screams. No one spoke. They knew that the noises were as likely to be some foul thing loose in the maze as it was to be one of their fellow captives. Of course, their imaginations were running wild, fearing that anything could be lurking around the next corner.

Derek faltered again and Carl caught him before he could hit the ground. "I need to rest, son," Derek said in a low voice, straining to get the words out. "I will rest here, and you and your mother will go on."

"No," Ellen exclaimed, "I will not leave you."

Derek tried to smile and for just a moment, his easygoing, lopsided grin almost had her convinced he was fine. Then his face contorted with pain and Ellen knew he couldn't go any further.

"Carl," Ellen said, forcing herself to look calm, to be strong for her son's sake, "I want you to find help after all. Your father shouldn't travel anymore, and I will stay here with him."

Carl looked at his mother, and while still weak from the effects of the venom, he knew he had the best chance of all of them of getting out and finding help. He also knew that if he didn't try, his father would die. "Dad, should I go?"

Derek nodded and beckoned his son to come closer. "Son," he said in a low voice, "I need you to be strong here. I want you to do what it takes to get out. I am not going to make it. I want you to lead an honorable life. My grandfather's actions have tainted our family, but I have always striven to be a good person. I want you to do the same."

"Dad, you're going to get out of here."

"Just promise me, son," Derek said, placing his hand on his son's shoulder. "Promise me, okay?"

"I promise, Dad," Carl said, trying to hold back his tears.

"Thanks, son," Derek said with a smile. "I'm proud of you. Always have been, always will be. Now give your old man a hug." Carl leaned in and hugged his father and then hugged his mother, tears now flowing freely.

"I love you, son," Ellen whispered. "Now go. Find help for your father."

As Ellen and Derek watched Carl leave, they held each other and prayed that he would make it out, and whispered that he would manage to lead a full and normal life. They also knew they would never see him again.

CHAPTER 29

Suze grabbed Kaufmann by the arm and hauled him to his feet. For a tall man, he was remarkably light. He was downright skinny, in fact. He'd also lost a lot of blood and was clearly hammering on death's door with both fists. Even worse, the man was a hate-monger who stood against everything that Suze held dear in the world. Still, she couldn't let him die, especially at the hands of the creature advancing towards them.

Suze dared a look back and in the gloom of the maze she was able to discern the outline of a man. His body seemed huge, wide and powerfully built and was covered in glowing symbols. It took a moment for what she was seeing to fully register.

"Holy shit," Suze cursed. "We've got to get moving. So get your ass in gear, mister."

Kaufmann coughed and spat a bloody mass of phlegm. "What the hell is that thing?" He looked at Suze, hating the fact that the fat dyke clearly had the edge on him.

Suze wrapped her right arm around Kaufmann's waist and began dragging him forward, and as far away as she could from the advancing horror.

Paul, the voice seemed to whisper, *come to me*. It seemed to come from everywhere at once. The voice whispered to him, telling him things long forgotten, of past agonies and triumphs. He heard the voice of his mother calling to him and telling him that she loved him and was waiting for him to join her. He shook his head and tried to focus on the task at hand, and that was survival. "Get out of my head," Kaufmann howled and pitched himself forward, landing hard on both knees before ending up face down in the dust. He clutched his hair and shook his head from side to side, but he could not stop the voices from whispering in his ear. He moaned and struggled to get to his feet, and eventually was helped by Suze.

Kaufmann looked up at her, and, for the briefest of moments, she saw something human in his eyes, which were brimmed with tears. "What did it say to you, Paul?" she asked gently.

Kaufmann coughed violently. "I heard the voice," he said, cracking with emotion, "of someone long dead. Things were whispered to me that no one could have known. What is that thing?" he asked while pointing with his ruined hand.

"It's a *golem*," Suze whispered, almost with reverence. Kaufmann looked at her, his menacing glare replaced by curiosity. "It is created by an old, apparently long- forgotten kind of magic which draws its strength from the world. See those glowing symbols all over its body?" She pointed to the approaching horror. Kaufmann nodded. "Well, those are runes inscribed on the body in a very old form of Hebrew. The letters, if I remember my folklore correctly, are supposed to spell out God's true name."

"So what is it doing here?" Kaufmann asked.

Suze snorted. "If I had to fathom a guess, I'd say it was created by the guy who made this maze as an insurance policy against our escape."

"What do you mean, 'insurance policy'?"

"Look at it, Kaufmann." Suze grabbed his face and turned it to gaze upon the advancing monster. "Don't you see? Is your mind so clouded by hate that you don't see?"

"See what?" Kaufmann roared.

Suze pointed to the glowing letters. "They are getting brighter with each step that the *golem* takes towards us."

"So? Make your point, you fucking dyke," Kaufmann screamed, the spit flying out of his mouth.

Suze wiped Kaufmann's spit from her cheek, hauled back and slammed her fist into Kaufmann's face. He fell back against the wall and grunted on impact. "The reason the letters are growing brighter," Suze said slowly, trying to hold back her anger, "is that we are all its targets. It was created to kill us, and it will never stop trying to kill us until it is destroyed, which is pretty much near impossible." Suze balled her fists and felt her rage grow. "We are all going to die here, Kaufmann, all of us. That means you, me and everyone we saw in the room where we awoke. I should just leave you to the *golem* and do the world a favor."

Suze started walking away when she heard the plea, barely above a whisper, come from Kaufmann. "Please," he croaked, "don't leave me here to die." Suze cursed herself. She always had a soft heart, even for miserable, hate-filled people like Paul Kaufmann who were worse than any monster loose in the maze.

"Damn it," she muttered, walked over to where Kaufmann lay and extended her hand. He looked up and smiled, and something in the smile triggered every early warning system Suze internalized, yet she ignored it and took his hand. He grabbed it firmly and with a speed she never expected from his frail and broken form, he lashed out with his right leg and kicked her forcefully in the knee. The pain was instantaneous and she felt something give in a way that wasn't meant to. She fell backwards and landed hard, her eyes filling with tears.

Kaufmann got to his feet. "By the time that thing finishes tearing you to pieces I'll be long gone from here. As if I would ever associate with the likes of you. Your kind is better off dead." Kaufmann did not even wait for an answer. He shuffled forward as fast as his injured body would allow and turned left at the next four-way split of corridors.

"You miserable prick," Suze screamed after him. She tried to stand and the dagger-like pain that lanced through her leg forced her to give up that option. Tears streamed down her cheeks. She couldn't understand how anyone could live the way Paul Kaufmann did. To have so much hate that they were blind to the lessons that life was supposed to teach you. This whole nightmare they were trapped in showed what hatred could lead to.

Suze pulled herself to a sitting position with her back against the wall. The pain was excruciating, but she would not let it stop her from dying with some dignity. She swore she'd face death the way she always faced life, full-on and with no regrets. She would not scream, she would not cry. What she never expected was that she'd pass out from the pain.

The *golem* noted that one of its targets was still while the other had fled. Neither soul mattered more than the other. They all had to be destroyed so its pain would end and it could finally rest and end the eternal agony it felt. It moved steadily forward, sensing that the one ahead of it was not awake. Just then it saw a shape emerge from one of the cross corridors ahead and come running over to the prone woman. The *golem* heard it attempting to communicate with the woman, to no avail. Then the other figure picked up the woman, threw her over its shoulder and retreated the way that it had come.

The *golem* watched its target moving away, aided by another while, further ahead, and moving slowly, was the first man that had been with the woman. The *golem* weighed its options and selected the next target. It felt no emotion as it advanced towards that target. It had a task to complete and nothing would rob it of its reward. It was simple logistics.

Up ahead, down another tunnel, Paul Kaufmann leaned against the wall and tried to catch his breath. He had pushed himself in a bid to get away from the creature and the fat chick, so he should have bought himself some time. He supposed it wouldn't hurt to rest. He realized that he didn't hear that Suze woman screaming. He wondered if she had passed out before the monster tore her to shreds or if she had whimpered right to the end. Kaufmann chuckled at how he had played her, using her life as a buffer for his own.

Kaufmann decided it best to keep moving. He had no idea how long it would take to rip the woman apart, but he intended to be nowhere near the scene of the crime, so to speak. His goal was to escape this maze alive and to rally his followers back here to burn the place to the ground. It was this hate that kept him going.

Kaufmann staggered down another pathway and came, once again, to another intersection of passageways. He had never had a good sense of direction, and to be honest, in the gloom and shadows all the corridors looked alike.

A stabbing pain ripped through his side. Kaufmann knew he couldn't go any further. He had pushed himself too far. He slumped back against the wall and slid down to a sitting position. He leaned forward and violently coughed until he felt his body spasm. Blood dripped from his mouth and nose and Kaufmann wiped at it with the sleeve from his good arm.

Kaufmann wanted to laugh at the ironic situation in which he found himself. Last week he had been on top of the world. He was feared and respected and people knew his name. Now, he was destined to die alone in a maze. The real question was what would kill him first. Would it be the gas he had inhaled, which was slowly eating away at his lungs, or the creature coming after him?

Kaufmann suddenly felt a chill. A light mist swirled about him, filling his very fiber with cold. He heard his name whispered in his head, like the scraping of nails on cement. A torrent of memories came flooding back to him, as if his very soul were being extracted and judged. Kaufmann roared out a scream and looked up into the featureless face of the creature. It seemed to be looking right at him; it even tilted its head slightly as if studying him. Down each side of its body were symbols that Kaufmann recognized as Hebrew letters, and these were glowing intensely.

Suddenly, the creature plunged its hand deep into Kaufmann's ribcage. It shoved its other hand in immediately after and ripped the ribs apart as if they were chicken bones. Kaufmann howled in agony and the pain made him black out. His last thought as the creature tore him to shreds was that dying actually hurt a lot more than he had ever been led to believe.

Chapter 30

Allen and Judith had been wandering down the twisting corridors for what seemed like hours. More than once, they came to a four-way intersection and decided to keep going straight for fear of becoming completely disoriented. Despite this, Allen was convinced that they were going in circles.

Fatigue and hunger were setting in and they knew that finding food or water was more important than rest at this point. Becoming too weak to move on would not help anyone. They spoke little as they walked, both because they were lost in their own thoughts and also because they were wondering if they would manage to find help for Annie.

Eventually, they came to an open space. The corridor widened to a room that was more reminiscent of a cave. The walls were rough and the space looked more like a natural formation than one that had been created. Stalactites hung from the roof and seemed to drip water that pooled all over the floor. Stalagmites rose up from the ground like menacing sentinels, guarding the secrets that lay within the gloomy depths. The walls were lined with mold and lichen, both of which cast a slight phosphorescent sheen, bathing the cave in a greenish-yellow glow. There was a strong and overpowering smell which assaulted them immediately as they set foot in the cave.

Allen looked at Judith. "Do you smell that?"

Judith wrinkled her nose. "Smells like ammonia." She paused and put her hand to her mouth, as if to suppress her shock. "Do you know what else smells like ammonia, Allen?"

Allen shrugged, more concerned with what lay beyond the cave.

Judith took his arm and pulled him back from the cave to the hallway. "Allen, that ammonia smell, it can only be bat guano. The fact that it is so overpowering makes me think that there must be a huge bat population in the cave."

Allen chuckled. "Judith, bats do not attack people. Most species are herbivores. In fact, they tend to be shy and avoid people."

Judith glared coldly at him. "I'm not an idiot, Allen. But the vampire bat has been known to attack people when its food supply has been cut off. Look at this cave. Where do you suppose they are getting a food supply?"

"Do you have to be right all the time?"

Judith smiled. "Look, let's walk through the cave. There must be a way out on the other side. Just walk softly and don't speak. Let's just hope that if there are any bats in the cave, they are sleeping. Remember, the vampire bat is very small. It's about the length of your thumb so, individually, it would do very little damage. The concern is if there are hundreds stirred up at once; then there could be a threat. Are you ready?"

Allen nodded. "Let's do it."

They stepped slowly into the cave. Judith took the lead and glanced upwards. The ceiling was obscured in shadows, so there was no way to tell how high up the bats might be nesting if they were in the cave. They managed over a hundred paces into the cave, the smell of ammonia getting stronger as they penetrated deeper. They held their hands to their faces, desperately trying to breathe without choking on the stench. Allen kept wiping his eyes, which were now watering heavily. Judith looked over at him, and he saw concern etched in her features. They certainly had had some history in their years together, but nothing like this. It made him appreciate her even more.

Suddenly, Judith started coughing. Allen froze and looked at her. She finished coughing and wiped her mouth. Above their heads they heard what sounded as if paper were being rustled together, followed by a series of high-pitched cries.

"Run!" Allen yelled at the top of his lungs. He looked over at Judith, who seemed frozen on the spot. Grabbing her hand, he pulled her along as he ran deeper into the cave, guided only by the luminescent glow on the walls and floor.

Behind them, the rustling and shrieking noises grew in intensity and Allen turned to look behind him as they ran. What he saw nearly froze the blood in his veins. What must have been thousands of the tiny bats were flitting in their direction, driven into a blind frenzy by bloodlust and hunger. It looked like a living storm cloud was bearing down on them.

Allen ran as fast as he could, pulling Judith behind him. She wasn't able to quite match his pace and stumbled, falling forward and hitting the ground hard. Allen stopped and leaned forward to help Judith to her feet. She looked up, saw the thousands of bats bearing down on them and screamed.

Judith got to her feet and propelled herself forward, fueled by fear. Allen was right behind her, easily keeping pace. The bats were getting closer and they still hadn't seen the way out. Allen wondered if they hadn't made a huge mistake by coming into the cave. What if there wasn't a way out?

The first bat to reach them landed on Allen's back. It dug in with its claws but barely got through his shirt and didn't break the skin. Allen swiped at it, knocking it to the ground. The next bat flitted over and grazed Judith's cheek, drawing a thin line of blood. She quickly pulled it from her face and threw it to the ground.

The bats were soon attacking with greater frequency, landing wherever they could find purchase. It wasn't long before they both were covered in small scratches and bleeding from dozens of tiny cuts.

They kept running, dodging stalactites and trying to avoid the bats when Judith called out, "Allen, over to the right. There's a hallway leading out from the cave." Allen nodded and kept running, swatting at the bats, which now were more than two dozen strong and attached to his body in various spots, digging into his skin and licking at the warm blood.

Allen looked over at Judith as he ran and felt his heart go out to her. A third of her body was covered with bats, and he knew the pain she must be in, yet she never slowed her pace and kept running for the exit of the cave.

As they approached the far side of the cave, Allen noticed that the hallway leading away was bathed in light, and not simply the luminescence of lichen. He hoped the lights would be bright enough to deter the bats. As long as they did not succumb to the ones currently feeding off them, they could yet survive their current nightmare.

Judith wanted to do nothing more than to just lie down and give up. The pain was incredible yet she kept running and swiping at the foul little creatures. She needed to be strong for Allen. He liked to play the macho role, but she knew he'd be completely lost without her.

So they kept running. The bat attacks increased in frequency. Sometimes, they would try to affix themselves to their bodies and feed; other times, they just tried to claw at them, to open up a cut so the blood could flow for them to feed on a second pass.

They finally reached the other side of the cave and ran out into the light. The bats that were following them screeched and chattered, but very few followed as the light was almost blinding in its intensity.

"Stop, drop and roll," Allen yelled.

"What?" Judith called back.

"Watch me." Allen dropped to the ground and began rolling back and forth, crushing dozens of the tiny bats that clung to him. Judith did the same. When they were done, they both stood and shook off the few bats that still clung to them, many more dead than alive. The ground was covered with the pulped bodies of dozens of the tiny bats, as were their clothes, faces and hair.

"Well," Judith gasped, "we're alive. Although right now death doesn't seem half bad."

Allen hugged his wife. "We'll get through this. I promise."

"Liar," she said, her eyes welling up with tears as she kissed him, tasting his blood on her lips, "but that's why I love you."

"I suppose we'll need shots for rabies," Allen grinned and Judith smacked his arm.

They began walking down the hallway, which appeared to be a solid glass tube. Outside they saw snow, giving the walls a white, glistening look. The ceiling was over twenty feet high and while covered in snow in most places, it showed clear blue sky in others.

Judith began weeping. "Allen, look. It's the sky. What I wouldn't give..." She trailed off.

Allen took off his shoe and began pounding at the glass wall. He struck the wall as hard as he could and all he got for his efforts was a dull numbness in his hand. "Sorry, honey," he said, "these walls are several feet thick. I also wouldn't be surprised if they are some strong polymer to ensure that no one gets out this way. All this was a tease, to let us think we were getting close before taking our hope away later. What I do wonder is how no one has seen this tube from the air. They must have something like a one-way mirror so that from the outside it blends in with the scenery."

"How could someone be so evil?"

"This whole thing is about revenge. Yet what I fail to understand is how our captors can think they are righting the wrongs done in the past by torturing us before they kill us?"

"I just don't know, Allen. I just don't know."

As they walked, Judith noticed that Allen was moving with a slight limp. He caught her looking and shrugged it off. They had more important things to worry about than a twisted ankle.

"Do you think we can get rabies?" Judith asked after a few minutes of silence.

Allen laughed. "You sure know the right thing to say. Sorry I brought it up. Let's put it this way: if we get out of here in one piece, I'd suggest a series of injections right away."

They followed the glass hallway as it turned sharply to the right. Another fifty or so feet further, the hallway came to a dead end. At the end of the hallway was a glass ladder which led up to the roof, where there seemed to be an exit hatch to the outside.

"Think it's a trap?" Allen asked.

Judith looked at the ladder and the area around it. "No sign of anything visible to prevent us from climbing to the top of this thing, but after what we've seen, I wouldn't bet the rent on it."

Allen walked up to the ladder and put his foot on the first rung. Nothing happened. He carefully put his foot on the next rung. Again, nothing happened. *This is too easy*, he thought, yet somehow, the idea of climbing the ladder to the ceiling and opening the hatch that was there kept spurring him on.

Judith walked to the ladder and looked up at her husband as he slowly climbed up. Only two more rungs to go and he'd make it the top. "How's it going?" she called up.

"Almost there," Allen replied. He stepped up another rung and put his hand to the latch. He turned the handle and felt a current of electricity shoot through his entire body. Everything went black as he fell backwards and landed hard on the ground next to his wife.

"Allen!" Judith screamed. She leaned over her husband and tried to get a pulse, when the floor surrounding the ladder collapsed and they found themselves plunging downwards into the darkness. Judith lost consciousness before they even hit the frozen ground.

Chapter 31

They stood in uncomfortable silence. Kerry had not been that comfortable with Ryan from the start, and now she was asked to trust her life and hopes of escape to the man who had kidnapped her and forced her into her current predicament.

"Okay," Kerry said, "let's go over this one more time. First, even though you kidnapped us and forced us into this maze of horrors, it really wasn't your fault."

Ryan began to say something, but Kerry fixed him with a glare and raised her hand, warning him to keep quiet. Ryan lowered his eyes and remained silent.

"Second, the reason you were not at fault was that an evil sociopath threatened to kill your entire family if you did not go along with things. Third, this maze below the house is filled with deadly traps and other things that have their basis in the supernatural. Fourth, the maze is ever-changing so that passageways can move and that it's never the same maze, but each design forces us to go in the same direction, straight to the lair of a creature called the *golem*. Fifth, the *golem* is an indestructible creature made from magic, designed to kill each and every one of us. And finally, sixth, you came to your senses, are trying to save us, and we are all on the run from the same evil sociopath who had blackmailed you and your grandfather. Do I have all that correct?"

Ryan nodded. "I suppose, in context, it does seem completely unbelievable."

Kerry sighed. She stood there, hands akimbo, and glared at Ryan. "So, you saved our lives in the last room. I suppose that gives you some credibility. But you do realize that you put us in this place. You're responsible for every death that happens in this maze."

Ryan looked from Kerry to Eric, his eyes wet with tears. "Do you think I don't know that? Do you think I'll be able to live with all this on my conscience? I am very well aware that, no matter whether I had free will or not, I am responsible, and I will pay the price for the crimes committed here."

Kerry glanced at Eric. "You've been pretty quiet this whole time. What do you think?"

"While I doubt I'd ever have a beer with the guy," Eric remarked, "it does seem like he's being honest with us and that, if he had been blackmailed, he's trying to make things right."

"And what happens if he's really just here to make sure we don't survive this nightmare?"

"That's a chance we have to take, Kerry. Frankly, if he wanted us dead, he had his chance in the last room. The whole thing is messed up, but if he is giving us a chance to get out of here, I say we take it."

"Let me ask you one more thing, Ryan," Kerry demanded, "why us? Why didn't you save someone else?"

"I honestly don't know. I could always say you two were the closest, but to tell the truth, you two seemed like you needed my help the most."

Kerry threw up her hands. "Alright, we'll follow you. I hope we're not throwing away our lives by trusting you, but we'll follow. Where do we go from here?"

Ryan scratched his chin for a moment and ran his hand through his hair. "As I mentioned, the maze is a technological marvel. My grandfather was brilliant. He designed the maze to work in three dimensions and to be a dynamic creation, using sensors to detect non-movement, allowing the tunnels to change, making sure no one could possibly remember the route they had followed. Plus, all doors were designed to work one way so that once they were passed through they could not be opened from the other side. The rationale behind this was similar to role-player video games. Each participant would be pushed towards the final confrontation which, in this case, is the *golem*."

"So, if the maze is always changing and forces us towards the *golem*," Eric asked, "how can you possibly help us?"

Ryan grinned. "Good question, Eric. Well, there is one wild card. There are access tunnels at various points across the maze. These tunnels were created for maintenance purposes so if we use those, we can bypass the majority of the traps and evade the *golem*'s lair. Also, with all of you here in the maze, the *golem* will have awakened and is likely moving about the maze searching for each of you. It might not even be in its lair anymore."

"Couldn't we use the maintenance tunnels to get back into the house and get out that way?" Kerry asked.

"In theory, yes, we could," Ryan added, "but the problem is that Jason likely has either blocked off the exits or placed some kind of lethal trap. We can try, but it looks like the maintenance tunnels to the exit at the end of the maze are our best option of escape and of evading Jason, who will not hesitate to kill us on the spot. As far as I know, Jason doesn't know where the maze ends."

"Let's go then, Ryan, "Eric added. "The quicker we're out of here, the better."

"Okay," Ryan said, "follow me, but stay close."

Ryan led them down a series of twisting corridors, using a small flashlight to give them enough light to see a twenty-foot circle of light. Several times at intersections he had to stop and pause to reorient himself. Conversation was virtually non-existent, as each was lost in his or her own thoughts. Eventually, they came to another intersection, with one direction heading to a dead end forty feet down, and the other opening up into a larger cave.

Ryan led them down the corridor and came to a stop before the wall. He removed a key ring from his pocket, pulled a specific key from the ring and inserted it into a keyhole that was virtually invisible in the stone wall. After he pulled the key from the lock, the door slid soundlessly open, revealing a long corridor running in both directions. Unlike the rough, rock walls that made up the maze, the maintenance tunnel walls were of smooth and polished stone. Overhead recessed lights made the access corridor both warm and inviting after the dark and dank maze.

Ryan entered first, followed by Kerry and then Eric. He turned back and said, "If by some chance Jason is still in the house and has found the control room and is now monitoring the cameras, we're as good as dead as he can be here in minutes. I'm working on a democracy here. Are you sure you're okay trying the access corridors?"

"What was in the cave we just left?" Eric asked.

"It was full of giant carnivorous rats that were enhanced by Jason's black magic to be the size of lions or bigger."

"No shit?" Eric stammered.

"No shit," Ryan replied.

"Okay, then. I think that we're going the right way," Kerry insisted.

Ryan led them down the brightly lit corridor, the only sound the clicking of their shoes on the tile floor. Eventually they came to a door where Ryan once again produced a key. He paused and glanced back at Eric and Kerry. "Okay, here's the deal. Once inside, follow me and stay very quiet. If Jason is anywhere in the house, he can't know that we are, too. The plan is to go straight to the garage where Jason keeps his car. He keeps the keys in the glove compartment, so take those and get the hell away from here."

"What about you, man?" Eric asked. "You said this Jason guy will kill you if he sees you, so why not split with us?"

Ryan shook his head. "I can't," he said softly. "I have to go back for the others."

"I'll stay with you," Kerry added. "I don't want it on my conscience that I just ran."

"Are you for real?" Eric shouted, pointing a finger at her. "This is our big chance. We can get out, call the cops and be sure we'll live to see the next morning. Going back is suicide."

"He's right, Kerry," Ryan said. "You need to get out."

Kerry looked at Ryan and then at Eric. "I can't leave. There are too many other innocent people here, like that sweet old couple. And don't forget about Suze. We don't know if she's alive or not. My mind is set. I'm staying."

Eric spat on the ground, slowly pacing in a small circle, and muttered, "Do as you please. Once I see the outside, I am gone from here."

"I've made my choice, Eric."

"Kerry, are you sure about this?" Ryan asked. "I can't guarantee your safety once we're back inside. And trust me, it's a death trap." Kerry simply nodded.

Ryan put his key in the door and turned it. He turned it again and jiggled it in the lock.

"What's wrong?" Eric asked.

"The lock mechanism isn't responding," Ryan replied. "All keys for this maze have built in computer chips, so only those who have these keys can get access to the maintenance tunnels and the house. If the door isn't opening, it can mean one of a few things. Either the key or the door is broken, or Jason manipulated it on the other end by overriding the locking program."

"So where does that leave us?" Eric asked.

"Well, there are several maintenance tunnels around the maze and a few do lead directly to the house. I think there is one that Jason is unaware of, so that's where we'll try next. I just have to warn you both that we'll be going right back through the maze to get there and it's not going to be easy. If that entrance is blocked, we'll have no choice but to go to the end of the maze and try for the way out there. That is a last resort because it will take us close to where the *golem* is likely to be and neither of you will stand a chance if we do. For now, I'll need you both to trust me and to do exactly as I say. If you don't, and I am deadly serious here, you won't make it out of the maze alive." Ryan fixed them both with a cold stare. "Got it?"

They both nodded and followed Ryan back down the tunnel to the maze.

CHAPTER 32

Carl ran until the stitch in his side was unbearable. He came to a stop, put down the woman and bent over, sucking in air in huge gulps. Even in the murky gloom of the maze, Carl recognized her as one of the other captives in this madman's game. If his memory served him, her name was Suze.

He cast a nervous glance back in the direction he had come from. He didn't know who or what that thing was, but he wanted to put as much distance between them and it as possible. He felt a cold tremor roll down his spine at the thought of that creature. It was so big and had such weird glowing symbols all over it. Even worse, Carl thought, was the air of something utterly soulless which surrounded it. Now Carl did not consider himself a coward, but the thought of seeing that thing again made his stomach clench. His father's words came suddenly crashing back and he realized now why his father had been so afraid. The creature was not only huge and powerful looking, but it seemed to evoke fear at a primal level.

Carl leaned down and looked at Suze. She was still out cold and even in the darkness he could see that she had been roughed up pretty badly. Still, her breathing was strong and nothing appeared to be broken. He also realized that he couldn't carry her through this maze and that she would have to be woken up, and soon, since time was not in their favor. If the monster came after them, they only had a few minutes' grace.

Carl gently patted Suze on the cheek until she emitted a soft moan and shook her head side to side. Her eyes snapped open and she scurried back against the wall, looking around in fear.

"Easy," Carl whispered. "You're safe, at least for the moment. But we do need to get going."

Suze forced herself to a sitting position, wincing as she did. "You're Carl, right?" Carl nodded. "So, what happened? Last thing I remember is Kaufmann throwing me to the *golem*."

"The *golem*? Oh God, then my father was right about what it was."

"So you have seen it. I studied a lot of folklore and they don't often even remotely look like this thing. This is some kind of testosterone-fueled freak. They aren't usually as big and imposing as this one. Rather, they are built to be more man-like. Whoever created this one made sure it could do as asked without a chance of failure. Did you see the glowing characters all over its body?" Carl nodded. "Well the glowing runes are written in Aramaic, which is an old language upon which Hebrew is based. The letters spell out the name of God, which is inscribed onto its skin, for lack of a better word. The fact that there are so many runes means the creator used God's full name. That scares the heck out of me since it implies the creature was created using very powerful sorcery and is extremely strong and, to us, very deadly."

Carl nodded. "I wasn't even thinking about how dangerous it could be. I just saw that thing coming for you, so I ran in, grabbed you and took off as fast as I could."

Suze smiled. "You saved my life, Carl. I owe you one." She tried to stand and felt waves of pain shooting through her leg. She fell back down.

"What's wrong?" Carl asked, his concern growing. He knew he couldn't carry her too much longer. But he also knew he couldn't just leave her, either.

"That prick, Kaufmann, kicked me in the knee to incapacitate me so the *golem* could get me while he escaped." Suze growled through the pain as she forced herself to a standing position. "He damaged something in my kneecap. Might be a torn tendon, I don't know. But whatever it is, it hurts like a bitch."

"Come on," Carl urged, "put your arm around my shoulders and use me as leverage. I'm not leaving you here, so we need to figure if this will work."

Suze obliged and put her arm around Carl's shoulders. She was grateful for the boy's strong, stocky stature. A born athlete, she was sure, and likely strong enough to help her get out. They took tentative steps forward and soon found that they had a steady rhythm going.

They walked for what seemed like hours, making slow and steady progress away from where they had last seen the *golem*.

"So," Suze asked, gritting her teeth against the pain, "how did you end up alone in the maze?"

"My dad is hurt really bad. We encountered a ton of giant rats and nearly died fighting them off. Then, just when we thought we were safe, the mother of giant rats came and attacked us. It did some serious damage to my dad and now he's too hurt to move. My folks sent me to get help. It's funny because even though I'm not a kid anymore, they still treat me as one. I know the real reason I was sent away was that they didn't want me to see my dad die. So I'm trying for the way out and praying I can get free and come back with help to save both my folks' lives." Carl wiped back a tear and looked over at Suze. "How did you end up alone? I thought you were with that good-looking girl and the guy who thought he was it."

"You mean Kerry and Eric. Well, not long after we all split up, we found ourselves trapped and then the tunnel flooded with water. I was sure I was going to drown. I remember trying to keep my head above water when everything went black. When I awoke, I found myself face down on a muddy floor in a darkened tunnel, all alone. I don't know why Kerry and Eric left me, but they did, so I wandered this maze of death for God knows how many hours by feeling my way along the walls and being extra careful to watch for traps.

"Then I had the misfortune to cross paths with Paul Kaufmann. The man is simply the worst human being I have ever met. I saved him and offered him help and even then, after I helped him, he tried to throw me to the *golem* to save his miserable skin. I was sure I was done fore. Then you came along and carried me away to safety."

Carl grinned. "Safety is really only a relative term here in the maze, right? It will mean more if I can get us out of here."

They walked in silence, focusing on the outline of the walls in the near-absolute darkness. Eventually, they came to a door with the word "Exit" embedded in the stone, glowing red, casting a beacon of hope through the gloom.

They felt along the stone, frantically looking for something with which to open the door.

"I can't find the handle," Carl wailed.

"I can't believe that this is just something to mess with us," Suze replied. "The other traps have been a lot more elaborate than this. It makes no sense to put the word 'exit' into the stone of the door."

"I know that, Suze. But we've been all over this door. Twice, I'd imagine."

Suze scratched her forehead as she thought it through. "How about checking the floor on the ground in front of the door? Or we can look on the ceiling? Or even check the walls alongside the door? There has to be a way in somewhere. It makes no sense to have this otherwise. The maze is a deathtrap, but there always seems to be some reason behind things."

Carl dropped to his knees and began pushing and prodding at each tile. Suze tried those on the roof. A half hour later, they had tried every inch of floor, wall and ceiling within ten feet of the door. Their search had been fruitless and where they had hope upon first arriving at the door, they now both felt anger and frustration building.

"What did we miss?" Suze shouted angrily.

"I don't know. We covered every inch of the damned door and the floor, walls and ceiling before it."

Suze ran up to Carl and grabbed him by his collar. "Actually, Carl," she replied, with excitement, "we didn't." Suze ran over to the door and ran her finger in the groove made by the word "Exit". The word glowed brightly for a second and then the door slid soundlessly open, exposing a brightly lit room beyond.

"Yes!" Suze said and did a quick fist pump.

Carl leaned in and made a sweeping gesture towards the light with his arm. "Shall we?"

"It's not like we have many other options."

Carl helped Suze through the door and once they were through the door slid shut behind them. Taking stock of their surroundings, they saw that the room was made of featureless white stone on the floor, ceiling and walls. Halogen lights were built into recessed sockets in the ceiling and while relatively low-wattage bulbs compared to the near total darkness of the maze, the lights appeared blinding to Carl and Suze, both of whom had to cover their eyes until they were used to the radical shift in lighting.

In the middle of the room were two stone benches that seemed built into the floor. Each bench was curved and pointed towards a featureless wall. Across from the way they had just entered, and to the right, were the outlines of two other doors. Aside from that, the room was devoid of anything else.

"So," Carl asked, "what do we do now?"

"Apparently," Suze remarked, "we sit. And from the looks of things, it's to be a show." Suze limped over to the front bench and was followed closely by Carl. She sat, breathing a quiet sigh of relief and Carl followed, sitting right next to her.

The moment Carl sat down, the lights slowly dimmed. Directly in front of them the stone wall slid open to reveal a screen. The screen began to glow and they found themselves watching a black and white film of a prisoner escaping from a prison camp in winter. The film started with the prisoner, dressed in filthy rags, standing outside the prison fence late at night. He looked at the camera with a haunted glance and started to run. Shortly thereafter, several guards appeared with large German Shepherds. They give chase, following the prisoner through the woods, never allowing him to get too much of a lead. Then the prisoner slipped while crossing a stream and fell into the water. Within minutes, the dogs were on him, biting him through the thin fabric of the prison uniform. A guard appeared and aimed his rifle at the prisoner, who raised his arms in a sign of surrender. The guard did not seem to notice or even care and took closer aim. The prisoner's eyes went wide and he whispered something, some final plea for his life before the guard shot him in the chest, sending him spiraling backwards into the icy waters. The guard fired twice more to make sure the prisoner was dead and then turned and walked back in the direction of the prison camp.

The film ended and the screen went blank once more.

"Jesus," Suze muttered under her breath.

"Think that was real?" Carl asked her.

"Shit. I mean, it looked old, but it also looked staged. As if the prisoner was put outside for the purpose of the film. But why do something like this? And who would benefit from such a horrific snuff film?"

Before either of them had a chance to answer, one of the doors on the opposite wall opened. Carl and Suze sat there frozen, anticipating some new threat. When none came, and the door remained open, they walked over and saw that it was a small vestibule with a computer screen built into the wall to their left, with a keyboard directly beneath it. Directly ahead of them was another door and to their right was a one-foot square hole was built into the other side wall.

Suze touched the space bar and the following words appeared on the screen:

```
Congratulations on making it this far. Would
you like to try and escape? Y/N
```

Suze looked at Carl, who shrugged. She typed in the letter Y on the keypad. The following appeared:

```
Please be advised that the way out is perilous
and success is not guaranteed. Would you still
like to try? Y/N
```

"I'm not so sure about this, Carl," Suze said quietly. "It feels like a trap. Let's go back the way we came."

"I need to get out, Suze, and I'm going to try. My parents' lives depend on it." Carl put his hand gently on Suze's shoulder. "Look, you're hurt. Why don't you wait here and I'll make a go at it, okay?"

"Carl, do you really think this will lead you out?"

"I don't see why not. While this maze has been a nightmare, the offer of freedom was dangled before us from the start. I need to believe that that Ryan guy was telling the truth about getting out. It's all I have to hold on to right now."

Suze sighed. "I have a really bad feeling about this. I think we were put in the maze not only to die, but to make sure we had all sense of hope taken from us before we did. Just like how the Jews were slowly marginalized in many of the European countries under Nazi rule. Slowly kill a man's hope and then there is nothing left to live for. While I wish I can say that I still feel hope, the sad truth is I've started to accept the fact that I will die here in this underground tomb. Besides, even if I wanted to go with you, my knee is ruined, thanks to Kaufmann. I'd never get very far."

Carl grinned. "You'd only hold me back as well. Now leave the room and let me see what hitting the 'yes' button will do."

Suze hugged Carl and gave him a quick kiss on his cheek. She then hobbled out of the room. "Please be careful."

Carl turned back to the keyboard and typed in the letter Y. The door to the vestibule slid shut, separating Carl and Suze. The following words appeared on the screen:

```
Please remove all your clothing and place it in
the hole in the wall directly behind you. You
have five minutes. All clothing must be removed
or a deadly gas will flood the room and kill
you instantly. Please hit the Y key when done.
```

A digital clock appeared on the screen, counting down the time from five minutes. Carl cursed and began shrugging off his clothes. When he was down to his undershirt and shorts, he threw his clothes into the hole and hit the Y key. The clock kept counting down. He realized that either there was some kind of sophisticated sensor or the room was monitored. Either way, he had less than a minute left. He quickly stripped down, threw the rest of his clothes into the hole and hit the key once again. The clock stopped at fifteen seconds, then dissolved from the screen. Beneath the keypad, a drawer slid open, revealing some clothing within.

Carl looked at the screen for more instructions and seeing none, he picked up the clothes. It was a concentration camp uniform, made up of blue- and grey-striped fabric. Carl noticed a shirt, pants and cap. An old pair of shoes was also provided, although they were clearly too small. Shivering slightly, he put on the shirt, noticing how rough and scratchy it was against his skin. Next came the pants, and he wished he had at least been given underwear. The shoes were next and while tight, he managed to put them on over his bare feet. Finally, he placed the cap on his head and turned back to the screen. He noticed the following:

Dressed? Y/N

Carl hit the Y key on the keypad and the door to his right slid open, revealing a wide tunnel, well over fifty feet wide. Although the tunnel plunged into darkness, far off in the distance he saw a small rectangle of natural light which he had a gut feeling came from outside.

Carl stepped through the doorway and the door behind him slid closed, enveloping the tunnel in complete darkness. Suddenly, the whole tunnel got brighter and it took a moment for Carl's eyes to adapt. Gone were the stone walls, and instead he found himself standing by the fence of the prison camp, the exact one he had seen just moments ago in the film he had watched with Suze. He took a moment, blown away by the realism of the effects. Twice he had to reach back to touch the wall in order to feel the cold stone under his fingers to know that the fence behind him and the woods in front and to either side were merely very sophisticated effects. From overhead, snow and ice began falling, and the temperature began to drop. He hugged himself for warmth, feeling his clothes already beginning to dampen and freeze. The snow began collecting on the ground and off in the distance he heard what sounded like an air raid siren followed by the excited barking of dogs and angry shouts in German.

It suddenly all came together for Carl and he felt his blood run cold.

The film they had seen, the fence around the camp, the woods the prisoner had escaped to, they were here in the tunnel. The film hadn't been staged at all but rather recorded some other unfortunate who had made it this far only to die cold and alone.

Carl felt tears welling up in his eyes. "I won't give in, Dad," he muttered under his breath. "I'll get out and find some way to get help." Steeling himself for the worst, Carl began to run through the woods, through the driving snow and rain, the yelps of the dogs not far behind him.

Suze had sat back down on the bench in the room when suddenly, the screen came to life. Once again, she saw the prisoner standing by the fence that surrounded the concentration camp. He looked up directly at the camera, his face set in grim determination, and began running. She held back a scream of pure horror as she realized that this time the prisoner was Carl, and that rapidly approaching him were two guards and their dogs.

CHAPTER 33

While her son was busy running for his life, Ellen held on to her husband. Even in the gloom of the maze, she could see that he was drenched in perspiration and that his skin had taken on an ashen pallor.

"Honey, are you there?" Derek whispered, leaning in close to his wife. He saw the tears in her eyes and his heart ached at what he knew he must do.

Ellen wiped her tears away. "How are you feeling, Derek?"

"To be honest, not too good," Derek said, forcing a grin. "I need you to do me a favor, Ellen."

"What is it?"

"I want you to try to find Carl and get out of here with him. If you can manage to find help, great, but I need to know that at least both of you will get out."

Ellen looked at her husband in horror. "I won't leave you here alone to die."

"Damn it, Ellen," Derek coughed, "I'm already dead. My brain just won't accept it."

Ellen felt her world slowly slipping away into a maelstrom of white noise and she had to grab onto her hair and pull just to force herself back to reality. "I'm not leaving you, Derek, and that's it."

Derek put his hands on his wife's shoulders and looked her straight in the eyes. "The wild card here, Ellen, is your life. I'll be dead, whether in an hour or six or even a day. I'm going to die. Every part of me hurts, and to be honest I just want to close my eyes and sleep, but I'm too scared that I won't wake up. But you still have a chance and your odds will be a heck of a lot better if you were with Carl than if you waited until I died before moving on. By then, Carl could have suffered a similar fate. I want you to find our son and watch over him."

"Derek, please," Ellen sobbed, "I can't just leave you."

"I love you, Ellen, but you have to go. And frankly, nothing would hurt me more than knowing that you watched me die like this. Please, just go."

Ellen knew Derek far too well to argue with him. He was as stubborn today as the day they had met and she knew that when he set his mind to something, nothing could get him to change it. She hugged him hard, not wanting to let go, her cheek on his, their tears mingling together. Then one final kiss and Ellen stood up. "I will bring back help, so help me God. Don't die on me!"

Derek smiled weakly and whispered, "I love you."

"I love you too." Ellen stood, cast a quick glance at her husband and hurried down the hallway in the direction Carl had taken a few hours earlier.

After Ellen left, Derek leaned back against the wall. He hadn't been kidding when he had told Ellen that he was hurting. He wanted to just close his eyes and rest. Nothing else mattered. He closed his eyes and let oblivion take him away.

Ellen worked her way down the winding passageways of the maze, moving on blind instinct in the direction she hoped Carl had taken. At each intersection, she had automatically chosen the right turn, remembering an old trick her mother had taught her if she ever got lost. She knew that, somewhere over the years, she had mentioned it to Carl and hoped that his brain had hard-wired the information so that his instinct would have kicked in and he would have gone the same route.

After a while, Ellen came to a turn in the maze, but something made her pause. She saw a faint glow and heard wet, rending noises from around the corner. She did not want to look and see the source of the noise because in her gut she knew it could not be good, but she did not want to backtrack without first seeing what lay ahead. Her biggest fear was that Carl was hurt and would need her help, and she vowed that she would find him and keep him safe.

Cautiously, Ellen peered around the corner and pulled back immediately. She saw a man kneeling near the far wall, huge by any standards, glowing in the darkness. He, or it, she thought, seemed to be bending over something, too busy in its purpose to even notice her.

This might be her chance. If the glowing man was too preoccupied, she might very well be able to use the shadows to sneak by. She took a tentative step forward, her shoe making a soft scraping noise on the stone floor. Ellen froze, and despite the overall damp chill of the maze, she found herself beginning to perspire.

The rending and shredding noises continued, so Ellen took another tentative step, then another and kept walking slowly until she turned the corner. She slipped soundlessly into the shadows, never once taking her eyes off the glowing man whose back was to her as he worked furiously on something on the ground.

Ellen started moving along the wall, keeping to the shadows, stealing an occasional glance back at the huge man. If he saw or even heard her, he gave no indication. Something made her pause, though. The man was so engrossed in what he was doing that Ellen's natural curiosity was aroused, making her want to know what it was that he was doing. No, she thought, she *needed* to know what he was doing.

As silently as she could, she crept behind the glowing man and peered at what was keeping him so busy. She felt her legs grow weak beneath her when she saw. The glowing man was in the process of tearing a man apart into tiny pieces. His ribcage was torn wide open and most of his internal organs were strewn over the maze's floor. The head was still attached to the body, but barely, held to the rest of the body by frayed strands of muscle and tendon, and it lolled to the side at an unnatural angle. Both arms were torn off and lay stacked alongside the body with the legs like firewood. Even in the darkness, the glow emanating from the huge man clearly identified the corpse as that of that hate-mongering racist Kaufmann, who had been imprisoned along with the rest of them, but not seen since they had first entered into the maze. While Ellen could not abide racism and saw racists as dangerous, she felt the sheer horror of the situation and had to clamp her hand over her mouth to keep from screaming. She began backpedaling and lost her balance, falling hard on her rear. She cried out, partly in shock.

The glowing man stopped what he was doing, turned and stood up to his full height. He turned his eyes to Ellen, who whimpered as she backed away. He advanced toward her and crouched down until his face was inches from hers. He smelled of freshly tilled soil and his skin had the damp appearance of mud or damp clay. She saw that his face was smooth and featureless, with small indentations where his eyes would be, a rudimentary nose, and a small slit for a mouth. The man had no ears and was bald. The only discernible features were the glowing characters embedded in his skin and some words written in what looked to be Hebrew on his forehead.

Ellen backed up to a wall, the man towering over her. She waited for the death blow, for the glowing man to rip her to shreds the way he did Kaufmann, but the blow never came. The glowing man tilted his head slightly to the side and almost appeared to be sniffing the air around him. He then stood to his full height, turned and disappeared into the maze in the direction from which Ellen had just come. She sank to the ground, hugged her knees and sobbed. She was alive, she would find Carl and they would get out of this nightmare. She swore that to her God and to anyone else who would listen.

CHAPTER 34

Ryan moved stealthily through the maze, followed closely by Kerry and then Eric, who brought up the rear. So far he had managed to evade two traps, and through his affable nature both Kerry and Eric were warming up to him. That helped fuel their trust, which in turn gave them hope of getting out alive.

Kerry walked up to Ryan, who had stopped at an intersection. She noticed the look of consternation on his face. "Ryan," she asked, "is everything all right?"

Ryan managed a weak smile. "I'm not sure if it's the stress or what, but I honestly am not sure which way to go."

Kerry's eyes went wide. "What does that mean, Ryan?"

Ryan sighed. "I told you that this maze is a dynamic creation. Its configurations are constantly changing. While I have a really good memory, eidetic in fact, I don't have all the configurations memorized. Sometimes the maze is simply in a state that I just don't recognize. So what it means is we do this the hard way. We go ahead blindly and hope to God I can locate one of the other access tunnels."

Eric came forward. He noticed Kerry standing there, hugging herself. "What's going on?"

Ryan stepped over to where Eric stood and said, "Change of plans. The maze has shifted and I don't know the way out from here. We're going to have to hope for the best and pray that the maze changes configurations to one that I know or go ahead blindly until we find an access tunnel."

Eric grabbed Ryan by the collar, his eyes blazing. "We trusted you, you son of a bitch! We put our lives in your hands and now you say you don't know how to get us out. I should just kill you here and now."

Kerry grabbed Eric and pulled him back. "Stop it, goddamn it. We need him. This is a setback that we didn't count on. Ryan may still find his way, and he does know the traps. Keep it in perspective, Eric."

Eric sat down hard, his back against the stone wall, panting. He put his head in his hands and sat there for a moment before he finally looked up at Kerry and then Ryan. "I'm sorry, Kerry. I just lost my head. After all we've been through, I'm just having a hard time holding it together."

Ryan extended his hand, which Eric grabbed, and he pulled Eric back to his feet. "I understand your frustration, Eric, really I do. And my goal is to get you out of here, so trust me when I say that this does not sit any easier with me. But we need to work together now, more than ever. I will need to know that I have both your and Kerry's support. If we don't work as a team, I can honestly say that we will not leave here alive."

"Understood," Eric added. Kerry cast him a cold glare and he averted his eyes, clearly embarrassed by his outburst.

"Okay," Ryan said, "time to get moving. But keep close, follow my every move, and try to keep quiet. Noise can trigger some of the traps as easily as body heat, so no unnecessary chatter." He looked at both Kerry and Eric, who each nodded. "Good. Let's go."

Ryan led them silently and quickly down a series of passageways. Sometimes he paused to survey the corridor ahead; other times, he made snap decisions and led them back the way they had come to make other choices in past intersections. So far they had not encountered any traps and they seemed to be making good distance.

Ryan came to a stop and held up a hand, motioning Kerry and Eric to stop. He signaled for them to back up. When they were far enough back, he whispered, "We have a small problem. The passageway ahead has a trap that is very difficult to evade."

Kerry leaned in close and whispered, "What's the problem?"

"I recognized the corridor up ahead," Ryan whispered, "and it's an ugly trap. It's two-tiered. We will need to follow a specific pattern, moving from tile to tile, and if we deviate too much, the trap will be triggered. Even worse is that the entire corridor is wired for sound and if we exceed the bare minimum decibel level, the trap will be activated."

"What happens if we activate the trap?" Eric asked, keeping his voice low.

"Most likely," Ryan whispered, frowning, "you'd be dead long before you knew what hit you. Are you guys going to be able to continue?" They both nodded.

Ryan gave the cue to Kerry and Eric to follow one at a time in complete silence. Ryan moved ahead five paces, paused, skipped to the space to his right, inched forward, shifted to the left, and then moved straight ahead. Kerry followed Ryan's footsteps and matched his path exactly, then joined Ryan at the end. Eric moved ahead next and followed the footprints in the dust and was nearly at the end when he sneezed. He froze and knew that he was in deep trouble. Ryan reacted almost instantaneously by yelling to him to run towards them as fast as he could.

Eric, being young and in shape, took off like a flash. On both sides, random holes appeared in the walls, and seconds later bullets were fired and crisscrossed the hallway. Eric dove forward over the spray of bullets. His jump was a bit short and he took two rounds, one to his left thigh and the other to his right calf. He hit the ground hard and was pulled to safety by Ryan, who reached forward to grab Eric by the wrists.

Kerry ran over to Eric, who was howling in agony. "How bad is it?" she asked Ryan.

"I'm not a doctor, Kerry," Ryan replied, "but it doesn't look good. The bullet that hit his calf tore through and is bleeding heavily. The other bullet, the one that hit his thigh, seems to have lodged in pretty deep and needs to be taken out. The problem is, we don't have anything on us that we can use. At best, we can stop the bleeding and pray that he doesn't get sepsis from the wounds. An even bigger concern is whether he'll be able to walk. With one bullet in him and a shredded right calf, our chances are not looking too good. Look, let's stop the bleeding and we'll see where we stand."

Eric was screaming in pain and Kerry rubbed his forehead in a desperate attempt to soothe him. Blood was pooling on the ground from his two wounds. "How are we going to stop the bleeding?"

Ryan crossed over to Eric, kneeled down and took a Swiss army knife from his pocket. He cut the pants around the wound in Eric's thigh and balled up the material. He then took a Zippo lighter from his other pocket and set the balled up jeans on fire. He put the blazing fabric on the ground and put the knife blade in the flames. "I'm sorry, Eric," Ryan said, "but this is going to hurt a lot. But if I don't do something, you'll likely bleed out and die. Do you understand me?" Eric nodded, so Ryan took the knife and pressed the blade to the flesh where the bullet had entered Eric's thigh. Eric screamed in agony and thrashed about as the knife sizzled and seared his flesh. Kerry helped Ryan hold Eric down. Ryan kept the knife pressed to Eric's thigh until he was sure the wound was cauterized and the bleeding had stopped. He then cut the jeans away from Eric's calf, balled up the denim and added it to the fire. Ryan then placed the knife back in the fire.

"Please," Eric moaned, tears streaming down his cheeks, "I can't take any more."

"Listen to me," Ryan said sternly, "either I stop the bleeding or you can die. It's your choice."

"Fine," Eric hissed, his face contorted in pain, "just do it, already."

Ryan nodded and placed the knife blade to the wound, and Eric screamed once more. Soon it was done. Eric had passed out from the pain and Kerry sat by his side, sobbing softly.

Ryan got up. "I'll go look around, see what our choices are." He walked down the passageway, disappearing into the shadows.

Kerry sat next to Eric, listening to his labored breathing. At least he was alive, although she had no idea how they would be able to carry him out of the maze. She tried to listen for sounds in the maze, but everything was completely silent. *Like a tomb*, she thought, and suppressed an urge to cry. The absurdity of her situation was getting to her, she realized. She could die in this maze and no one would ever know. She'd be buried forever, just another statistic of those who had gone missing, never to be seen again. Kerry had to fight to hold back the screams. What did she have to show for her life? No family, few friends and a boyfriend she wanted to get rid of but didn't have the heart to tell. She could die and she would barely be missed. The thought of how little a mark she had made in the world depressed her.

Ryan ran back a short while later. He looked flushed and out of breath. "We need to leave right now," he panted.

"What's going on?"

Ryan was busy shaking Eric, who was slowly coming to. Once Eric was awake, he helped him get to his feet, causing Eric to howl in pain. Ryan immediately urged him to keep quiet. He threw Eric's arm over his shoulder and started leading him down the hallway. Ryan looked back at Kerry and growled, "Come on."

Kerry grabbed Ryan by the wrist. "Wait one damn minute. What the hell is going on?"

"It's coming," Ryan hissed, "the *golem*. It's drawn to your life force. It's how it sees you. Even worse is your fear and depression and every other potent and negative emotion that makes it stronger, and if we don't leave now, you both are as good as dead."

Chapter 35

Carl stood outside the prison fence and surveyed his surroundings. The concentration camp was surrounded by dense woods, and with any luck those would serve as his means of escape. He looked up and saw the stars in the sky, and though the constellations looked different from those he was used to, he realized that he was seeing things from the perspective of being in Europe. Even though he suspected this was merely high-end technology, everything looked and felt real to him. It reminded him of the holodeck episodes from *Star Trek Voyager*. He wondered just what would happen if he walked sharply to his right or left. What would the trees feel like? Would they feel real?

A light rain had started, coming down in a slushy mix and adding to the snow that had already accumulated on the ground. Carl shivered and felt his prison uniform grow damp and then wet, the cold causing it to stick painfully to his skin. Even the air around him seemed to take on a crisp, wintry smell, completing the illusion of being in the woods.

From off in the distance he heard the barks and yelps of dogs, followed by guttural shouts in German from the guards. He didn't know whether the guards and dogs were real or simply part of the effects, but he knew he didn't want to risk it by hanging around. A way out lay ahead, where he had seen that ray of natural light from a window or hole in a far wall before the woods appeared, and he was going to reach it, no matter what.

Carl took off at a run, his old, threadbare shoes slipping and sliding on the slick snow- and ice-covered surface. The woods were straight ahead and he knew that the way to freedom lay in that direction. True, he gauged it to be at least the length of a football field, but Carl was a star running back in school and an avid hiker and he knew he could do several miles in his sleep.

Carl entered the woods and stopped for a moment to catch his breath. His prison uniform was soaked through and was already frozen stiff in a few places. He felt the rain and slush still falling, managing to reach him even through the thick canopy of branches overhead. He shivered and felt his skin burn where the cold must surely be giving way to frostbite. After less than fifteen minutes in this nightmare, he knew that the elements were already holding a strong advantage.

Carl leaned against a tree and was shocked to find that it felt real. The wood was cold and wet and rough to the touch, as if it had been outside in the middle of winter. Carl didn't know what kind of technology was being employed, but the sheer realism took on a new dimension. If the trees seemed as real as they were, then the likelihood of the dogs and guards being real suddenly shot way, way up. And if the guards were real, then they wouldn't hesitate to kill him if he got caught.

Carl turned and ran, trying to get oriented in the direction of where he assumed the way out would be. Behind him, and noticeably closer, was the frantic howling and barking of the dogs. The guards' cries could still be heard, but they had dropped back. Carl pressed on, sprinting through the woods as fast as he could, ignoring the numbing cold as much as possible.

After perhaps another ten minutes, Carl came to a partially frozen stream that blocked his path. The water looked deep and Carl didn't wish to expose himself any more to the elements than he already had. He was just about to take a tentative step into the stream when he felt something hard slam into his back and throw him face forward into the water. Carl fought against the frigid water and managed to rise back to the surface, swallowing huge gulps of the freezing air. He twisted around just as the dog, a large German Shepherd, lunged and clamped its jaws down hard on his left shoulder. Carl howled in agony and began furiously punching the large dog in the head with all his strength, laying one powerful blow after the other.

The dog was a massive creature and easily weighed in at over a hundred pounds. Carl took solace that had it been healthy and alive it would have tipped the scales at one forty or more. Its fur was missing in clumps all over the body, exposing the grayish flesh and yellowed bone beneath. The dog's intestines trailed behind it, dangling from the gaping wound in its gut. Its face was nearly devoid of fur except in small patches around the eyes and snout. One eye was missing and the other was glazed over and milky. Carl's repeated blows were taking their toll, though, and the dog yelped roughly as if in pain. Carl reacted quickly by grabbing it around its ruined neck and squeezed and twisted. The dog thrashed and kicked, but Carl held it firmly in place until the dog stopped moving. He let go of the dog and watched its corpse fall into the river then float to the surface before he pulled himself to his feet and dragged his frozen body out of the stream on the other side. He was dripping wet and his clothes were beginning to freeze on his skin. He now knew that he had made a huge mistake. Sure, it was only the length of a football filed to freedom, but in the bitter cold, soaked through to the skin, with animated corpses of dogs and German soldiers trailing after him, it might as well have been a hundred miles.

What about the guards, he wondered, *are they corpses as well? Can they even be killed?*

Carl pressed on, each step proving harder and harder to take. He went to the nearest tree and pulled and twisted until he managed to break off a branch that would help function as a walking stick. His hands were raw and bleeding, but he held on and kept walking, using the branch to steady himself. He managed to go a little faster when he heard the furious barking of the dogs and the angry shouts of the guards.

With blind endurance, Carl kept moving towards the edge of the woods and to promised freedom. Suddenly, another German Shepherd came from behind him and knocked him to the ground. This one was even larger than the first, and in a much greater state of decay. Even in the crisp, frigid air, he smelled the fetid stink coming from the beast. He swung the branch with all his might and connected squarely with the dog's head. Gaining the advantage, he hammered the dog's skull again and again until it was nothing more than a sticky pulp. The hind legs twitched for another minute before they finally stopped.

Carl sat there in the snow, the dog's brains and fragments of skull sprayed all over his chest and face, and he sobbed. He always had dogs growing up and having to kill two, even ones that were clearly dead, was more than he wanted to bear. He began questioning whether it was worth moving on. He couldn't feel his toes and his hands were frozen and raw. He placed his hands to his mouth and blew some warm air on them in the hopes of getting some feeling back. All that he managed was to feel the stinging pain from his fingers as some vestige of sensation came back to them. He then touched his fingers to his ears and nose and felt nothing, hoping the lack of sensation wasn't frostbite. Even the part of his body where the first dog had bitten him no longer hurt. He smiled grimly and supposed he should be thankful for small blessings.

He stood back up and with the aid of his branch kept walking, ignoring the numbness to his limbs and the fact that he no longer felt his extremities. Freedom was up ahead. He kept repeating this in his mind, his mantra, to keep him moving and to keep his resolve high. Carl heard a shout and turned to see a German soldier standing a distance back. The soldier was dressed in full military garb and was aiming his gun at Carl. Like the dog, the soldier clearly looked as if he had been plucked from the grave. His uniform was filthy and soiled and hung loosely from his lanky frame. The soldier's face was nothing more than a grinning skull with thin strands of rotting muscle and flesh hanging from the bone. His hat was worn and faded and pushed forward so that the brim covered its eyes, but Carl was sure that there would be none there to see. The soldier fired and the bullet whizzed close to Carl's head, a little too close. Carl turned and ran, two more shots striking the trees around him, as he raced deeper into the woods. He knew he'd never outrun this soldier who had been created by whatever eldritch means had brought him forth. Carl knew that it would never need to pause or rest. Even worse, he thought, the dead soldier seemed oblivious to the elements, since warmth was something it had ceased needing many decades earlier. *So much for keeping the playing field fair*, Carl thought.

Carl knew his only chance was to outthink the creature. He didn't know if the soldier had been brought back from the grave or was some high-end technology, but if he wanted to stay alive, he needed to out think and outlast his adversary. He thought back to the many hours of video games he had played. Surely there must be some strategy he could use to his advantage. He kept running and ducking between trees, putting a small distance between him and the soldier. He climbed the next large tree he saw and pulled himself up high enough to avoid being spotted unless the soldier looked up. Carl hoped the snow and ice on the branches, plus the height, would be enough to give him the advantage he clearly needed.

A few minutes later, the soldier came creeping stealthily through the woods, his rusting Luger held tightly in his hands as he scanned the terrain in front of him. He paused and tilted his head upwards, as if he were trying to sniff out Carl's scent. When he got below the tree in which Carl was hiding, Carl grabbed his branch, let out a primal roar and leaped from the tree at the soldier. The soldier looked up and squeezed off a shot, but it wasn't enough, only clipping Carl in the side before he landed hard on the soldier, his branch skewering the man clean through the skull. The soldier gazed at Carl, his eye sockets nothing but empty black holes, and opened his mouth. A viscous gray fluid oozed out. He twitched and then fell back, unmoving.

Carl leaned over the soldier and was repulsed by the foul smell. It smelled of a mixture of rot and soil. It was mostly skeletal, except for some skin and muscle tissue, grey and tinged with greenish-black mold. It still clutched the rusted Luger in its black leather-gloved hand, refusing to let go, even renewed in death. A bloated maggot crawled out from one eye socket and moved back into the skull through the ruined nose of the soldier. Carl had no doubt anymore that this was a reanimated corpse. There was nothing mechanical about the creature. He shivered, more from fear than the numbing cold. If he had to face zombies as well as everything else, what chance did he really have?

He looked down at his own body. His left shoulder was torn and bloody from the dog bite and he hoped that the movies about zombies and the undead were just made up, because otherwise he surely would become infected. He also had a raw, red furrow in his right side, running from near the hip to just below his arm, from the soldier's shot. In addition, he was underdressed and soaked to the skin, and would surely die of exposure. *To hell with this*, Carl thought. He peeled off his prison uniform and then undressed the dead guard, trying not to look at the moldy and grey corpse. He took perverse pleasure in putting on the dry shirt and slacks, not even minding the foul stench of decay that permeated the fabric. He then donned the jacket and was thrilled by the small degree of comfort it offered. Even better was putting the boots on his soaked and severely frostbitten feet. Carl had no idea whether his feet would ever be the same, but at least the boots stopped it from getting worse. Finally, he put on the hat and took the soldier's gun, which, though rusted, clearly was in working order. Standing up, he felt invincible.

Carl knew that there was at least one other reanimated soldier as he remembered the shouts from earlier. They had come from more than one man. So he dragged the body of the first soldier behind a copse of trees and covered it as best as he could with snow. All he needed to do was to wait patiently until the other dead soldier caught up. He hoped that at least from a distance he'd pass for one of the soldiers. His entire plan hinged on that one fact. But, he reasoned, it worked in video games, so why not here?

Perhaps five minutes later, he spotted the other soldier coming towards him, his gun held out, ready to shoot. Like the first, the soldier was a shambling corpse, a grim parody of life. Carl swallowed his fear, lowered his hat to hide his face and walked towards the soldier with his head down. The soldier uttered a shrill series of growls and hisses, mingled in with some German. All of this was gibberish to Carl, so he kept his head down and said nothing. When no response came, the soldier again uttered the sounds, a bit louder this time. When he got no response from Carl after the second attempt to communicate, the soldier walked over, put his hand under Carl's chin and lifted his face up. Before the soldier could react, Carl shot it twice in the face, shattering the skull and ensuring that it was quite dead before it even hit the ground.

This was the break he was looking for. Carl took off in a run and headed for freedom. He ran, even though he could not feel his feet, and the wounds in his side and shoulder were burning. But freedom was never to come without a price, as Carl soon saw. The snow began falling in thick, wet flakes and the wind picked up, whipping the snow around as hundreds of frosty daggers sliced into the exposed skin of his face.

Visibility was near zero, and Carl fought every step of the way. He had known that the way out was not going to be easy. He just never imagined it would be nearly impossible. He kept going, fighting against gusting winds and stinging snow and sleet. He fell on several occasions but each time he refused to lie down and die and got back up. Yard after yard, Carl pressed on, stumbling more and more, with every fiber of his being begging him to just lie down and rest.

Soon Carl was on his knees and could not find the strength to get back up. Even with all the years of playing football and the instinct to win so powerfully embedded in his psyche, he knew that he simply could not push any longer. He felt tears welling up and freezing as they did. He was letting his parents down. He was condemning them to die. In the distance, he heard more barking and cries in German. Were the same guards and dogs being reanimated or was this a second wave? He didn't want to find out either way.

"No, goddamn it," Carl yelled and forced himself to his feet one last time. He took step after painful step, moving on sheer blind rage when he saw it. Up ahead, like a glowing beacon, was a bright square that seemed carved into the air at the back of the woods. Car stumbled forward, screaming in pain, and stood before the hole. It was perhaps two feet by three feet, but it was a window looking out to a frozen field, clearly outside. Carl looked out and saw the blue sky and felt the fresh, wintry breeze. He heard a bird singing off in the distance. He wanted to cry. He had made it. He could get help and save his family.

He saw that he would never fit through the window with the German's heavy coat, so he shucked it off and pushed it through the hole to the outside. He then shimmied through, flopping to the ground outside. He turned back and remarked at how nobody would ever notice the hole being there unless they were right next to it, it was so expertly carved into the terrain. He looked around and saw far off in the distance a huge mansion and miles and miles of nothingness. Carl smiled weakly, bent down to retrieve the coat and gently put it on. He started walking towards the mansion, step after aching step until he could simply go no more. Exhaustion, hunger and his wounds took their toll. Carl looked up at the bright blue sky and then collapsed face down in the snow, the word "freedom" echoing in his brain as everything went black.

CHAPTER 36

Judith awoke with a splitting headache. She looked around through the gloom and called for her husband. She could barely see and felt along the ground until she reached a wall. She inched her way along the wall, her fingertips brushing the cool, smooth surface of the stone. It soon became clear that she was in some kind of circular room. A bit more frightening was that she hadn't felt any doors as she familiarized herself with her surroundings.

"Allen," Judith called again, panic slowly creeping into her voice. He had to be here somewhere. She moved from the comforting perimeter and moved towards the unknown middle of the room. She advanced on her hands and knees, desperately trying to determine if her husband was lying somewhere on the floor.

"Allen, please. Answer me," Judith screamed. She crawled about on the dusty floor, touching nothing as she did. She was growing increasingly more frustrated. Where had Allen gone? There was no visible way out, so he had to be somewhere in this room. She kept crawling about on her hands and knees until her hand suddenly brushed against something. She reached up and it felt large, like a person.

"Allen," Judith whispered, the tears already starting, "is that you?" She moved her hand over the shape and was convinced that it was, indeed, a person. Moving her hand to the face, she found it to be cold and slightly rubbery to the touch. The features were not Allen's and it slowly dawned on her that she was touching a human corpse. Judith began screaming as she backed away from the body and fell over another one lying on the floor behind her. She stood to run and then tripped over a third. She collapsed to the ground, shrieking.

Judith felt a hand on her shoulder then Allen's voice. She kept screaming and it took several minutes of Allen holding her close before she stopped hyperventilating and was able to regain her composure.

"It's okay, honey," Allen whispered, holding Judith close as he rubbed her back.

"I was sure I lost you," Judith sobbed, "because you didn't respond when I called. And then I felt those dead bodies. Why didn't you respond, Allen?"

"I was knocked out. I guess it was the shock or the fall. When I woke, I heard you screaming and zeroed in on your voice. Now let's focus on the task at hand. We need to find a way out of here. I can't believe that the madman who built this maze would allow his lab rats to simply die of starvation in a pit."

Judith rolled her eyes, but in the darkness the gesture was lost on her husband. "I think," she began, "that there must be a hidden door somewhere along one of the walls."

"I agree. Okay, honey, why don't we go to the wall, and each move in a different direction, examining the wall as closely as we can from the bottom to as high as we can reach, looking for any switches, levers, buttons or anything which could trigger opening a hidden door. We'll meet back where we started. Hopefully we'll find the way out."

Judith smiled weakly. "Sounds like a plan."

They found their way to the wall, careful not to trip over any of the bodies on the floor. They both got down on their knees and began running their hands over the wall's surface from bottom to top. The process was painstakingly slow, especially in the dark, as they used their hands to try to find what their eyes could not. Hour after hour, they searched the wall, sometimes getting their hopes up when a rough patch was felt, but always to no avail. "I need a break," Judith called across the room.

"Take as long as you need," Allen called back, his voice reassuring to her in the darkness, "but I plan on searching until I drop. I'm losing it slowly, and if I stop, I'm sure I won't have the heart to get back to the task. Also, the dead bodies in here with us are starting to smell. I'd rather get out of here as fast as possible."

Judith let out a long sigh. She knew her husband was right, and damn it, she thought, he always knew how to make her feel guilty.

They examined the walls for another two hours, both of them exhausted and growing increasingly frustrated. Allen was set to call it quits when Judith began screaming for him to come over. He ran in the direction of her voice, accidentally tripping on one of the bodies in the process, causing him to land hard on the ground.

"What did you find, Judith?" Allen asked, brushing himself off as he got to his feet and joined his wife.

Judith took Allen's hand and guided it to the wall. She placed his fingertip in a small groove in the rock and a cover popped up. Inside he was able to feel a small button. "Push it, Allen," Judith urged.

Allen scratched his head. "Are you sure, Judith? Pushing this button may mean more misery for us."

Judith released a low giggle that grew into full-blown laughter. "And what the hell do you call this then, Allen?" She paused. "I'm sorry. I'm tired, and I'm hungry and I just want to go home. So, please, just push the fucking button, because I just can't bring myself to do it."

Without another word, Allen pushed the button. The room suddenly flooded with light. While the light wasn't that bright, hours spent in near darkness caused them both to cover their eyes and howl in pain.

Eventually, their eyes adjusted to the lit room and what they saw had them wishing that they were still immersed in total darkness. In the center on the room, which was round and featureless, were at least a dozen corpses in varying stages of decomposition. A quick glance at the bodies proved to be a relief since they were all unknown to them. They were all dressed in jeans and plaid shirts and looked like construction workers.

"I suspect these might have been some of the guys who built this maze," Allen said.

"So what do we do now?" asked Judith.

"Well, the light makes it easier to find a secret door." Allen gestured to the walls. "If there is a door hidden in the stone, we stand a far better chance of spotting it than feeling for it. Come on, let's keep looking. The idea of being trapped in here with the dead is really freaking me out."

Allen and Judith trudged back to the wall and once again set to the task of finding the door. After a good hour, neither of them had found anything. Judith was about to give up when she noticed that the button that Allen had pressed earlier was now glowing.

"I'm going to push the button again," Judith remarked. And she walked over and pushed it. A section of the wall next to her slid back, exposing a door with a keyhole below a handle and an LCD screen set in the middle of the door. Judith tried the handle and found it locked, as she suspected it would be. She touched the LCD screen and it began glowing softly. The following words were written in bright letters:

```
To open the door, you must find the key. The key
can be found in the stomach of one of the corpses.
But you must choose quickly because you only have
ten minutes. After that, the floor will be pulled
back and all the corpses, and any unfortunates who
happen to the room, will be dropped into the ovens
below for cremation. Your time starts now.
```

The digital clock read ten minutes and began counting back. Allen grabbed Judith by the arm and said, "Come on. That leaves us less than a minute per corpse. Trust me, forget that it's not going to be pleasant, it's also not going to be easy since we have nothing but our bare hands to rip open their bellies."

"I can't do it, Allen," Judith wailed. "You know me. I just can't do this. You know how I am around dead bodies. I've had this issue my whole life, ever since I found my grandmother dead in the guest room in my parents' house when I was a kid."

"Is dying a better option? You've got to try!"

Allen ran to the nearest body, pulled back the shirt and began tearing into the stomach with his hands. It was far rougher than he had expected, for he only seemed to be scratching the surface of the flesh.

Judith came over and sat next to a very visibly frustrated Allen. "I can't do it," he cried. "It's not possible to do this with our bare hands." He looked at Judith. "I think this is it, then."

"No." Judith stood up. "There has to be a way. The trap is complex, but doable. We just need to figure out the key."

Allen ran over and hugged his wife. "That's it. You said the magic word, key. Quick, let's check the pockets of every body and see what we can find." They ran from body to body rifling through pockets. Within minutes, Allen had a small knife and Judith a nail file. While neither was ideal, both seemed sufficient for the task.

Allen ran to the closest body and Judith to the one next to it. He plunged the knife deep into his corpse and then quickly into the one Judith was going to work on, to at least facilitate the use of the nail file. Soon both had their hands stuffed into their respective corpse's bellies, fishing around for the key. The smell of the gases and rancid flesh made Allen gag and Judith followed by vomiting on the floor.

Allen finished and moved to another corpse. Judith did as well, moving to the body next to the one Allen was starting to work on. As before, Allen plunged the knife deep into the stomachs of both corpses. As before, their search was truly horrific, and again futile.

Allen ran to the next corpse, quickly followed by Judith. "Time," he yelled.

Judith glanced back at the clock and nearly screamed. "Just over four minutes left. We need to step this up."

Allen smiled. Nothing like a challenge to get his Type A wife to deal with a long-standing phobia. They managed the next two corpses in their best time yet, still yielding nothing. Allen looked back to the clock. They had time for maybe four more bodies, two each. That made ten of the twelve. If they guessed wrong, they were dead. Plus, he figured, they needed time to get to the door and work the lock. The key, he reasoned, would not be placed at random. Therefore, it was probably the furthest away from the door, since most people would start at the door and work their way outward.

He ran to the furthest two bodies and plunged his knife deep into both. They frantically began to search. Luck was with them, and he found the key in the stomach of his corpse. He yelled for Judith to head for the door and he quickly followed. The key did not fit the lock smoothly, but soon he got it in and the door slid open. Allen noted that they still had nearly a minute left and grinned triumphantly.

They ran through the door, which immediately slid shut behind them. They found themselves in a well-lit, clean corridor, with fresh plaster on the walls and tile on the floor. After the dark and damp tunnels and caves, they both found it a welcome change. The tunnel wound to the left, then to the right and came to another door.

Allen tried the handle and the door opened easily. They stepped inside and saw a short, fairly stout woman watching something on a display screen. Her eyes were red and rimmed with tears. Judith recognized her immediately from their time together at the start of the maze. "Suze," she screamed.

The woman turned around and her face lit up when she saw Allen and Judith. "I'd come over and properly welcome you to my private place in this hell," Suze remarked, "but my knee is really messed up and I can barely walk."

Allen and Judith walked over to where Suze was sitting. "What's on the screen?" Judith asked.

Suze sighed. "I think I just saw Carl, you know, the Martins' son, manage to get out but I think his injuries were too much and that he'll simply die outside."

Allen scratched his head. "Why don't you start at the beginning, Suze? And don't leave anything out."

Suze began with her separation from Kerry and Eric, and her subsequent encounter with Kaufmann and the *golem*, and finally, how Carl saved her life and his attempt at escape through the woods. When she was done, Judith sat down next to her and put her arm around her shoulders to comfort her.

Allen was the first to speak. "Okay, so it seems that the way Carl took is not the best option. Between the elements, dogs and soldiers, our chances look grim. Also, Suze can barely walk with her damaged knee. That leaves us only one alternative. We need to go back to the maze. Now, Suze, tell us about this *golem*."

Suze filled them in on how a *golem* was created and how it was virtually indestructible. She mentioned her hypothesis that the creature was created to hunt them down and that it wouldn't stop or rest until they were all destroyed. Even worse was that with each life it took it grew in size and strength and even its level of ferocity.

"Can it be stopped or killed?" Judith interjected.

Suze grimaced. "It can. There are two ways to destroy a *golem*. I hesitate to use the word 'kill' since it has never truly been alive. Remember that this is a soulless, animated being created to destroy and nothing more. Now, the two main ways to destroy a *golem* are based upon its mode of creation. In one method, where the creator of the *golem* wrote instructions in blood on calfskin and placed it in the creature's mouth, simply removing the parchment would deactivate the creature. Of course, that would involve getting close enough to the *golem* to remove it.

"Frankly, I am more convinced that the creator of the creature used the method of inscribing the name of God on its body to bind it Usually, written on the forehead would be the word 'Emet,' which means 'truth' in the Hebrew language. Well, by erasing the first letter of the word 'Emet', the letter aleph, it then forms the word 'Met', which means 'dead' in Hebrew. So, there you have it. All we need to do is get close enough to the *golem* to either erase one letter from its forehead or take a piece of parchment from its mouth."

"Let me ask you this," Allen said after Suze had finished. "One, will it be easy erasing the letter from the forehead? And then what happens if the creator wrote 'truth' on the forehead and *also* placed a piece of parchment in the monster's mouth?"

"Well," Suze paused, "erasing the letter will not be easy. It will involve moving right up to the monster and gouging it from its flesh. The characters will be deeply inscribed. And if the creator managed to also add the parchment of instructions, it means this thing will be virtually indestructible."

Judith looked at her husband, then at Suze. "What happens if we manage to get out without encountering the *golem*?"

"It will follow us out without stopping and will not rest until we are dead."

"Then we have no other option," Judith said grimly. "We need to track it down or die trying. Of course, getting out of this maze would allow us to get weapons and help. Here we have nothing but our wits."

"Is there a way out of here?" Allen asked, and glanced towards the direction that Carl had taken, "besides the way we can't use."

Suze nodded and pointed to the doorway. "Take me with you."

"Are you sure?" Judith asked. "It won't be easy, especially with your knee. It's safe enough here for you to wait. It's warm and well-lit."

"I have a feeling that you may need me," Suze replied. "Besides, I won't let others take risks I am not willing to undertake."

"All right, then," Allen growled, "let's go find the way out or, at the very least, find and kill ourselves a monster."

CHAPTER 37

Ryan ran as fast as he could with Eric slung over his shoulder in a modified fireman's lift. Eric was only slightly bigger, but Ryan never claimed to be that strong or fit and was feeling the strain. Kerry kept pace and Ryan believed that she could have easily left him behind.

They'd been running for the better part of half an hour, stopping only sporadically to rest and catch their breath. Each time it seemed harder and harder to pick Eric up and resume running. Even worse was the fact that Eric kept drifting in and out of consciousness and his dead weight slowed them down.

"Ryan, I appreciate not being left behind," Eric managed to say while they were catching their breath, "but I think I can manage to walk if I lean on you."

"Eric, I'm not sure you really get the magnitude of our situation," Ryan said sternly. "The *golem* will not give up. It will not rest. It is an unstoppable killing machine. With each kill, it gets bigger, stronger and faster. While it has no intellect to speak of, it can learn and adapt and will only become more dangerous. While not programmed to kill anyone except those it was created to kill, the moment it senses a threat to its being it will react with as much force and violence it deems necessary. Nothing will stop it from completing its task because only then can it rest."

Eric let out an exasperated sigh. "I know we're in trouble. It's just that I feel helpless being carried like a kid. And I can't imagine how your carrying me will get us away any faster. Besides, I'm bigger and stronger than you and can carry my own weight."

"Eric, just let him carry you," Kerry chimed in. "Ryan gives us our best edge to get out of this mess, and we need to trust him unconditionally. So take your posturing and just shove it. We need to think with our heads, not our genitals."

Eric looked as if he were slapped. "I just want to carry my own load, Kerry. There's no time for misguided man-bashing. I can manage fine enough."

"Stop it, both of you," Ryan hissed. "I know the situation is getting to all of us but if we don't stop lunging at each other's throats, we won't need the *golem* to finish us off, we'll end up doing it ourselves. Now listen to me and listen good. The *golem* tracks by something like sonar. It senses when it's close to its target and will take the shortest path to reach it. Since this section of the maze is the most complex, there are many pathways and corridors that bisect. We may run our asses off and still it can find itself ahead of us. So we have to keep moving. Got it?" Both Eric and Kerry nodded.

"I meant what I said," Eric added. "I can manage a good pace by leaning on you. The pain seems to have dulled somewhat to a tolerable level."

Ryan thought about it for a second. "Okay, Eric. Let's try it your way for a bit."

Eric leaned on Ryan and they moved on as best as Eric could manage. Ryan noticed Eric wincing, but he had to give him credit for not complaining even once. He supposed that Eric did not wish to give Kerry the satisfaction of being right. He reasoned that Eric was the true epitome of a frat boy, constantly trying to show bravado around his peers and especially around pretty girls. Little did he realize that such acts did little to impress women like Kerry, who clearly tended to be more partial to men who were intellectual and sensitive.

"It just came to me," Ryan said as they turned a corner, "that I know of another maintenance tunnel nearby." He pointed to a tiny red square on one of the walls. "See that marking?"

"Yes," Kerry replied. "What is it?"

"The last part of the maze was designed to be static," Ryan said. "Since this part of the maze also served as the *golem*'s lair, it doesn't change. But because so many of the passageways look alike, my grandfather placed these symbols to indicate that the exit to a maintenance tunnel is near."

"Can the *golem* follow us into the maintenance tunnels?" Eric, asked his face contorted in pain.

Ryan smiled. "No. The entrances to the tunnels are solid steel doors embedded in rock and concrete. The *golem* is extremely powerful, but nothing short of a tank could get through those doors."

"Then let's get to it," Kerry urged.

Ryan led them down the corridor to the hidden door. He pulled his key ring from his pocket just as the *golem* lumbered around the corner. It glowed brighter with each step it took towards them.

"Open the fucking door!" Eric screamed.

The *golem* charged at them, swiping at Ryan with a solid backhand that sent him hard into the wall, his key ring tumbling from his hands. Kerry leaped for the keys, just barely avoiding a vicious blow.

Eric turned and began limping down the corridor, trying to put as much distance as possible between the *golem* and himself.

Kerry picked herself up and ran over to Ryan. "We have to help him."

Ryan stood and regarded the *golem*, which stood between the fleeing Eric and themselves. He grabbed Kerry by the arm and pulled her in the opposite direction. "We need to go," he screamed. "Now!"

"We can't just leave Eric!" Kerry cried, refusing to be pulled away.

Ryan pointed towards Eric. "He had no such problems about leaving us. Besides, if we go towards him, we also go towards the *golem*. Hopefully, it goes after Eric, I can open the door to the maintenance tunnel and get you to safety and then go back after Eric and try to save his hide."

"I want to help, Ryan," Kerry pleaded.

Ryan slapped Kerry hard across the face. "I don't care what you want, Kerry. You are going to listen to me and do as I say. Got it?" Kerry nodded, lowering her eyes, fighting hard to keep the tears at bay. Ryan took her by the hand and pulled her away, cognizant that the *golem* was within striking distance.

Ryan ran as hard as he could, initially pulling Kerry along, but soon she had recovered and was running alongside him, perfectly matching his stride. After a few minutes, he motioned for them to stop.

"Okay," he told Kerry slowly as he got his breath back, "wait here for a second. I'll backtrack and see if it followed us or Eric." Kerry started to speak and Ryan held up his hand. "The *golem* doesn't sense me. I wasn't part of its programming. It would only see me as a threat if I made an overt move towards it." Ryan placed a hand on Kerry's arm. "I'll be right back. I promise." Ryan started down the tunnel, stopped and turned towards Kerry. "I shouldn't have hit you. I'm sorry."

Ryan turned and ran back the way they had come. Thankfully, their footprints were visible in the dust, because due to the twists and turns they had made escaping *the golem*, Ryan had doubts he'd be able to find his way back. Halfway back, he saw that the *golem* had followed them instead of Eric but had turned off into another passageway.

Ryan felt his blood run cold. The *golem* was after them and he had left Kerry by herself. He cursed and ran back to get her. He found her waiting just where he had left her and felt relief flood over him. He doubted he had ever felt so glad to see another person in his entire life.

Kerry saw the mixture of relief and fear on Ryan's face. "What is it?" she asked.

"It's the *golem*," Ryan whispered. "It didn't follow Eric. It followed us. I don't know the logic that drives it, but it decided you were next. The thing is, it turned off on another passageway, but that doesn't mean it's not circling around. It might be driven by some sense to the proximity of its target, which means it may be coming for you by another way. If we go now, we can make it back to the maintenance tunnel, hopefully before the *golem* realizes we changed our escape route."

Ryan and Kerry ran back to the tunnel without incident. Wherever the *golem* was, they didn't see it. Ryan got the door open and ushered Kerry into the well-lit tunnel. "Okay," he said, "I'll close the door and ask you to wait here until I come back. It's safe here since nothing can break through these walls. They can withstand a tank, so I doubt the golem can match that."

"What happens if you don't come back?" Kerry asked, her voice low and trembling.

"You will have to try to get out," Ryan replied. "This maintenance tunnel will run to the end of the maze and let you out near the exit. The problem is still the *golem*. If I don't make it back, it means that it is still loose and that you are probably safer in here than anywhere else. It might make sense to just wait here and hope help arrives. Still, if it comes down to it and I don't come back, remember two things that you will need to know in order to escape. The first is you must choose the middle door with the wrought iron handle, and second is the number 155. That's the pass code. Remember that, because if I don't come back, it's your only hope."

"I have it. Middle door with wrought iron handle and pass code of 155. You'd better make sure to come back, Ryan."

Ryan smiled and left Kerry in the maintenance tunnel. He heard the door slide slut behind him and he took off in search of Eric. Following the footprints proved easy enough, and a short while later he found Eric slumped against a wall.

"Eric," Ryan asked as he cautiously approached the younger man, "are you okay?"

Eric looked up, his face pale and drawn. His eyes were wide and his expression looked like he was in shock. "Ryan?" he mumbled.

"Yeah," Ryan replied, his anger at Eric replaced by pity and concern, "why did you run, Eric?"

"I don't know," Eric sobbed. "When I saw that thing, something just snapped inside me. I don't want to die down here, man."

Ryan kneeled down in front of him. "That's why I'm in here. I'm trying to get you guys, and anyone else I happen to find, out of this mess. By having you run off like that makes it that much harder for me to help you."

Eric's eyes grew wide. He opened his mouth to speak and forced out one word: *golem*. Ryan turned around just in enough time to feel the *golem*'s huge fist connecting with his head. He saw a bright flash of light and then everything went black. Eric watched, frozen in fear as the *golem* lifted Ryan's prone body and hurtled it down the corridor.

The *golem* then grabbed Eric by his arms and pulled him to a standing position. Eric felt a cold breeze blowing and a cold whisper inside his head caressing his deepest memories, stroking them back to life. He relived each valued moment of his life as if he were experiencing them all first-hand, while the voice of his tormentor whispered truths and lies into his ear. He saw every terrible thing he had ever done in his life. He saw all the pain he had caused and everyone he had ever hurt.

"Please," Eric whispered, the tears flowing freely.

The *golem* pushed Eric up against the wall, one large hand on his sternum. It moved its face mere inches from Eric's. The creature had no facial features except rudimentary indentations for eyes and mouth. Its forehead glowed with some pulsating pale green symbols. The creature appeared to sniff at Eric's cheek, gently touching its face to his. The *golem's* skin was cool and dry and smelled of earth. Eric felt his bladder let go and cringed as the warm urine flowed down his leg. He screamed, desperately trying to push his attacker away. The *golem's* crush was like steel and Eric felt the pressure steadily increase until the creature's hand managed to pierce his ribcage.

Ryan came to, his head throbbing and feeling completely disoriented. Blood from an open cut on his forehead dripped into his left eye, blurring his vision. Eric's screams brought him back to his senses and he got himself painfully to his feet. He rushed back to help Eric and saw the *golem* pulling its fist from Eric's chest, dripping with blood. It then placed both hands inside the gaping wound and effortlessly ripped Eric's ribcage in half. Ryan screamed in horror and if the *golem* heard him, it didn't show it. It methodically kept tearing Eric apart as if only his complete dismemberment would suffice.

Ryan turned and ran. He knew that there was nothing he could do to help Eric. He wondered if he could save any of them from the unstoppable force of the monster and whether he'd be forced to watch Kerry die in a similar manner. He didn't know how many souls the creature had already destroyed, but it seemed larger and more ferocious and its runes were glowing brighter than he had previously seen.

Ryan let himself into the maintenance tunnel and saw Kerry sitting in a corner. She looked up and saw the expression on Ryan's face and the blood flowing from the gash on his forehead. She mouthed Eric's name and Ryan just shook his head, the tears forming in his eyes. He didn't have any words, so he just stood there, his head hung low. She stood up, walked over to Ryan and held him close. She trembled slightly. "Are we going to make it?" she whispered.

"I don't know, Kerry," Ryan rasped, his eyes wet. "I wish I could tell you that we will, but I honestly don't know. I can't stop it, but I'll do everything I can to help you evade it."

CHAPTER 38

Allen led the way, walking slowly so Suze could keep up. Her knee was in bad shape and the best she could do was limp. Judith followed close behind. The plan was simple: try to find a way out. That was Plan A. Seemed simple enough, on the surface anyway. They had been told that a way led out at the end of the maze. Allen rationalized that maybe there were other exits. Suze mentioned that Carl had managed to get out, but the extreme circumstances he faced likely cost him his life. No, if there were closer ways out, then there were also traps, so their best option was to find an easier escape route, and that was at the end of the maze.

Plan B was not so simple. To succeed with Plan B, they had to kill an unstoppable monster. They all knew deep in their hearts that if they were forced into Plan B, their chances of succeeding were slim to none at best. So they moved on, hoping for one option but steeling themselves for another.

They walked for a while in silence until Suze finally spoke. "Know what I've noticed?"

Both Allen and Judith turned to her. "What is it?" Judith asked.

Suze grinned. "I may be wrong, but have either of you noticed that we have not seen any traps for a while?"

"Actually, I haven't. What of it, Suze?" Allen replied.

"Don't you see?" Suze continued, "We must be nearing the end of the maze, the part that would serve as the *golem*'s lair. You see, they couldn't have traps if the *golem* was wandering around, now could they? So we have to be getting close. We may just manage to get out of this in one piece after all."

The growing sense of well-being was to be short-lived. As the group turned a corner they came upon a gruesome discovery. Just a short ways down the corridor they were able to discern in the gloom what looked to be a corpse sprawled out against the wall.

Allen motioned for them to stop. "Okay, we can see that there is a body up ahead. From here, it's not possible to know whether it's real or a clever fake."

"Why would someone put a fake corpse in a maze, Allen?" Judith said sarcastically.

Allen grimaced. "To make us turn back. So we won't go forward and perhaps find, I don't know, the way out? This entire maze is filled with lethal traps. What about a more subtle trap?"

"Well, before we take such leaps of faith," Judith remarked, "let's make damn sure that the body is real and hope that it isn't someone from one of our groups. They could have littered this place with corpses to discourage us."

They advanced slowly upon the body. When they got close enough, Suze let out a gasp. "That's Eric," she said, her voice trembling. She surveyed the carnage and turned away quickly before vomiting. The body had been ripped open from the sternum and each internal organ was laid out in front of it, almost reverentially. The other thing readily apparent was that the eyes had been removed and were nowhere near the body. Suze began sobbing, her breath coming in short, erratic bursts. "He was a decent guy," she said slowly. "He didn't deserve to die like that."

Judith held Suze close and rubbed her back. "No one deserves that," she whispered, "no one."

Allen knelt by the body. He touched Eric's face. He then put his finger into the pool of blood around the body. Grimacing, he stood up. "I've got more bad news for you both," he said. "The body is still fairly warm. The blood is the same and hasn't begun to congeal. I'm no forensic examiner but it's pretty clear that whoever or whatever did this to Eric did it only a short while ago. Which poses the big question: if Eric was killed recently, where is his killer? Because we all know that it can't be far."

Suze forced herself to look at what was left of Eric and got painfully down to one knee. "There," she pointed to the ground, "if you look close, you can see the footprints in the dust and dirt. The creature stood over Eric while it tore him apart but a few feet back there's another set of footprints that are smaller. They look human and they seem headed away in that direction." Suze gestured down the tunnel.

"We need to follow them, because there is strength in numbers," Judith added. "Whoever else is still alive may need our help."

"Or us theirs," Allen said glumly. "But I do agree. We need to find out if anyone else may still be alive."

"It may be Kerry," Suze added. "We were all traveling together. Kerry, Eric and I were in a tunnel when I was separated from the group. I hope to God she's okay."

Allen helped Suze to her feet and she leaned against him as they walked. "I hate to say this, Suze, but I don't think God has anything to do with this."

They followed the footsteps, which came to a stop at a wall. Judith looked at her husband and whispered, "Someone knows the way out. I'm not sure if following these footsteps is such a good idea since they may belong to the people who put us here."

"Wait," Suze said, pointing to the ground. "There's more than one set of footprints. Look, there are two larger sets, which we can assume belonged to Eric and our mystery guy, but there is a smaller set, too, and these are clearly a woman's. In the entire time since our abduction, did any of you see a woman?"

Allen and Judith looked at each other and shrugged.

"Well, neither did I," Suze exclaimed, "and I'll bet that the woman who went through this wall was imprisoned here just like us. It might be Kerry. We need to find a way to open the door, and fast."

Allen and Judith began searching the walls and Suze scanned the floor, looking desperately for a lever or switch, anything they could use in the hopes of getting the door opened.

Allen kicked at the wall in frustration. He fell to his knees, pounding the wall with his fists, uttering a stream of curses. Judith ran over to her husband's side. "It's not the end, honey," she whispered, "we can still work our way through to the end of the maze."

"I suppose you're right. For once, though, I wish we would simply catch a break."

Judith stood and stared down the hallway. Suze limped over and stood next to Judith.

"Do you feel that, Suze?" Judith said, "Like something is furrowing around your brain, whispering and taunting."

"Yes," Suze replied, "I do feel it. Ever since we stumbled upon Eric's body, something seemed to be scratching at the back of my mind. It seems to be calling me by name. And I don't know why, but it's getting so very cold."

"What's happening?" Allen asked, his panic rising at seeing his wife and friend standing there, as if in a trance.

"Don't you feel it, Allen?" Judith asked.

"Feel what?" Allen screamed. "What's going on?"

"The *golem*," Suze answered, "and it's coming for us."

CHAPTER 39

Jeremy tripped and fell to his knees. Jason cursed and kicked him hard in the ribs, causing Jeremy to cry out in pain.

"Please," Jeremy begged, "I can't take anymore." He was bleeding from several wounds, the result of not being quick enough at the two traps they had encountered on their way through the maze. Jason had saved him each time because, after all, he needed Jeremy to be the one to go through the traps first.

"Quiet," Jason hissed, "or I will tear you apart right here. The only reason you are still alive is I may need you before this is over. Ryan and your beloved Kerry are traveling together, and you may still come in handy."

Jeremy stood and brushed himself off. *How did he know that Ryan was with Kerry?* As much as he hurt, he didn't want to give this monster any more satisfaction. Also, as long as Jason felt that Kerry was still alive and being helped by Ryan then he knew that Jason would keep him alive. Jeremy was no fool and he knew that Jason would kill him as soon as his usefulness was at an end. What he needed was a plan. He realized that he might actually have the beginnings of one, and if timed well he'd still be able to still get out of this alive. The plan was still raw in his mind, but it made sense.

"I will not be the guinea pig for any more traps," Jeremy said, hoping his voice did not shake and that it showed more conviction than he actually felt.

Jason grinned and ran a hand down Jeremy's cheek. "Well, the kitten has grown claws." He clapped his hands. "Bravo. Well, I do have some good news for you, boy. We are now past the traps and are in the final phase of the maze. Welcome to the lair of the *golem.*"

"W-what's a *golem*?" Jeremy stammered.

Jason's predatory grin grew wider, exposing his sharp teeth. "The *golem* means nothing to you or me. We are not on its radar. Your dear sweet Kerry, on the other hand, will be torn to shreds once it gets its hands on her. I'd like to watch that happen."

Jeremy threw himself at Jason, hammering him with the hardest punches he could manage. Jason took a few then grabbed Jeremy by the throat and applied pressure. Jeremy gasped for air and flailed weakly at Jason, trying to get him to loosen his grip.

Jason dropped Jeremy to the ground, where he lay gasping in a heap. "Don't forget your place, boy. While these little outbursts are mildly entertaining, you must never forget your place. You live because it's my whim to allow it. And right now, with your usefulness coming to an end, I will expect you to be more servile. Understand?"

Jeremy nodded sullenly.

"Do you understand?" Jason roared, his voice booming.

"Yes, I understand," Jeremy replied. He would do whatever it took to see Kerry again, and if it meant swallowing his pride, he would do so. But he swore that he would kill Jason the first chance that he got. And as he got to his feet, he began thinking through his plan, carefully refining the way he'd make this monster pay.

Chapter 40

Allen glanced at his wife. She had a faraway look in her eyes. He looked over at Suze, who stood next to Judith, and she wore the same glazed expression. He shook his wife by the shoulders; she seemed not to notice until she let out a short gasp.

"Allen," Judith said, shaken. "I felt like I was a million miles away. This voice seemed to whisper in my brain, like a cold caress, stroking the lobes until I was in a kind of numbness. I still hear it, Allen. It's the *golem*. I don't know how I know, but I do."

Judith shook Suze, who also seemed in a bit of a trance. "The voice seemed to be inside my head, too. It knows me, seems to threaten and taunt me, and yet there is a sense of pain in the voice. Didn't you hear it, Allen?"

Judith looked over at her husband. "Didn't you hear the voice in your head?"

Allen shook his head. "All I saw were both of you going into a slight trance, as if you were focused on something else."

"Don't you see?" Suze cried. Allen and Judith both stared at her. "You are not a target of the *golem*. Clearly it's Judith's bloodline that the *Golem* is after. You can get out."

"I can't leave her, Suze. I'd rather die."

Suze looked at Allen and smiled. "We can use this. When the *golem* comes, try to get behind it, and while Judith and I keep it preoccupied, you leap on its back. Try to scratch off the aleph, the first letter of the word on its forehead.

Meanwhile, I'll try to get my hand in its mouth to take the parchment."

Judith shrieked and both Suze and Allen whirled around. Down the hallway, rounding the corner and heading towards them, was the *golem*. It came to a stop as if considering its options. It glowed brightly from the characters inscribed on its body. It stood at least seven feet tall and was very broad and muscled. It looked much bigger than Suze remembered, as if it were growing with each life it snuffed out. It stood there as if frozen and tilted its head towards the group, as if sensing them instead of seeing them. The air around them got cooler and a thick, viscous mist seemed to come from everywhere at once.

"Now!" Allen yelled. "Suze…Judith, I need you both to be ready. I'll work my way around and get behind it."

"Allen, don't!" Judith yelled. "What if Suze is wrong?"

"Then get ready to move," Allen growled. "Don't let me act in vain."

Allen walked gingerly to the wall and pressed himself flat against it, edging slowly towards the *golem*. The creature did not move and stayed in place, even as Allen passed behind it. If it saw him, it paid him no heed. Once behind it, he waited for Suze and Judith to act.

The *golem* began advancing on the two women, with Allen following closely behind it. It moved slowly, purposefully, and though it was over seven feet tall and easily weighed over three hundred pounds, it moved as if it weighed nothing at all. It came to a stop in front of Suze and Judith, and both charged it at the same time.

While Suze and Judith threw themselves at the golem, Allen leaped on its back and reached around to gouge off the first letter on its forehead. The *golem* swung its left arm and knocked Judith hard to the ground. Suze, noting that the creature did not have a mouth, jammed her hand into the creature's face where the mouth would be.

Allen, meanwhile, had begun scratching at the first symbol on the left when Suze let out a bloodcurdling howl. She pulled back her right arm and Allen saw in horror that Suze was missing most of her hand. Blood was flowing freely from the wound.

"It bit my hand," Suze wailed. "The fucker bit off my hand. I had it…I had the parchment in my grasp. "

The *golem* swung at Suze and connected with her head, knocking her to the ground. Judith, meanwhile, was getting back on her feet. The *golem* reached behind it, grabbed Allen by the hair and pulled, wrenching Allen over its shoulders and sending him crashing to the ground next to Judith.

Suze roared and leaped back at the *Golem*. She grabbed it by the head and saw what Allen had been trying to erase. *Moron*, she thought. He had tried to erase the first letter, but on the wrong end. She cursed herself for assuming that he knew that Hebrew was written right to left. She began using a nail from her good hand to gouge the *aleph* and found the *golem's* forehead to be more like rock than clay. As she was trying to erase the *golem's* life, it wrapped its arms around her torso and began to squeeze.

Suze screamed as the pressure around her waist intensified. She had begun thrashing and kicking and trying to break free when she heard the snap. It took a moment to register that the creature had broken her back. It tossed her on the ground, knowing she was finished, and turned its attention to Allen and Judith.

Allen rushed the *golem*, trying once again to erase the letter that would end the creature's existence. It proved too fast for him and grabbed him by the leg as he attempted to climb up the creature.

"Run, Judith!" Allen screamed. "It's too strong. Run. Please, for the love of..." But his pleas were cut short as the *golem* swung him by the ankle into Judith with inhuman ferocity. His head struck her in the leg, and the force of the swing shattered her tibia and nearly severed it at the knee. Allen, meanwhile, was left discarded on the ground, his skull caved in and leaking blood and cerebrospinal fluid onto the dusty dirt floor. He twitched and convulsed and then lay still. Judith began dragging herself away, pulling with her arms, blood spurting from her exposed femoral artery, and screaming for help.

The *golem* looked at Judith then turned its attention to Suze, who was lying prone, making low mewling noises. The creature moved closer to Suze and with one hand propped her up against the wall.

"Get away," Suze rasped, her voice barely a whisper, her gaze clearly focused on Judith, who was dragging herself away. Suze knew that Judith could not hear her. Certainly not the way she was screaming. But it did

offer Suze some solace, hoping that perhaps her death would give someone else a chance.

Suze turned her gaze back to the *golem*, which seemed to be studying her. It leaned in close and Suze saw its lack of features clearly for the
first time. Even though it had mere indentations for eyes in the packed
clay and earth, it cocked its head at an odd angle, as if watching her. She
smelled the damp earth and clay and it reminded her of that horrible day
in the woods when she had been left to die. As it moved its face closer
to hers, Suze managed to spit a gob of bloody phlegm into the creature's
face. It made no attempt to wipe it off, nor did it show any reaction to
Suze's defiant act. She heard voices in her mind, exposing her all fears
and mistakes, as if she were being judged. She cried for her life and for all
those things she would never accomplish.

The *golem* reached down and placed one hand on Suze's chest, feeling
for the heartbeat. It moved its hand slowly to the sternum and pushed
inwards until it broke through. Suze shrieked in agony and felt her consciousness slowly slipping into away. The *golem* paid her no heed as it
wrenched apart her ribcage and methodically began taking her apart. It
laid out her organs in front of her rapidly cooling corpse, and when done,
it plucked her eyes out and crushed them in its mighty hands. It then
stood. There was another close by.

Judith, meanwhile, had gotten a good distance away from Suze's
slaughter. Even though she was bleeding copiously from her ruined leg,
she forged on, screaming for help. As she passed the spot where they
had earlier noticed the footprints going into the wall, the door slid open
and a man and a woman stepped out. The man looked concerned as he
scanned the gloomy hallway from where she had come. The woman saw
Judith's ruined leg dangling behind her, held on by strips of cartilage and
muscle, and vomited. Judith looked up and began to weep. "Please," she
croaked, her throat raw from screaming, "please help me."

Ryan looked up and saw the *golem* bearing down on them. Kerry noticed as well and began to scream. "Get back inside," Ryan urged. "I'll
take care of her."

Kerry stepped back into the maintenance tunnel. Ryan grabbed Judith by the arms and pulled her quickly into the tunnel. He let her go and shut the door from the inside, mere feet from the advancing *golem*. The creature pounded on the door and wall outside the maintenance tunnel, powerful blows that echoed within the tunnel. It wailed loudly and mournfully, its pain evident in its cries.

"Make it stop," sobbed Judith. "Please...make it stop."

Ryan knelt down beside the injured woman. He noticed her leg and realized that there was nothing that he could do to help her. She had lost too much blood and they had nothing to properly staunch the bleeding. He was amazed at her willpower to have even made it as far as she did.

"Who are you?" Judith asked, her eyes beginning to gloss over.

"Shhh," Ryan whispered, placing Judith's head on his lap, gently running has hand over her head, trying to make her as comfortable as possible. "Don't talk. Save your strength."

"I need to tell you something," Judith continued, her eyes half closed and the words beginning to slur. "The monster can be killed. Suze," she paused, and choked back tears, "Suze figured it out."

Kerry sat down on the other side of Judith. "Did you say Suze?"

"Yes," Judith replied, struggling to become a bit more lucid. "The monster...she called it a *golem*...killed her." Judith coughed and bloody spittle darkened Ryan's jeans, her lips and mouth bright red with blood.

Kerry put her head in her hands and cried. She had only known Suze a short while but had felt a strong kinship with her. Anywhere else, and under normal circumstances, they could have been friends. She cried for Suze, for their current mess, and what would never be.

Judith coughed again, and continued, her voice weaker. "Suze told us how to kill the *golem*. On its forehead," she said and paused, forcing the words out, "is a word. I don't remember what it is, but by erasing the first letter..." Judith slipped out of consciousness.

Ryan shook her gently. "What does erasing the first letter do? Grandfather told me that the only way to stop it was when it completed the task that brought it to life. Nothing else would cause it to fully cease." He shook her harder.

"Ryan!" Kerry shrieked, "She's dying. Let her be. She doesn't need this in her last moments."

Ryan looked at Kerry, cognizant of the pounding still going on outside the door. "Don't you get it?" he yelled. "If she knows something to give us a chance to save you, I'd try to resurrect her from the dead if I thought it would help."

"She deserves better," Kerry replied.

"We all fucking do," Ryan answered curtly. "My family was nearly destroyed years earlier. It drove my uncle mad with anger and hatred and allowed him to be manipulated into making this nightmare. Then I got dragged into this and was led to believe we were wronging a right. But it wasn't wronging a right. The soldiers who did this are long dead. All of you were decent people and did not deserve this, and now I have to fix it. I can't allow this creature to take another life. I can't..." he trailed off. He shook Judith again and her eyes opened.

"Tell me," Ryan said urgently, "how to kill the *golem*."

Judith coughed again. Her spit was now bright red and it trickled down her chin. Her eyes were already glazed over, half-closed and she had a faraway look. She continued speaking, her voice weaker than ever. "There are...two ways to kill it. First....erase the first letter from the word on...forehead. Changes...meaning to the word 'death'...in Hebrew." Judith paused. Her eyelids fluttered and her breath was short and raspy.

"Please," Ryan pleaded. "What is the second way?"

"...mouth," Judith coughed again, spitting more blood. "In the mouth is...paper. Take it out...take it out...and it dies." She closed her eyes again, her breathing becoming more and more labored. Ryan and Kerry did their best to make her comfortable despite the frantic pounding on the door.

Two minutes later, Judith gasped her last breath and was still. "She's gone," Ryan said. "I'm so sorry for Suze, for my family, for the *golem*, for everything."

"Just get us out of here," Kerry replied, her tone stiff and mechanical. "We now know how to kill it, so if we meet up with the monster we will do just that. But you will stay by my side until this nightmare is over. You owe me that. Got it?"

Ryan nodded his head. "You have my word. I swear on my life."

Chapter 41

"Ellen had been walking for hours. So far she had been following the *golem* by its footprints, keeping a safe and secure distance behind. Whenever she came upon carnage, she said a prayer for the dead and kept on. She did not wish to ever get within eyeshot of the creature again. The two times she had accidentally crossed its path, it had ignored her. She hoped her luck held, but she didn't want to push it. She knew that sooner or later she'd find the way out. Until then, she would follow the monster and maybe it would lead her to the exit. For now the maze seemed trap-free, so it was just a matter of time until providence showed her the way out. And when she did find her way out, people would pay.

Her top priority was finding Carl and then getting out and getting help for Derek. She knew that she should be doing more to find the others and offer whatever help she could, but her first focus was her son. She didn't feel guilty or that her actions were selfish. She was being a good mother and wife, and she was taking care of her own.

Ellen kept walking, her focus single-minded. She would find Carl, no matter how long it took. She said a silent prayer and kept searching. She had never failed once in her life, and she did not intend to start now.

CHAPTER 42

Ryan and Kerry ran through the maintenance tunnel as quickly as they could. The *golem* was still pounding at the door, making no headway, and they realized that if it were at the tunnel's door, the way out would be clear. Therefore, the faster they got to the exit, the better their chances would be of escaping the maze and returning to the outside world.

"I have a plan," Ryan said while they were running.

Kerry, matching his pace, raised an eyebrow and replied, "Well?"

"Well," Ryan began, pausing to catch his breath, "according to what Judith told us, we know that we can kill the *golem* by erasing the first letter of the word on its forehead or by destroying the paper in its mouth. My thought is that first we escape from the maze then I'll return with a flame-thrower, or something along those lines, and turn it on the *golem*."

Kerry looked at him, a skeptical expression on her face.

Ryan stopped running and took a moment to catch his breath. Kerry stopped next to him. "Here's the deal," Ryan said, "a flamethrower will work in two ways. It will burn up the parchment in the *golem*'s mouth and it will melt the clay to the point where it's soft enough for me to wipe off the letter and kill the monster once and for all." He grinned, pleased with his reasoning.

"Look," Kerry replied, "while it sounds like a great plan, this is a supernatural creature. Are you sure fire will do the trick?"

"Fire cleanses everything, Kerry. Besides, if you have a better idea, please feel free to suggest one. I want this over as much as you. The creature won't initially attack me, so I should be able to at least get close enough for a shot at stopping it."

Kerry sighed. "We'll play this your way but once outside, I want to get help."

"Like who?" Ryan asked. "I can't go to the police. They'll lock me up for murder, and the *golem* will track you down and destroy you. Let me kill it, and then I'll face the music. Okay?"

Kerry nodded. She couldn't help herself, but she believed him. She believed his story about making a bad judgment based on emotion, and she truly believed he wanted to save the other people in the maze. Most importantly, she believed his remorse was real. Something in his eyes and expression told her that he was good person. That earned him the benefit of the doubt. "Okay," she said, "let's keep going. I want out of this place big time."

They came to the end of the maintenance tunnel. Ryan stopped at the door and turned to face Kerry. "Okay," he said, "here's the deal. We will have to run the final stretch. It's a twisting series of passageways that are static in design. What that means is they do not ever move. So, if we've beaten the *golem* here, and I have every reason to believe that we have, we should be home free. I'll open this door, check if the coast is clear, and then we run. Got it?"

Kerry nodded.

Ryan pushed the button on the door and peered out, looking in each direction. Even through the murky gloom, he could see that the passageways were empty. He motioned for Kerry to come out, then he closed the maintenance tunnel door.

Ryan took off in a quick sprint, closely followed by Kerry. He maneuvered around a series of twists and turns and finally came to a stop at the entrance to a short, well- lit hallway. At the end of the hallway was an open foyer space with three full-sized doors, spaced about six feet apart.

"We're here," Ryan sighed with relief. "This is the way out." He gave Kerry a quick hug. "Come on," he said, beaming, "let's go outside."

Ryan led Kerry to the three doors. Each one was unique. The door to the right was solid mahogany with a golden French handle. The door on the left was made of solid copper and had a copper-inlaid handle. The one in the middle was more basic. It was a simple wood door, painted white, showing some age, with a black wrought iron handle.

"Which one do we choose?" Kerry asked. She was clearly out of breath, and after what had happened to Eric, Suze and Judith, Ryan was surprised she was holding it together at all.

Ryan walked to the door in the middle. "Don't you remember what I told you? This whole maze centered on the pain in his life. When you consider that the happiest time of his life was during his childhood, then the door itself should be symbolic of that as well. This was the actual door to my grandfather's house. Grandfather purchased the house decades ago in a nostalgic moment when he wanted some ties to his birthplace. He then had the door shipped here after Jason convinced him to build the maze to fulfill his final solution. Putting the door as the way out seemed cathartic to my grandfather and that if anyone did escape, it was a symbolic cleansing of his past." He pulled the door open and motioned for Kerry to follow him. Ahead lay a well-lit corridor with a cream- colored carpet, walls painted a soft gray and recessed lighting going the length of the corridor. At the far end was another white door.

"What would have happened had we chosen the wrong door?" Kerry asked. Ryan just shook his head. She realized that not only did she not want to know, she didn't care either. All she wanted was to go home.

"That's the way out, Kerry," Ryan said, pointing to the door. "Freedom is less than fifty feet away."

"I think you may have other issues to contend with, Ryan," came a silken voice from behind them. Ryan and Kerry spun around to see Jason standing there with a gun trained on a young man that Ryan did not recognize.

"Kerry!" Jeremy exclaimed happily. "I never thought I'd see you alive again." He moved toward Kerry when Jason grabbed him by the collar and pulled him back. He grabbed Jeremy by the head and with a deft twist snapped his neck. He let Jeremy fall in a heap at his feet. His head lay to the side at an unnatural angle and his eyes were wide open and staring.

"Jeremy!" Kerry screamed. "You fucking animal! You didn't have to kill him!"

Ryan grabbed Kerry around the waist and held her back. "Kerry, keep away from him. He's extremely dangerous."

Jason moved towards Ryan and Kerry with a slow and purposeful stride, as if he were relishing their fear. His features seemed to change as his grin widened, showing more teeth than was normal. Ryan pulled out his gun, the one he'd been holding for worst case emergencies, and fired three shots, two striking Jason in the chest and one in the face. Jason staggered a bit, then fell back and lay there in a widening pool of blood.

"You did it, Ryan," Kerry exclaimed as a broad smile crept across her features. "For someone supposedly so dangerous, he sure went down easy."

Jason shuddered and slowly got to his feet. He leaned forward and let forth a scream that was more horrible than anything either Ryan or Kerry had ever heard before. He then stood up straight and glared at them. Jason pointed at Ryan and hissed, "You can't kill me with bullets. All they do is cause momentary discomfort. I've read every book on the black arts. I have sold my soul for abilities you will never understand. I can no longer die. Now that we've come to the end of the line, there is no need to maintain the charade of the doting manservant any longer. Since you are of no use to me, there is little reason to expend any effort in maintaining the charade. For the pain and trouble that you've caused me, I'll make sure you die very slowly."

Ryan moved himself in front of Kerry and began slowly backing them towards the hallway behind them and the freedom that it offered. "I don't understand, Jason," he said, in part to buy as much time as possible, in part out of curiosity of his role in this whole mess. "How did my grandfather ever get involved with the likes of you?"

Jason grinned. "I don't see any reason not to tell you. You can't stop me, nor will you ever leave this place alive. So if it gives you comfort thinking that you are buying time to plan a way out, feel free to do so. You see, your grandfather found me through a secret society. He was looking for someone who understood arcane magic to help him with a task of a sensitive nature. Turns out he wanted someone to help him create a *golem*. While I was a master of the dark arts, the teachings of your people were something I always found elusive. So I agreed to help him because I wanted to learn how to raise a *golem* as well. We raised a creature in Europe many years back and set it to task. Each time the target was terminated, we needed to rebuild the creature. The final iteration of the *golem* is what you see in the maze. By this point, your grandfather knew how to create the creature by himself. He made it bigger, stronger and far more lethal. So while I spent years whispering in his ear, convincing him that his vengeance was just, this final solution of killing all the remaining descendants of the men who killed his family was more for me. I wanted a test environment on how the creature would act with so many targets."

"I don't understand," Ryan replied. "What could you possibly gain from inciting my grandfather to kill these people?"

"Like I said, Ryan, your grandfather's petty revenge meant nothing to me. He needed help from someone with a background in arcane lore, and I needed help in learning the magic of your people. To learn to raise an unstoppable killing machine like the *golem* was too good an opportunity to resist. So I stayed with your grandfather all those years, and while he learned from me, I learned from him. I could now do what I could not those many years ago. I could create a *golem* and get it to do my bidding. This maze was important because it allowed me to see how the creature would respond in a non-linear environment with multiple targets. Unfortunately, just before we actually brought everyone here, your grandfather began to see how I had been manipulating him into maintaining his revenge for all these years. I had been using simple magic along with a mild drug to make him very open to suggestion. I suppose after all those years he was developing a tolerance. So I upped the dosage. Unfortunately for him, the added drugs reacted poorly with his illness and ended up hastening his death.

"The reason for the *golem* test run here in the maze is simple. Once I am convinced it will work, I will unleash an army of these creatures on this country with instructions to kill everyone that lives."

"You're insane," Kerry screamed. "What purpose could you possibly have to want to kill millions?"

"I doubt it will be that many," Jason replied. "The military should manage to destroy the creatures before the death toll gets that high. A couple of hundred thousand dead should be about right."

"Why?" Ryan interjected. "We get it. You're using the creatures to kill many, many people. But for what purpose?"

"Years ago, my family was killed by a suicide bomber in Tel Aviv. No one claimed responsibility for the bombing which claimed eleven lives. I watched as attack followed attack and nothing was done because there was no one source to pin the blame on. I realized that we needed to eliminate the problem at the source. To stop terrorism, we'd need to wipe out Egypt, Syria, Libya, Iran, Iraq and every other nation in the Middle East. The only country that could possibly do that was the United States. So I watched and waited and looked for a way to get my revenge. After helping Michael Carson prepare his *golems*, it occurred to me that unleashing dozens of the creatures on American cities and sending video to all the major news networks claiming responsibility from every known terror group would stir the American population into a frenzy. People would demand blood, and the government, which is so weak in international affairs, would retaliate with the full force of our military strength."

"Jesus Christ," Ryan said. "You're willing to start a world war for vengeance."

"And how is what your grandfather did any different?" Jason replied with a grin.

"First off, he wanted revenge on the men who brutalized and killed his family. I would have as well. The revenge that followed on the families was more a result of your influence. You're talking about starting a war that will kill millions and if nuclear weapons are used might render large portions of the planet inhospitable for years to come."

Jason spat on the ground. "They are a pestilence on the entire human race. The world will be better off if they were all dead."

"I won't let you do this, Jason," Ryan said and aimed the gun.

Jason threw his head back and laughed. "And how will you stop me? You saw the effect bullets have on me. Fire away. I will leave you broken but alive and aware to watch as I rape and torture your precious girlfriend."

Ryan cringed at the thought of what this animal planned to do. He kept slowly backing up, casting casual glances backwards in an attempt to find the right moment when he could get both himself and Kerry away.

"Ryan," Jason growled, his voice getting coarser, "I would advise you not to even attempt making a run for the door. I am far stronger and faster than you are. I will tear you both to shreds before you get within ten feet of the door."

Ryan stopped. He knew he had to keep Jason talking while he thought of how they could get away. "Noted," he replied, his voice barely a whisper. "I need to know, where do I fit in this whole mess?"

"Your grandfather was dying, Ryan," Jason said, "and while I managed to extend my influence over his life through sorcery, I could not cheat death. He loved and trusted you and I felt that I could put that to use and easily enthrall you with simple magic to finish what we started here. I knew that I'd need your help to get everyone here and to make sure that things ran smoothly. Little did I realize that your strong will would prevent me from controlling you for any extended period of time. No loss. All are dead save you two, and that will change shortly. And I would like to add that after watching such a successful trial run here in the maze, I'm looking forward to seeing what my *golems* will do outside in the cities."

Kerry dropped to her knees, cupped her face in her hands and began crying. She looked up at Jason, almost as if she were pleading. "Is everyone really dead? I'm the last one?"

Jason grinned and replied, "Yes, Kerry. You are the last one. But don't worry because that matter will be corrected shortly."

"What do you gain from killing us, Jason?" Ryan asked.

"Nothing. This is simply for my own amusement," Jason replied, his voice low and raw. "I will render you helpless and let you watch while I rape the girl. Knowing that you are powerless to stop her debasement, especially seeing how strongly you feel about her, will be my pleasure. Then I will kill her slowly. After, as I take your life from you, I'll walk away from this house and set the wheels in motion of my plan to wipe the vermin of the Middle East off the face of the Earth."

"Your plan would work," Ryan said with a twisted smile as he backed further away, "except you forgot one important variable."

"What's that?" Jason roared.

"That," Ryan said, pointing to the *golem*, which was slowly advancing behind Jason. A grey frost swirled about its body and the runes that were so carefully inscribed glowed with a fierce brilliance.

Jason threw his head back and roared with laughter. "Ryan," he said, regaining his composure, "I was with your grandfather when he created the *golem*. I saw the names that were put on the list. And I know that the only ones who have reason to fear the creature are those related to the men who massacred your grandfather's family."

The *golem* came up behind Jason and grabbed him under his arms, lifting him in the air. Jason screamed in agony as the creature began applying considerable pressure to his ribcage.

"I forgot to tell you, Jason," Ryan grinned. "Your control over my grandfather was weaker than you thought. While you went to get me, he had a moment of lucid thought, free and clear of your drugs and control, and tried to destroy the creature. He was not powerful enough to destroy the *golem* or to cancel its programming. When I arrived he told me everything, and with my help we performed an addendum to the ritual and added your name to the target list."

Jason began thrashing about. He roared in rage and pain and tried to cast a spell to either stop or incapacitate the *golem*. None seemed to have any effect as the *golem* threw him against the wall, shattering the stone and sending up a pile of dust. Jason tried to get up but found that he could not move his broken frame. "Damn you!" he screamed, not sure himself if he meant Ryan, his grandfather or the *golem*.

Ryan, meanwhile, grabbed Kerry's hand and pulled her towards him. "We've got to go now," he screamed, "while it's distracted with Jason. This will be our only chance." Kerry nodded and they ran down the hallway towards the last door. Jason's screams followed them.

To the right of the door was a keypad. Ryan typed in a three-digit number. "The address of my grandfather's house, as I told you earlier," Ryan remarked to Kerry as a pneumatic hiss sounded and the door swung open. Ryan stepped through and immediately fell to his knees and screamed. Kerry followed and looked at Ryan and then at the five-by-five foot room they found themselves in. There was no way out.

"What's going on, Ryan?" Kerry sobbed, tears welling in her eyes.

Ryan looked up at her and knew he had failed. "This was the way out, Kerry. I saw the blueprints, and Grandfather confirmed it earlier this week."

"Then why is this stone wall blocking our way?"

"It had to be Jason. He must have known the exit was here and decided not to take any chances. Even under Jason's manipulations, my grandfather had a sense of honor and wanted a way out for those who would make it to the end. Someone like Jason apparently has none and lives only for the pain and suffering of others. This way if anyone ever made it to the end, he'd still ensure that no one escaped to alert the authorities. Oh, Kerry, I'm so sorry."

"I don't want to die, Ryan," she wailed.

Ryan stood and held her for a moment. "Our only chance is to go back and fight the *golem*. Judith told us that Suze figured out how to kill it. While I was hoping to do this on my terms, it seems as if our backs are to the wall."

Kerry stared at him, her eyes widening. "We'll never make it."

Ryan didn't even have time to argue. He felt the icy mist before the *golem* became visible. It stepped out of the mist, a harbinger of death, ready to claim its last soul and earn its eternal rest. "Get behind me, Kerry!" Ryan screamed.

Kerry Ramirez, the creature whispered. Its voice seemed to come from everywhere at once, yet was low and seductive. *I have come for you. I come for retribution.* Its voice seemed to caress her mind, to sap her will to resist as it teased and taunted her with her own memories.

Kerry looked around, desperately seeking a way out. The *golem* was large and filled the passageway. She knew she would never escape. She crossed in front of Ryan and ran her hand gently down his cheek. "You tried," she whispered, her eyes red with tears, "and I forgive you. I know this wasn't your fault. You're a victim like the rest of us. You can't beat this creature any more than we can. Look how easily it destroyed Jason. Just please try to remember me if you should make it out." She then turned and walked towards the *golem* to face her final destiny.

Ryan howled in anguish and threw himself at the *golem* before it could get to Kerry. It swatted at him, but he ducked under its blow and launched himself onto the creature. He pulled his keys from his pocket and began feverishly working on the *aleph*, desperately trying to kill the creature. The *golem* pummeled Ryan with powerful blows, wracking him with numbing pain, yet Ryan held firm to the creature's neck. Ryan was close to removing the aleph when one of the creature's flailing arms found purchase, striking him squarely in the head and hurling him clear down the hallway, tossing him aside as if he were nothing more than an irritating insect. "Run, Kerry," Ryan coughed, fighting the pain and struggling to maintain consciousness, "please…run."

Kerry looked at Ryan, then at the *golem*, which was advancing towards her, but somehow a bit slower and less steadily than before. She reasoned that Ryan must have removed enough of the letter to do some harm. She made one final attempt to dodge the creature, but it moved with a surprising swiftness, catching her by the arm. She struggled to free herself, but the *golem* held on tightly and threw her into the wall. She hit with a sickening crack and was still. Ryan looked on, helpless, as the blood pooled around Kerry's prone and twisted form. He tried to move, but the pain was too much. He looked up at the *golem*, which just stood there, as inanimate as a statue, and wept.

Epilogue One

Ellen worked her way down the dimly lit hallway. She was tired and hungry and her body ached. She had seen the remains of two people and while one of them clearly belonged to the hate-monger Kaufmann, the other corpse was mutilated beyond recognition. At a minimum, she suspected that it was a woman.

Turning a corner, she walked down another hallway and came to a room with three doors. One was open and led to a well-lit hallway beyond. She stepped through the door and froze when she saw the scene in front of her. There was a man on the ground who had been torn to shreds. Next to him was another man who Ellen did not recognize, his neck clearly broken. Further up the hallway was the *golem*. It stood there still as a statue. Ellen noticed that the runes on its body no longer glowed. She wondered if the creature was dead. She approached it cautiously. If it sensed her approaching it didn't show it. She reached a hand out and lightly touched the creature. Its flesh was cool to the touch, feeling like clay and also like dried leather. It smelled of freshly tilled soil with an undercurrent of rot or decay.

Ellen gently stepped by the *golem* and saw the two bodies on the ground in front of it. She recognized the girl, Kerry, from their group. She ran over and felt for a pulse. The skin was cold and she couldn't feel anything. Her heart ached seeing someone so young with their life snuffed out so needlessly.

Across the hall was the young man she had seen on the screen and who had imprisoned them all in the maze. She approached him carefully and touched his neck. There was a pulse. Ellen shook him until he opened his eyes.

Ellen put her face inches from the young man's and said, "Get me out of here or I will kill you now." He nodded and looked over at Kerry's body. A tear trickled down his cheek.

"I'm so sorry," he said, his voice cracking. "Please help me up."

Ellen helped Ryan to his feet and put his arm over her shoulder. "Tell me where we need to go." He nodded.

"Come on," Ryan rasped and stole one last glance at the still figure of the *golem*. "Let's go."

Epilogue Two

Boston. Two days later.

Danny Conlon slowed his car, turned into the deserted lot off Atlantic Avenue and drove behind the old building. Parked behind an old dumpster, so it would not be noticed from the street, was Liam's Dodge Durango. He must already be inside.

He picked up his BlackBerry Storm from the cup holder next to his seat and cursed silently. Still no message. What was Liam doing? He was supposed to contact him when he arrived. It was three forty-five in the morning and the city was silent and deserted. After the amount of snow that had hit the Boston in the last month, at least the night was clear and bright for a change.

Danny buttoned his coat and pulled on a pair of thin Isotoner gloves. Not the best thing to keep out the chill, he thought, but better not to be limited by something like mittens. He patted his pocket and felt the reassuring bulge of his Glock. Better to be safe than sorry, Danny's father had always said, and Danny took such things to heart.

He hurried to the back of the building and saw the faint traces of footprints in the powdery snow. The footprints led to the back door, which had been once locked up but now swung open, exposing the darkness within.

Danny gritted his teeth. He was going to give Liam a swift kick in the ass when he found him. Although they had known each other for twenty years when they ran together in their gang in Southie, Danny had always been the alpha and Liam the follower, roles both seemed to very comfortable with.

He pulled a small flashlight from his coat pocket and turned it on as he walked into the building. The light glowed a weak yellow orange and Danny cursed for not having the foresight to get fresh flashlight batteries. Liam could not have been here long, Danny mused, since the snowy tracks were still visible on the ground.

This was supposed to be a simple job, Danny thought. The hard economic times had forced many companies into bankruptcy, and that left a glut of furniture and equipment for sale to those who had money to spend, often for pennies on the dollar. One such person who had money to spend was Jackie Dooley, who was well known to both Danny and Liam. Jackie was a few years older and when they were boys had taken it upon himself to beat Danny and Liam mercilessly, warning them to keep off his streets.

The years might have passed, but the decades-old humiliation had not, and when Liam came to Danny with word that Jackie had a fortune in computers and servers stored in the basement of the building he owned on Atlantic, Danny saw this as the chance to get even...and rich in the process.

Danny followed the footsteps to the staircase and saw them trail off into the gloom below. He wished he could at least turn on a light, but the last thing he wanted to do was attract attention. Bostonians did not typically get involved, but it only took one to call the cops. The weakening light from the flashlight would have to suffice.

In the basement, Danny heard a faint rustling followed by a slow dripping noise coming from his left. "Liam?" he hissed between clenched teeth, "that you?"

When he heard no response, he pulled the Glock from his pocket and advanced carefully. Turning the corner, he saw someone kneeling down against the far wall. Danny lifted the flashlight so he could get a clearer view.

The man was crouched over Liam, or at least what was left of him. Liam's chest was ripped open and his organs strewn before him in a macabre tapestry of death. "Liam," Danny whispered, and fired three shots into the back of the man's head. The bullets seemed to be absorbed and the man stood and turned to face him. It was over seven feet tall, and while powerfully built, that was where all human similarities ended. It had glowing characters all over its body and a blank, featureless face with glowing characters written across its forehead.

The creature began advancing towards Danny, who fired two more shots into the thing's chest. When that did nothing to slow or stop it, Danny turned and ran, bounding up the stairs two at a time.

He ran outside, slipped on the icy ground and fell painfully to his knees. Danny stood and felt his leg give out beneath him, the ankle buckling under the weight. He leaned on his good leg and limped painfully to the car. He dared a glance back and saw the creature framed by the doorway of the building. Out of the gloom on the basement, he saw it a bit more clearly. It seemed to be made of earth or stone, and the face was blank with subtle indentations where the mouth and eyes would have been. Its hands were little more than elongated stumps, the fingers looking more vestigial than functional. It was also splattered with blood.

Liam's blood, Danny thought and felt his bladder go.

He made it to the car and climbed in. He said a silent prayer that he hadn't taken the time to lock his doors. He started the car easily enough and slipped the transmission into reverse. The car did not move. He looked around wildly but could not see the creature anywhere. Suddenly the rear of the car was lifted up and Danny had to push back on the steering wheel to avoid being thrown against the windshield. He floored the gas pedal again, and the engine roared, but the car still did not move.

The car was flipped over and landed on its roof, trapping Danny upside down, belted in his seat. He didn't even have time to unlatch the belt before a powerful blow to the driver's side of the windshield caused the glass to explode inward. Danny had a moment to scream before the creature pulled him from the car and then everything went black.

The *golem* finished dismembering Danny and felt a surge of energy ripple through its body. The runes along its skin glowed brighter for just a brief moment. It looked out across the parking lot to Atlantic Avenue and the buildings beyond. There were people in those buildings and it could not rest nor would the pain abate until they were all dead.

The *golem* did not need to eat, nor sleep. It moved single-mindedly towards its one purpose. It was to destroy every living thing it encountered, and nothing save its own destruction would sway it from its chosen path.

Across the country in Los Angeles on the outskirts of the city, another *golem* felt the stirrings of life from its counterpart in Boston. Blood has been shed and it too must now come to life and fulfill the purpose for which it was created. As in Los Angeles, similar awakenings were occurring in New York, Philadelphia, Chicago and over a hundred other cities. One hundred and forty *golems* in total came to sentience at the same time and moved out towards their respective slumbering cities, towards their programmed destinies of unending destruction.

Epilogue Three

In a darkened tunnel beneath the sprawling mansion in Maine, all was still. The maze was effectively disarmed so that all traps had been rendered inert. Not a soul stirred in the maze or the home above.

The *golem* stood still as an inanimate statue. The bodies of its recent victims surrounded it. It was for all intents and purposes dead. The runes on its body were dark and no thoughts worked their way through its rudimentary consciousness.

Suddenly one of the runes on its lower arm began to glow a faint and luminescent green. Then the adjacent runes also began to glow weakly. It took over ten minutes before all the runes on the creature's body were glowing. It raised its hands before its face and roared as surges of pain worked their way through its body. Its rudimentary consciousness was awakened and with it came the searing pain. There was one from the list that still lived. It could not be at peace until they were all eliminated.

The *golem* felt the presence of the other. It was not far but moving away from its position. With increasing fluidity in its limbs the creature moved, driven by the need to complete its task. It would follow the one to the ends of the Earth if needed and then it would welcome the sweet oblivion it craved.

Gordon Anthony Bean was born in Laval, Quebec but now lives and works in New England. He is married with one daughter. He has published the short stories 'From a Whisper to a Dream' in the *Sinister Landscapes* anthology by Pixie Dust Press and 'Out of the Corner of His Eye' in the *From Beyond the Grave* anthology by Grinning Skull Press. *Dawn of Broken Glass* is his first novel. He is currently at work on his second novel, *Bloodlines*, and is editing a horror anthology forthcoming from Guardian of Forever publishing. He is also a member of the New England Horror Writers Association.

www.ingramcontent.com/pod-product-compliance
Lightning Source LLC
Chambersburg PA
CBHW020614260626
47157CB00003B/1004